LETHAL PURSUIT

Also by Will Thomas

Some Danger Involved

To Kingdom Come

The Limehouse Text

The Hellfire Conspiracy

The Black Hand

Fatal Enquiry

Anatomy of Evil

Hell Bay

Old Scores

Blood Is Blood

LETHAL PURSUIT

WILL THOMAS

MINOTAUR
BOOKS
NEW YORK

First published in the United States by Minotaur Books, an imprint of St. Martin's Publishing Group

www.minotaurbooks.com

Library of Congress Cataloging-in-Publication Data

Names: Thomas, Will, 1958– author.
Title: Lethal pursuit / Will Thomas.
Description: First edition. | New York : Minotaur Books, 2019. | Series: A
   Barker & Llewelyn novel ; 11
Identifiers: LCCN 2019029068 | ISBN 9781250170408 (hardcover) |
   ISBN 9781250170415 (ebook)
Subjects: GSAFD: Spy stories. | Suspense fiction.
Classification: LCC PS3620.H644 L48 2019 | DDC 813/.6—dc23
LC record available at https://lccn.loc.gov/2019029068

Our books may be purchased in bulk for promotional, educational, or business use. Please contact your local bookseller or the Macmillan Corporate and Premium Sales Department at 1-800-221-7945, extension 5442, or by email at MacmillanSpecialMarkets@macmillan.com.

First Edition: November 2019

10   9   8   7   6   5   4   3   2   1

I would like to dedicate this book to Forrest Elliott,
my friend, my instructor in several martial arts,
and an enthusiastic fan of my work.

Kamsahamnida, Saboonim

ACKNOWLEDGMENTS

It takes a lot of work by a lot of people to turn out a novel like the one in your hands. Agents, editors, copy editors, publishers, and artists have turned it from a stack of seemingly random pages into this finished product.

I'd like to thank my agent, Maria Carvainis, who has shepherded me to this, the eleventh volume of the Barker and Llewelyn novels. My editor, Keith Kahla, both an enthusiastic fan and a careful critic, lays hands upon the manuscript and the process begins. Alice Pfeifer stays in close contact with me as the edits travel back and forth. Meanwhile, my publicist, Hector DeJean, uses his craft to get the book out before you, the public.

You expect the author's name on the front of a book. Many thanks to the people who helped put it there.

A special thank-you to my wife, Julia, without whom nothing would get written. She's my encourager, my inspiration, and my helpmeet.

It is useless to deny, and impossible to conceal, that a great part of Europe, the whole of Italy and France, and a great portion of Germany—to say nothing of other countries—is covered with a network of secret societies, just as the superficies of the Earth are being covered with railroads.

—Benjamin Disraeli

LETHAL PURSUIT

PROLOGUE

The express from Dover was still coming to a stop when Hillary Drummond leapt onto the platform. He staggered a moment, coming close to falling, but righted himself, balanced like a tightrope walker, with a suitcase in one hand and a satchel in the other. Once assured of his footing, he began to sprint along the platform at Charing Cross Station, heedless of the scores of men and women judging him for his lack of decorum. Drummond cared not a whit for their scandalized glances. After all, no one was trying to kill any of them.

WAY OUT, the sign said on the wall of the Underground. Drummond felt relieved. He'd been looking for a way out since the ferry at Calais. He stumbled on the third step of the staircase leading to the street level, and looked back over his shoulder. There were no blue coats in sight, not yet, anyway, but he knew better than to think he had outrun his pursuers. Did he have time to do the one thing he had to do? Perhaps he could lose himself in the vast cavern that was Charing Cross Station.

He passed the familiar green kiosk of a W.H. Smith's and it made him glad he was in London again. He longed to look up at Admiral Nelson perched above Trafalgar Square. He'd lost his taste for Wiener schnitzel and goulash. If he survived, he'd stop at the Red Lion, glut himself on roast beef and pud, and drink himself senseless. It seemed a proper reward for six months' labor.

Drummond looked over his shoulder again. There was still no sign that anyone was following him, so he darted into the public toilet. It was a gamble, since there was only one entrance. He could not hide in such a public place, because this group had no compunction about being seen. Death provides its own anonymity.

Ten minutes later he came out into Charing Cross Road. Nearby the bell known as Big Ben began to play its preamble. When it tolled, he counted the peals. It was just after nine in the morning. What day was it? Tuesday, he thought. Or perhaps Wednesday.

London was in his nostrils. It was a reek, but it was a good reek, a familiar one. It was coal and soot and steam engines, horse sweat and night soil. Whitehall was just ahead. He could see it. Then he noticed a man with a blue coat at the corner. No, not a man. A youth. Drummond wasn't certain whether he had been spotted or not, but he did not take the chance. He ducked through the nearest door for safety.

He was in a public house, by all appearances. The wood was ancient and gray, the smell of the room hoppy. Patrons and even the publican himself looked at him without interest. He stayed just long enough to doff his coat and hang it on a hook before stepping out a second door. The youth had passed by. With nerveless fingers he pulled a cigarette from his case. Before he could pull a box from his pocket, a hand came forward with a match.

"Thank you," he said.

"Bitte."

His training came instantly to hand. He caught the fellow with the heel of his pump just above the hipbone, where the ball of the femur met the socket. The young man folded like a regatta-day lawn chair. To add insult to injury, Drummond kicked him in the ribs and stepped over him. A hand clutched at his ankle but he shook it away.

Yet another youth came pushing his way through the crowd of men and women leaving the station. It was Drummond's first full view of the uniforms the young men wore. The boy wore a dark blue peaked cap and a matching long coat with a high collar. The coat was cut very tight around the body, but loose in the arms. Above the left side pocket was a kind of leather bag buttoned to his waist. The coat fell to his knees and the top of his boots, but in the middle it tapered to a point almost a foot lower. Every bit of trim on the blue coat, the collar, the sleeves, and the apron of his coat, was piped in an almost festive red.

Drummond realized for the first time that it was snowing. He'd been too occupied to notice it before. Clouds of vapor wreathed the boy's head and the pedestrians pinched their collars about their necks. A fine layer of snow lay on the pavement ahead. It had probably begun that very morning.

All would have been fine and he'd have waited for the youth to come after him, but instead the boy's hand reached for the leather holster at his waist. Drummond couldn't take the chance. He leapt forward and caught his attacker's forearm with his heel, savagely breaking the bones. The youth's limbs shot out from under him and he fell. Nearby, a woman gave a scream of alarm, but no one stopped to help. It was too cold.

"Acne," Drummond muttered to himself. The youth had acne. Were there no men in their country willing to make the journey? Surely someone older must be leading this band of well-dressed youths. The prize he brought with him was worth a fortune, after all. It could also start a war. For all he knew, it already had.

Drummond burst into Whitehall Street and his head naturally turned right, where Admiral Nelson watched sagely over London from his one-hundred-sixty-foot pedestal. The admiral still stood, one-armed and wily as ever. England still reigned. Drummond himself finally had something to show for it, this work he'd been doing for so many months. Now all he had to do was survive another eighth of a mile.

His head turned left. At the far end of the street, across from the Houses of Parliament and hiding Westminster Abbey from view, were the Home and Foreign Offices. He'd come hundreds of miles by rail to get here, used many a stratagem to survive, took such resources as he could in order to make it this far. His last meal had been a bun pinched from the kitchen of the Orient Express. He dared not be so open as to have a meal in the dining car. By then he knew every inch of the train, from roof to undercarriage, and every place he could squeeze his six-foot frame into.

There was no one about in Whitehall Street, no one dangerous. No dreaded blue coats. How many had followed him? It was impossible to tell.

Drummond knew this area like the back of his hand. When he joined the Foreign Office as a clerk, he'd delivered messages to almost every building in the street: the Admiralty, the Horse Guards, Scotland Yard, Downing Street. Now he skirted an alley hurrying to Great Scotland Yard Street. Surely no one could attack him in front of the gates of Scotland Yard.

He trotted south. There were too many pedestrians on the pavement and a crush of vehicles in the street. Hay had been strewn on the dirty cobblestones to give the horses traction in the snow. It was frigid cold. Not too much farther, he told himself. The Foreign Office was growing bigger and bigger ahead of him.

He bumped shoulders with another man.

"Beg pardon," he murmured.

A pain went through him, a flash of heat like a poker. Then he felt something being drawn out of him. Immediately, he had trouble breathing. Air simply would not be drawn into his paralyzed lungs. He looked over his shoulder. A man stood there regarding him, the man whom he had bumped into. There was a sword in his hand. As he watched, a drop of blood fell in the snow, as bright red as the piping on the youths' coats.

He must get away. The man was behind him and two more blue coats were running toward him from the other side of the street. There was only one choice. Drummond leaped into traffic.

Horses snorted in his face, affronted by his sudden appearance. He scrambled past them, hugging his suitcase to his chest. He wheezed. No air. No air.

There was a median between the lines of traffic, a thin strip of grass covered in dirty snow and a few bare trees like hands grasping vainly for the heavens. Out of the corner of his eye he saw two of the youths reach the same median, one on either side. What must it be like to have such youth, to have fleet limbs that do what one tells them to? Drummond was only thirty-four, but now he felt twice that. He jumped into traffic again, but this time he encountered a layer of hard ice. His feet slipped out from under him and he hunched forward, suitcase extended, trying to keep his balance. A horse bellowed in his face and he fell under an oncoming growler.

An iron-shod hoof came down on his chest, crushing his ribs like matchsticks. Another stumbled on his knee, shattering it, causing the horse to slip and tumble down on top of him, half a ton of warm horseflesh. Lastly, as if an afterthought, the front wheel of the cab rolled over his ankle before skidding to a stop, straddling him.

Everything hurt at once, an excruciating pain as he had never experienced before. There was a ringing in his ear that would not go away. He understood he was dying. One didn't recover from such injuries. He gasped for breath, but he had to stay alive for one more minute to savor one final sight.

The man and the two youths stood over his body, looking down on him without pity. One of the boys held his suitcase and was undoing the clasp. The lad reached in and drew out a shirt and undergarments. And socks, lots of socks. The man's face clouded and he began yelling at the boys.

Drummond tried to chuckle, but it was beyond him. He'd stowed the satchel in a locker in the station. He'd never reach the Foreign Office, but others would come, his brothers in the service. He was only a pawn, really; but even a pawn can threaten a king.

CHAPTER ONE

Mac!" Cyrus Barker bawled from his bedchamber at the top of the house that morning, the tenth of January 1892. My wife was already down in the kitchen helping Etienne Dummolard, our chef, but I was shaving, so I turned to hear what the disturbance was all about. One rarely heard a word of criticism about Jacob Maccabee, and certainly not from our employer. I heard our factotum's soft footfalls on the stair overhead.

"Sir?" he said, a trifle coldly.

"Mac, what are these?" Barker rumbled.

"I believe they are hose, sir."

"To be more precise, they are silk hose," Barker replied. "What are silk hose doing in my drawer? Where did they come from?"

"From Paris, sir. I ordered them for you. They are very fine and in fashion. All the butlers in London are suggesting them to their gentlemen this year."

"Mac, I am a humble man and I prefer humble hose. Plain

woolen socks are good enough for me. I am no fashion plate, and have no need of silk hosiery."

"I'm sorry, sir," Mac said. "I was only trying to keep you looking modern and professional, like contemporary enquiry agents."

"Who, pray tell, wears such frippery?"

"Mr. Llewelyn does, sir. His wife chose them for him specially, I understand."

"Well, that is more than enough silk for one household, then. The silkworms may toil for Mr. Llewelyn, but they need not do so on my account. Take this box and post it back to Paris, before it taints the rest of London with French decadence."

"Yes, sir."

I heard Mac sigh as he came down the stair a defeated man. I donned my jacket and followed him to the ground floor. Going into the kitchen, I kissed Rebecca on the cheek and she handed me a hot cup of coffee. Etienne was teaching my wife the proper way to bake a French tart, which I found ironic. I wondered if our chef had heard the Guv's remark about French decadence. His voice does tend to carry.

Etienne waved me to a chair and slid a warm pastry my way so that I wouldn't interrupt his lesson. I looked out at the cold, austere garden, enjoying the peace while Barker still grumbled in his bedchamber. Things were topsy-turvy. Everything had been subtly derailed, like a train engine that had jumped the track but was still rolling forward parallel to the rails. One knew something bad was coming, but did not know when or how.

I heard Barker's heavy tread on the stairs, pecked my wife on the cheek, and took a large bite from the tart before sprinting to the front hall. Mac opened the door to his butler's pantry and gave me a forlorn look, holding a flat white box in his hand. Poor Mac. The man was very nearly perfect and unused to being scolded by the headmaster. Unlike me, for instance. I opened the door and Barker sailed through it into another day. In black woolen socks, of course.

I went in search of a cab. Perhaps my employer's fit of pique was due to his injury, I thought, as I directed the vehicle to our home to pick him up.

Barker had been badly injured six months earlier, a compound fracture of the tibia, which left him with a leather brace and a cane. It meant that he was confined to his desk more often than either of us preferred. It must have ached, but the man was a stoic of the first order. In true Scottish form, he would not complain. It was up to me to note when his limp became more pronounced and suggest we take a hansom. The cold of a London January, which seeps into one's bones, did nothing to aid in his recovery.

This meant, of course, that most errands, from delivering messages to bringing lunch from a local public house, fell to me. It also meant should either of us be attacked, it was my duty to defend us both. It hadn't happened yet, and I sincerely hoped it wouldn't, not for my sake, but for his. The Guv's pride would be damaged, being defended by his subordinate, and the man does tend to brood.

"Lad, what are you ruminating over?" he asked as our hansom reached Westminster Bridge.

"Nothing important, sir. This and that."

Recently, Barker had remarked that I was less talkative than I had been as a bachelor, which was for the better. Things were more complicated now that I was married. I had two completely different people to please, sometimes with contradictory expectations. There was less time to read, or to soak in the bathhouse in our garden. These were prices I gladly paid, since I'd never been so happy in my life. Rebecca was perfect for me, and as I learned more about her every day, I appreciated her all the more.

"Here we are," he rumbled.

I would not help him out of the cab, but I hovered nearby in case I was needed.

"Morning, Mr. B., Mr. L.," our clerk, Jeremy Jenkins, said as we entered.

"Good morning, Jeremy," I replied.

Cyrus Barker grunted in greeting, crossed our chamber to his desk and sat in his green leather swivel chair. Jenkins and I had a sort of signal as to how the Guv was faring on any particular day. I shook my head. Storm clouds approaching.

Lifting our ledger book, I began going over our accounts, or pretended to. I'd gone over them the day before. In reality, I fell back to thinking about my wife.

During our honeymoon, Barker had renovated the first floor for our private use. The guest bedroom had become ours, a lumber room beside it had become a sitting room, and my old bachelor quarters were now a study-cum-library. We could not fault his generosity, but I was aware that he did so partially to have me on hand should he need me. If Rebecca had her wishes, we would have moved into her house in the City, which she still kept. We had reached a temporary compromise: each morning after breakfast, she would go to Camomile Street in order to receive callers and friends, and then the two of us would return, separately, to Barker's house to have dinner together and retire for the evening. It was not a perfect arrangement, and as much as I enjoyed the routine, I knew it was only a matter of time before we moved permanently. A woman needs a house, to choose cushions and drapes and add countless small details. A husband is there on sufferance, to pay for everything and to keep his opinions to himself.

Cyrus Barker and I were installed in our offices in Craig's Court. Unfortunately, there was no current case under our scrutiny. Between his aching limb and the lack of mental stimulation, I feared he would take to growling at me much in the way he had growled at Mac that morning.

There was much more in me with which to find fault and I was an easy target to hand.

"Please, Lord," I prayed to myself. "Something to keep him occupied. Anything. He needs it. I need it. We all need it."

I assumed, in my sins, that God hears a lowly Methodist who had married a Jewess and was now attending a Christian-Jewish church. I was still working out if we were satisfied in Reverend

Mordecai's church-synagogue, but whatever we were, we were more satisfied than the Guv.

Cyrus Barker had lost his faith. Well, perhaps not his faith as such; according to Baptist doctrine, no man is able to pluck the believer out of his Father's hand. Still, he drew little comfort from the Scriptures as he once did, and I knew him well enough to see that it pained him. Fewer verses came from his lips. The old ship's captain was at sea.

Charles Haddon Spurgeon, that prince among evangelists, whose sermons were published worldwide and who preached at the Metropolitan Tabernacle but a few streets from the Guv's house, had had a dispute with his congregational and denominational leaders. He withdrew from the Baptist Union over what he saw as a growing apostasy and they censured him. He retired to the South of France. As a deacon, Barker was called to an immediate meeting, which lasted long into the night. Two days later, he resigned. That was in 1887. Spiritually speaking, he was never the same again.

Barker glanced my way and I became industrious, typing notes from our last case. There was a flutter in the waiting room outside and I caught a glimpse of military braid, one of the old soldiers who delivers telegrams and packages in London. Jenkins signed for whatever was delivered, then stood. I knew what would come next: he would enter with the missive on a silver salver with as much dignity as could be mustered by a clerk who'd spent the previous evening pouring neck oil down his gullet.

In he came, of course, stopping with the salver at Barker's desk. We live but to serve.

Cyrus Barker stared at the salver as if it were an adder that might bite him. He seized the edge of the package with his hand and raised it, testing its weight. By the way he hefted it, the package contained something heavier than mere paper. He set it down again and ran his fingers over the irregular object, trying to deduce by touch alone what it was. He nodded decisively. His hand went to his desk drawer where he kept an Italian dagger for use as a letter opener, then he slit the top and dropped the contents of the envelope into his hand. It was a key.

I rose from my desk and leaned over his, examining it as my employer turned it over in his hand. It was an old brass key, thick and long, the kind of door key that existed before locks became such fine and complicated mechanical marvels. I saw a letter stamped into the ferrule on one side, the letter *Q*. It was not in an elaborate script, just a simple oval with a tail. There was no way to tell if it was originally stamped thereon or if it had been a later addition.

Barker sat back between the high wings of his green leather chair, deep in thought. He spread his arms wide and placed his hands prone on the desk. Then he began to drum on the spotless glass sheet that lay upon it. He looked at his hand. He looked toward our bow window. He looked down again and then up. Then he stood.

"Let us take a walk, Mr. Llewelyn," he said, coming out from behind his desk. Though officially we were partners in the agency, my opinion was not requested.

We passed through the outer office and I informed our clerk that we would be out. We donned our coats and stepped outside into the bitter wind. I fixed my hand to the brim of my hat, walked into Whitehall Street, and regarded the vehicles passing by. Cabmen perched atop their cabs, huddled in their thick coats, looking miserable. Their fares hunched over inside the open vehicles, no less despondent. I turned to make some commonplace remark to Barker and found that he wasn't beside me.

I turned and saw him striding deeper into Craig's Court, heading east toward the Telephone Exchange. I hurried until I was beside him again. His breath came in white plumes, as if he were smoking one of his innumerable meerschaum pipes. We came to the cul-de-sac, which veers right, and faced Harrington House, a wide circle of tall gambrel-roofed buildings. They had been built a few centuries earlier to provide the Earl of Harrington access to a Palace of Westminster that was never built. One felt sorry for the earl in his powdered wig, dejected that his grand scheme was thwarted by Henry VIII, that old spoilsport. But I digress.

There was a tall, thin building of indeterminate age on the right hand just as one reached the court. It had an old, yellowed TO LET sign in the cobwebbed window. Barker walked up to the door and put the key in the keyhole. It fit. It took a little jiggling, but the door came open with a protest of both the wood of the door and the aged hinges. Barker inclined his head toward the side of the entrance. In the wood there a crude letter had been carved, Q, as if by a jackknife. It did not look recent, and may even have been a hundred years old.

"I've never noticed this building before," I said as we stepped inside.

"No, you haven't," he replied.

It was cold in the vestibule, so cold one wondered if what was floating in the air were dust motes or ice crystals. A set of steps led up toward the first floor and we found a door at the top. The Guv tried the key, but it didn't work. We turned to the stairway leading to the rooms above, but it had been roped off: a dusty, aged piece of rope was hanging between the two bannisters. Immediately, Barker plunged down the stair to the ground floor again and I followed after.

We descended another pair of steps to the bottom of the stairs, barred by yet another door. The key unlocked it. We went through and found practically the last thing I expected to find: a long brick tunnel.

"Down the rabbit hole," I said, quoting Carroll.

More pragmatic, Cyrus Barker lit a match and found an old-fashioned candlestick with a brass ring on a shelf. He lit the candle, and without hesitation headed forward into the tunnel. I was glad to see that it was both dry and warmer than the house we had exited. I hazarded that it might be some kind of sewer tunnel that had been abandoned. It was too narrow for even the oldest carriages of the Underground.

"Built by the earl, I'll warrant," the Guv said, his voice echoing in the tunnel. "A private entrance to the palace."

"The one that was never finished."

"Precisely."

We plunged deeper. I don't do well in tunnels. They are too enclosed for my liking. It was what kept me from following my father and brothers into the coal mines of Gwent. Ten minutes there and I would be in a blind panic, convinced the ceiling would fall in and crush us or a wind would come through and snuff out all the candles attached to our helmets. I tried everything, but nothing could be done. The miners considered it a curse. I half believed it myself.

Though the tunnel was perfectly dry, my face became clammy and my lungs felt waterlogged. I tried not to reveal it to my senior partner, but he misses nothing.

"Forward, Thomas. One step in front of the other. This tunnel has to end somewhere soon."

"Yes, sir," I said.

During the first week after formally becoming partners in the agency, we had both attempted to have me call him by his Christian name, but it was a resounding failure. He would always be "Sir" and I would always be "Thomas." I was lucky to get him to stop calling me "lad" now that I was six-and-twenty and sometimes he still forgot.

We had walked perhaps five minutes before we came to a fork in the tunnel. By this point it had widened and the ceiling became higher overhead. What was the purpose of this tunnel? I wondered. I guessed that we had been going south, but the second tunnel headed west and there was a gate blocking it.

"The key?" I asked.

It had been a rhetorical question, but Barker put the key in my hand. I tried it in the keyhole of the barred gate and it opened easily. That meant it had been oiled in recent memory. We stepped inside.

"South," I continued, pointing down the first tunnel. "That's roughly where the Houses of Parliament are. Perhaps this is some sort of escape tunnel for them, in case of emergency. Dangers such as Guy Fawkes's attempt to blow up the House of Lords, or Old Boney making a landing here from France."

"You read at Oxford, lad, not I," Barker said.

"So, where will this tunnel end? Westminster Abbey?"

"Not so far south," he said. "Look at the brick."

I studied it by the flickering of the candle. I ran a hand along it and found it smooth. The brick was made more recently. Possibly much more recently.

I ducked a cobweb unsuccessfully and brushed a spider from my shoulder.

"There it is," Barker said.

We came to a door, which opened easily to my associate's hand, even without the key. The two of us stepped inside and found ourselves in an ordinary broom closet.

Barker opened another door and we found ourselves in a large, well-appointed kitchen. The chefs and assistants glanced up from their work, then returned to it. A man in livery stood waiting for us.

"Good morning, gentlemen," he said, whisking our outer coats with a brush. He helped us doff them and took our hats, then whisked our suits, as well.

"Come this way, please. You don't want to be late."

We followed him, or tried to. The man was quick afoot. I've seen Mac glide about, but this fellow would have done himself proud at a field event.

We were led through several corridors, past innumerable rooms. I had a memory of walls and moldings in a warm marble. There was a good deal of renovation going on; canvas was on the floor and there were buckets of paint I had to skip around, and I heard someone sawing wood nearby. It looked like a typical nobleman's home, but currently a little dowdy and neglected. Still, the owner must be rather wealthy, for the rooms went on and on.

Then we came upon a room full of people working, some typing and others writing or talking, like a newspaper office. It was jarring. Perhaps it wasn't a residence at all, I thought. London is like that. A residence becomes a shop. A shop becomes an office, which becomes a public house, which eventually becomes a residence again. London reinvents itself every morning.

Barker and I trotted to keep up with the fleet-limbed servant. I felt sorry for the Guv on his injured leg. Were I to collide with a chance individual, limbs would be broken. Once the young man turned without warning us, and we shot past and had to retrace our steps.

Finally, we reached a pair of doors. Our guide knocked, then threw them open quickly and stepped aside, allowing us to pass through. In fact, the young man gave me an encouraging push in the back.

There was a desk and a man behind it, a heavyset man, balding, with a long beard. Cyrus Barker stepped forward and bowed his head in greeting. I was a little slower. It isn't every day one meets the Prime Minister.

CHAPTER TWO

Y our Lordship," the Guv said.

I wasn't sure his usage was correct. For some reason that no one has successfully explained to me, the Prime Minister was also the First Lord of the Treasury as well as the Foreign Secretary. The third Marquess of Salisbury, as he is called, was practically the British government all by himself.

I barely noticed the man behind the desk. I was looking at the rows of books behind him and feeling green with envy. I'd work there for nothing to lay hands on a volume every now and then. The cases were inset from floor to ceiling, each shelf stuffed haphazardly with books. There were no crockery or souvenirs, no honors or trinkets to spoil the view, just paper, paste-board, and leather. Unless they were inherited from the previous occupants of the building, they showed a keen mind. Inevitably there were legal and governmental books any politician might need, but there were also Greek classics, Dante, Adam Smith and David Hume, and a complete set of the novels of Disraeli, no doubt left behind by the author himself. I wanted to take down some of those volumes and sit in a chair unobserved, reading the day away. Unfortunately, that wasn't why we had been summoned.

Salisbury pulled a watch from the depths of his waistcoat and consulted it.

"Fifteen minutes," he said, as if he'd lost a bet.

"Sixteen," Barker said, consulting his own. "Your timepiece must be fast. I, on the other hand, was culpably slow."

"It was my fault, sir," I said to the Prime Minister. "I did not realize we were going into a tunnel. I don't perform well underground."

"You are Mr. Llewelyn, are you not?"

He had glanced at a piece of paper on his desk, one of thousands in stacks and piles fanned across the large expanse and spilling over onto a table nearby. The chamber smelled of tobacco. Cigars, I imagined. Dunhills. Only the best for our Prime Minister.

"I am, sir."

"Have a seat, gentlemen. We have much to discuss and very little time before my next appointment."

The Prime Minister wore a long beard, dark brown, laced with strands of silver. His eyes were gray, and his cheeks gaunt. He possessed one of those occupations that ages a man before his time. Did he have such strands of silver when he first accepted Her Majesty's request? I wondered.

"Grave" was the word that sprang to mind when I saw him in person. I could not determine if the work suited the man's natural solemnity, or if his temperament was bowed down by the sheer weight of the office he held. In either case, he would not be the sort to accept a flippant remark, which only made me want to make one all the more. Best to say as little as possible, lest such a remark slip from my lips unbidden.

"I imagined the task impossible, but you are here and so we must begin," he said. "Sit."

Barker and I slid into a pair of Chippendale chairs in front of his desk.

"How may we help you, sir?" Barker asked.

Salisbury sat back in his chair and scratched his forehead. I noted he was not currently parading the whole of Her Majesty's government before us.

"A Foreign Office man was found dead yesterday morning in Whitehall, not fifty yards from your door. Were you aware of this?"

"No, sir," Barker said.

"Pity," he replied, as if our not knowing it was a failure. "As I understand it, his body was taken to Scotland Yard, only a few steps away, where a key was found in his shoe. It was a railway locker key as it happened, and after the Foreign Office got wind of the matter they took over the operation and tracked the key to Charing Cross Station. There they found a satchel containing . . . well, never mind what it contained. The curious thing was that Whitehall Street was temporarily occupied by a dozen or more men in blue uniforms, for what purpose, I cannot say. Drummond, the agent, had just returned from somewhere. Germany, Austria-Hungary, Poland, possibly even Russia. The fellow was a good man, one of the Foreign Office's best, and he was a law unto himself, drifting here and there and sending regular and informative telegrams back to England. He arrived on the Dover Express. Some of those young men must have followed him from the train and killed him."

"How?" the Guv asked, keen as mustard. "By gun or knife?"

His nose was twitching, figuratively speaking, and I think he wished Salisbury were not being so cryptic.

"No, Mr. Barker. With a sword. Then he was run over by a cab."

The Guv had been sitting forward in his chair, but now he leaned back and brushed a hand over his long mustache with something almost resembling satisfaction.

"Eastern Europe, then. What country did he last visit?"

"We have no idea, sir," the Prime Minister admitted, eyeing my employer.

I'm sure he found Cyrus Barker interesting. Most people do.

"These men," my employer continued. "Did anyone get a proper description?"

"All we know at this time is that there were a number of men in blue coats and peaked caps. One witness said they were young."

"University lads, then."

"Perhaps," Salisbury said cautiously.

"May I assume you wish us to find these young men and their leader?"

"No, Mr. Barker. The Foreign Office will deal with that. I have a special assignment for you, if the two of you are up to the task."

"The item in the locker at Charing Cross Station," I said.

"Yes," the Prime Minister said, nodding. "We have the satchel and we need you to deliver it safely out of the country. Well, just barely. You will take it to Calais, where it will be handed over to someone else to take it out of harm's way."

"So, it is to be courier work, then," my senior partner said, his face falling. He did not like courier work. There is no one to grapple with and it's generally much ado about nothing. To be frank, he found the work beneath him.

"No, sir. The Home Office will make a show of carrying the satchel in which the package will be delivered. They will act as decoys. You will deliver the actual item yourself. In my opinion, our adversaries will be quick to spot the ruse and begin searching London. Already too many people know."

"That is why the key and the tunnel were necessary."

"Yes, Mr. Barker. I fear it is already too late. The worst has a way of happening."

"Your Excellency, we are a humble agency. We have but two men, perhaps four if I can muster them. You have the Foreign, the Home, and the Colonial Offices at your disposal. You have

Scotland Yard. You have the best army and navy in the world. Why would you choose us?"

"A private agency will be more difficult to spot than the more obvious government agencies. You are the last men they would expect."

One of the Guv's eyebrows peeked over the hill of his dark spectacles. "The last they would expect? Why, pray tell?"

"Because, sir, you would not be an agency our government would naturally choose. The commissioner of the Metropolitan Police despises you. You have a poor reputation among both the Home and Foreign Offices. Your methods are considered unorthodox, haphazard, and impulsive. Most of your cases end in bloodshed."

"I see."

"On the other hand, they admit you have a reputation for being successful in most of your endeavors and many detectives in London consider you worthy of respect; either that or they were leery of the secretive work we offered and suggested you instead. Somehow you manage to be both highly successful and a general risk at the same time."

"Which is exactly the sort of agency you were looking for."

"As you say."

Barker pushed his lower lip up into his mustache and his brows settled into the quartz spectacles again. "Interesting."

"I'm not certain we have the same interpretation of the word," Salisbury said. "Are you willing?"

"Perhaps. This package might be a bit of a problem. Can you be more specific?"

"I cannot."

"You must be able to say something about it. Is it alive and breathing? Tell me I am not delivering a dog of the King of Italy's favorite child."

The Prime Minister grunted, whether a chuckle or sound of annoyance I could not say. "I believe I can tell you with some degree of certainty that the package is not alive."

"Then I accept." He looked at me. "We do accept, do we not?"

"Of course," I said, knowing he had asked me out of politeness alone.

"Done, then."

"I suppose I should ask about our fee," I remarked.

Barker looked pained. He did not like to discuss fees.

"Our agency would not charge Her Majesty's government for our services," the Guv said. "It is our duty."

The Prime Minister was not prepared for such patriotism. He looked at Barker doubtfully, as if he were making a joke.

"Ah," he said. "That is very good of you."

"Not at all," my employer said.

I had read in *The Times* about Salisbury, one of the most pessimistic men in all London. He had such a strong belief that the world was sliding into inevitable chaos that his only work was to kill any reform bill in Parliament that might represent change or progress in any form. Even if he succeeded in all his endeavors, it would make no difference. Time stops for no man, even if he is a Conservative.

"May I ask if either of you is Catholic?" he asked.

"I was raised Methodist," I told him.

"And I am Baptist," Barker rumbled.

Our host scratched his balding head again. Perhaps he was thinking the Guv was not only unorthodox, he was nonconformist, as well.

"Can't be helped, I suppose. This may surprise you, gentlemen, but Europe is in trouble. Worse than trouble; it's crumbling. Russia, our old enemy, is slowly falling in upon itself for internal reasons, but the Germans are smelting any metal they can find into munitions. The young Kaiser, that little popinjay, is attempting to build an army and navy to threaten ours and if possible to capture some of our colonies in Africa. He may keep them, as far as I'm concerned. Damned nuisance, these little African countries, always fighting over something, or needing money best spent elsewhere. However, we took charge of them and now we cannot give them up without appearing weak. How did we find ourselves in this situation? Someone like Burton goes out in the jungle and discovers a tribe, then plants a flag in the ground for Her Majesty, and we are expected to pay for its upkeep until it becomes a modern, prosperous country, which it never shall!"

He coughed and frowned as if we had forced him to betray his own confidences.

"Where was I? Africa. No, not Africa, Germany! They are an association of ancient fiefdoms and vassal states loosely welded together by Bismarck. They all appear to work in concert, but that is merely how they present themselves to the world. Each of them wants to enjoy all the benefits of being a powerful country, but they want someone else to pay for it. They'll call themselves German if it suits them, but a Westphalian always considers himself a Westphalian."

"Do you think," Barker asked, "that Drummond's death was related to this?"

"No doubt. I despise spy work, but how else can one find the information? Purchasing it is far less reliable. It's a quandary, gentlemen, but then, all Europe is in a quandary these days. I have an ulcer paid for by Eastern Europe."

"Did you trust Drummond?"

The Prime Minister nodded his domed head. "He was among the Foreign Office's very best. He read history at Oxford, specializing in Eastern Europe. Learned all the languages. Wrote a brilliant paper on Chancellor Bismarck and the ramifications of unification. Apparently, he was a fine athlete, a three-quarter in rugby, and he could get on with practically everyone. The Foreign Office sent him east and found it was easier to give him his lead. Then he began sending information to us, either in letter form, or sometimes in code. It was like a treasure trove."

It was time to make Salisbury understand that I was not a silent partner.

"Was there any indication that Drummond's life was in danger or his position vulnerable?" I asked.

"Nothing from his missives."

"You sound as if you knew him," Barker said from his chair. His stiff limb was out in front of him, resting from being hurried along.

"His father was a dean when I was chancellor at Oxford. Clever lad. He left a wife and son. The only comfort one can derive is that he died on English soil and not in some godforsaken spot like Hungary where his widow would never recover his body."

"Does Her Majesty know about this matter?" the Guv asked.

Salisbury frowned. "Mr. Barker, I'm afraid that does not concern you."

"It might if Drummond came from Germany."

"You are speaking of the ties between Her Majesty and the German royal family?" Salisbury asked.

"I am, sir."

"Let us attempt to keep this case from royal ears, shall we, gentlemen?"

Salisbury pushed his chair back, bent down, and set a leather satchel on his desk. It was lumpy, stained, and scuffed. It had seen better days, but appeared to still offer good service or it would not be in use. Barker stood, as eager as a pointer.

"May I?" he asked, reaching for the satchel. The Prime Minister looked reluctant, leaning forward so that the handle was between his hands. Finally, he leaned back enough to let Barker examine it.

"Thomas, your notebook. Gladstone bag, approximately twelve by ten by ten. It is heavy. Three-quarters of a stone or more."

He raised it to his ear and listened as he moved it about. "I hear shifting. Is this package fragile?"

"It is," His Excellency admitted.

"We must be careful with it, then."

"Please do. Do you have any questions?"

"Several. To whom will I report?"

"To me, of course."

"Not the Home Office?"

"No. They shall not be involved in this matter."

"Do they know that we have the satchel?" I asked.

Salisbury leaned forward and clasped his hands on the top of the desk. His beard wagged just over them. "No."

Barker and I looked at each other with the same thought: *In a pig's eye*. None of the agencies mentioned had a reputation for being silent. They leaked like an old boat.

"When shall we meet you?" Barker said, continuing his last question.

"When the bloody package is delivered. I should think that was obvious."

"Your Excellency, may I not investigate this fellow's murder, as well?"

"We have the Foreign Office for that. They are quite keen to avenge the death of one of their own. I suppose once this package is delivered, you might aid them in the investigation, but that is a matter for them to decide."

Barker nodded, a trifle glumly. "What about Scotland Yard?"

"What about them?" The Prime Minister was starting to grow impatient.

"Were I to be arrested, for example, should I keep silent about this operation?"

"Why would you be arrested?"

"I have no idea," the Guv said, "the possibility exists."

Something was wrong here. Barker was pestering him with questions. That was the sort of thing I did.

"Well, don't let it."

"But what if—"

"Damn it, man! Just go about your duties. I don't care how you do them!"

"Yes, sir."

Then I saw one end of that thick black mustache go up just a fraction. It was the Guv's idea of a smile, but only about five people in London knew it.

You old devil, I thought.

"Mr. Barker, do you know what you are about? Are you prepared for this work?"

"I am, sir."

I wanted to warn the Prime Minister that this was not the way to speak to Cyrus Barker. Then I asked myself why I felt the need to protect Salisbury. He had insulted the agency. I owed him no allegiance at all.

The Prime Minister rose with finality. "There you are, then. Good luck. Deliver it as soon as possible. I believe a train leaves for Dover in an hour."

Barker lifted the bag from the desk and put it under his arm like a rugby ball and we turned to leave.

"Swithen!" Salisbury cried.

"Here, sir!" our guide said, stepping in the door, so close that I inferred that he must have been listening.

"Show these gentlemen out."

"The same way they came, sir?"

"Yes, yes!" Salisbury said, waving all of us away with the back of his hand. He turned and reached for another folder. We had been dismissed. We were led to the pantry door again without a word.

CHAPTER THREE

We made our way back through the tunnel. Now that I understood that it had a beginning, a middle, and an actual end, I was not as paralyzed with fear as before. Barker clutched the satchel in his hand as if weighing it, as if trying to work out what it was, as if the bag in his hands would help him decipher why he had been given this assignment. It is difficult to know what he is thinking. Perhaps he regretted taking the assignment.

Coming out of the house marked *Q*, we turned into the narrow alley that was Craig's Court. I looked about sharply. Was anyone suspicious looking? Were there youths in blue coats around? Did anyone notice the bag in the Guv's hand? Not so far, but we were headed toward Whitehall Street. Someone, or even a group of men, could step into the alleyway as we approached and face us, carrying anything from a dirk to a Martini-Henry rifle.

We were up to our noses in mufflers. The wind would cease for a moment as if waiting for someone to pass, then scurry along afterward like it was late for an appointment. Barker did not notice, taking all in stride: cold, heat, tempest, or flood. Even temperamental PMs.

Reaching the corner without danger to life and limb, we turned right and then right again into Cox and Co., Barker's bank. The building is heated by boiler and the warm air envelops one like a blanket as one enters. We had to stop while the condensation on my employer's spectacles dissipated. Then he turned away from the row of diligent tellers and began to ascend a wide staircase. I followed after.

When we reached the offices of Mr. Humphrey, the manager, the Guv turned and put a hand on my shoulder.

"Sit, Thomas. I need to speak to Mr. Humphrey privately."

I shrugged. He gripped the satchel tighter and a secretary took him in at once. Barker has a substantial amount in this bank so close to his offices. He also had money in a half-dozen other banks as well, but they need not know that.

I sat in the chair and attempted not to sulk. Some partner, eh? Forced to sit and wait like a truant boy? I removed my gloves and hat, scarf, and overcoat due to the heat. The latest issue of *Blackwood's Magazine* sat on a table in front of me, glossy and new. It provided no diversion. I detest *Blackwood's*.

I wondered why we'd come to Cox and Co. If the Guv was going to put the satchel in a private vault we couldn't very well take it to Calais. But then why carry it about, risking life and limb when it could sit snug and secure in a bank until the morning.

The wait took longer than expected. A half hour of precious time slipped away. I wondered if we would be back from Calais in time for dinner. There was still something strange about being separated from Rebecca for more than a few hours. It was like slow asphyxiation. Even then I was trying to create an excuse to see my wife before we left, in and around her social calls.

The Guv and Mr. Humphrey came out of the office shaking hands and promising some sort of fellowship that would never happen. There was no sign of the satchel, but Barker looked pleased with events.

"That's sorted, then," I said when he had finished. "Was it necessary to have me wait out here?"

"It was," he rumbled. "There was information discussed to which you are not privy. Also, I needed to know that anyone outside attempting to take the satchel would have to get by you first."

I suppose that my vanity was flattered a little, not that I would accept that as an excuse.

"Do you think someone could be that desperate?" I asked.

"A man is dead already. Shall we go?"

A few minutes later, we found our chambers much as we left them. Jeremy Jenkins was sitting at his desk in the outer office, but he was listing to one side, propped on an elbow. I passed into the office proper and pulled my Webley from a drawer of my roll-top desk. I opened it, saw that it was fully loaded, and put it in the waistband of my trousers against my spine. Barker nodded and filled his British-made Colt, setting it on the glass-topped desk in front of him. We sat. Then we both sighed.

"Was it the right decision?" I asked.

"To lock the case in the safe? Who can say, since I haven't fully worked out what's inside it."

"Haven't fully worked out?"

"Don't pester me with questions, Thomas. I need to think." He turned toward the door of the outer office and caught Jenkins's eye. "Jeremy, be certain you are fully armed. From now until the satchel is delivered, this office may be attacked at any moment."

"Yes, sir."

Jenkins opened a lower drawer and lifted a dusty pistol. It was an old Adams revolver, silver, with an octagonal barrel. I'd never seen it before, and I would bet a pound to a penny it hadn't been fired in a dog's years.

I was watching through the doorway. My desk was on the right as one entered; his was on the right as one exited. Now he turned and looked at me. The last he knew we had received a key, but he would not ask about the aforementioned parcel. I was to explain everything later.

Barker was already seated behind his desk. He was scratching the flesh under his chin, which he often did when deep in thought.

"When are we leaving for Dover, sir?" I asked.

He didn't answer. In fact, he didn't even verify that he had heard the question.

We all heard the outer door open, however. We jumped from our seats and reached for our pistols. The visitor had slipped into the office so quietly, so smoothly, he was like a swimmer slipping off a ledge into a pool. He was perhaps five-and-thirty, slender, clean shaven, lank haired, and bland. He nodded at Jenkins as if he'd been in our chambers a dozen times, and we were mates, but we'd never met him. He walked past our clerk and came to a stop only when he met the heavy solidity of Barker's desk. There, he bowed his head gravely, like an actor at curtain call. He somehow knew that Barker preferred not to shake hands.

"Home or Foreign Office?" Barker rumbled from the depths of his chair.

"Home," came the reply. "Hesketh Pierce, at your service."

The Guv reached out a palm, offering him a chair in a way I have always considered a remnant of his days in China. Pierce sat. That is, he receded into a chair. He glanced over his shoulder and nodded and so did I.

"So, we are to work together, then," Pierce said.

"To be more precise, separately, but parallel," Barker responded. "Did you take precautions not to be seen?"

"I did. No one saw me enter."

"Not even someone in the Silver Cross?"

"I just came from there. I was waiting for you."

The Silver Cross was a public house on the south corner of Craig's Court. The windows wrapped around the corner and into our alleyway, so that one can get a view from the closest chair of our door across the street.

"We were a foregone conclusion, then," I said.

"You were—Mr. Llewelyn, is it?"

"Yes, Mr. Pierce. How did you come to know about our involvement? I thought it was a secret."

"Scotland Yard told us. Am I interrupting your work?"

"No," Barker replied. "How may I help you?"

"I wanted to know; that is, I need to know what hour you shall be leaving for Dover tonight. I have to prepare my men. I considered taking the same express, but I didn't wish to disturb your operation."

"That is very kind of you, Mr. Pierce."

"I see no reason why we should be antagonistic toward each other, especially since our association will only last a few hours. What time do you intend to leave? It might be useful to join with the crowds of workers returning to Kent at five, but there are challenges, as well."

Barker cleared his throat and stood. He crossed to his smoking cabinet, chose a pipe and began stuffing it with his own blend from a wooden jar. He looked over his shoulder.

"Oh, I certainly don't intend to start today. There is plenty of time."

For a moment, Pierce's urbane mask slipped. His eyes started from his head. However, he recovered quickly. Quicker than I did.

"I hope you know what you're doing, Mr. Barker. I believe the Prime Minister asked you to take it tonight. That was what I heard he told you."

"He suggested it," Barker said between puffs, the flame reflected in his quartz spectacles. "However, he told me I could handle it as I please. Did he not, Mr. Llewelyn?"

"Yes, sir," I said.

What are you up to, Barker? I thought to myself. Did you pull that caveat out of Salisbury in order to give yourself space to maneuver?

"I think it unlikely that the Vatican is champing at the bit just yet."

"No," Pierce countered, "but Monsignor Bello will be waiting."

"I am not particularly concerned with how the Jesuits feel. Calais is a lovely port. Let them enjoy the wine, at least."

Wait, what's going on? I asked myself. The Vatican? Jesuits? Neither had come up in the conversation with the Prime Minister.

"The satchel is safe, then?" Pierce asked, shifting in his chair and taking in the room with a casual glance that I was certain was not casual in the least.

"You saw me take it to Cox and Co. from the first floor of the Silver Cross. It is secured in the vault as we speak. No German spies or young men in blue coats could penetrate those walls under any conditions."

"You were in there awhile, Mr. Barker."

The Guv shrugged his burly shoulders. "Mr. Humphrey is an old friend of ours and a naturally gregarious fellow. The exchange between us was brief for one who knows him."

Stuff and nonsense, I thought. Humphrey is as dry as a British Museum mummy and as friendly as a wounded badger. Also, we hadn't known the fellow for more than a year.

"Will you keep it there?" the Home Office man asked. "For tonight, I mean? I'd like to know it is safe."

"Pray tell me your exact duties, Mr. Pierce. I was told you would provide a diversion so that Mr. Llewelyn and I might deliver the satchel. Now you seem to want to safeguard it."

"It should be everyone's duty to safeguard it."

"Perhaps." A smoke ring rose to the ceiling, growing larger until it came apart. "Meanwhile, who is investigating the murder of Hillary Drummond? Scotland Yard?"

Pierce gave a discreet chuckle at the thought. He pulled a cigarette from a silver case and lit a wax vesta with his thumbnail.

"Hardly. Don't get me wrong. The Yard is the best in the world at what they do. Spying is something else entirely."

"Is it you?" my employer asked. "Are you the investigating officer?"

"No, I'm merely the diversion."

The Guv lifted a knee and sat on the corner of his desk. "You a diversion and I a courier. This is not proper work for gentlemen. Do you know who is in charge of the investigation?"

"Of course, but I am not at liberty to give his name."

"A pity. I'd have liked to bring the murderer of one of our best agents to account. He was a competent spy, was he not?"

"Drummond?" Pierce asked. "Top-drawer. A good man. He was Foreign Office, of course, but we muck in together when we can."

"Tell me more about him. I'm trying to work out what I can secondhand, you see. Would you say he was the best agent in Eastern Europe?"

The Home Office man sucked the smoke of his cigarette up into his nostrils before blowing it out again, and lifted his chin in thought.

"I'm not close enough to know where Foreign Office spies are based, but the fact that he was itinerant is a sign that they trusted him fully. You know, they don't like you over there at the Foreign Office. Apparently, you discredited one of their best."

"Are you speaking of Trelawney Campbell-Ffinch?" I interjected. "Is that actually one of their best? The mind reels!"

A year before we were instrumental in exiling Ffinch to the far reaches of India.

"Anyway, I was surprised to discover on the plaque on the door that your given name is Cyrus. All I've ever heard is 'Bloody Barker.'"

"I don't take cases some agencies would, and I do take some that others would not. I don't have enough associates to protect the rest of the country, but I care what happens in my own back pocket. Foreign agents stabbing an operative at my front door unsettles me."

"I don't think they took you into account," Pierce said.

"They will by the end of this, I assure you," my employer responded.

"What are you going to do? Sit here on your heels? Hunt about all over London for young men in blue coats?"

"Who can say?" my employer replied. "I might poke a stick into some hornets' nests and see what comes out."

"Since you have nothing else to do," Pierce said. "Just a satchel to deliver to the South Coast."

"Exactly."

"Child's play."

"Amateur work."

"You could do it anytime."

"Aye."

"But you're not," the Home Office man said.

"Not today, no."

"Because?"

"The stars are not aligned," I guessed.

Barker nodded.

"Tell me," Pierce said. "Is it because you want to find the beggars who killed Drummond? You want to investigate?"

Barker dug around in the bowl of his pipe with a small tool he kept in the ashtray on his desk. "If I have time. It would be helpful to have a list of possible suspects, as an exercise, you understand."

The laugh came out of Pierce's throat so fast he was not prepared for it.

"You've got brass, Cyrus Barker, I'll give you that," he said. "So I'm supposed to help you with a list out of the goodness of my heart and without the sanction of my superiors?"

"Aye, that would do."

"In exchange for what? You're an interesting fellow, I'll agree, but I'm not in a position to offer you anything, even if I had it."

Barker nodded sympathetically.

"What do you need?" the Guv asked.

"The satchel would be nice. This scheme to act as a decoy is rather beneath our skills."

Barker almost smiled. His brows rose above the rim of his spectacles and settled down again like a brief eclipse.

"A tall order. I could be left with nothing. However, I will consider it."

"We could protect it better and leave you free to investigate the murder of Drummond, which is your forte."

"Am I speaking to the Home Office now, or Hesketh Pierce? Will you report everything I say to your superiors?"

"I will," he admitted. "I'll repeat every word. That does not mean I will do so tonight."

Barker turned over his pipe and tapped it on top of the cork plug in the center of the ashtray. Fine ash poured out. He considers dottles an affront to his smoking abilities.

"I couldn't do what you do," he told Pierce.

"Work as a spy?"

"No, work for a superior who has a superior, who has one of his own."

"It is not necessarily a choice," Pierce remarked. "Some of us are not independently wealthy."

"Ha!" I laughed. "Strike me for a fool if you're not an earl's son. I know a tab when I see one."

"Very well, Mr. Llewelyn, my father is a baronet, but I'm the third son. No one will be offering me the family seat anytime soon, and even if they did it's probably in debt." Pierce rose effortlessly to his feet. "Anyway, you are now working for a superior who has a superior. In fact, Salisbury has thousands of them."

Barker looked amused. "So I am, Mr. Pierce. At least for the present. If you could get me that list, I would be in your debt. Good day."

The Home Office man nodded to us and left.

"So much for anonymity," I said. "We should not trust him."

"Agreed. What, pray tell, is a 'tab'?"

"A Cambridge man, sir. I am an Oxonian and he is a Cantabrigian. The enemy, so to speak, at least during the annual boat race. 'Tab' is a shortened version of the name."

"The things you know, Thomas!"

"Yes, well, the more I know, the more I know how little I know."

"'Happy is the man that findeth wisdom.' Proverbs 3:13."

"He was an interesting fellow, Pierce. Very urbane. Professional."

"Indeed."

"What was that about the Vatican?" I asked. "The Prime Minister didn't mention it. I'd have remembered if he had."

"I inferred it. If the satchel contains sheets of glass, it can only mean one of two things, as far as I can deduce. It could be some sort of bacillus, and if so we shall both be dead by morning, or it is something of significance to the Church, perhaps a manuscript. I thought it more likely to be the latter. If so, the most obvious destination for it would be the Vatican Library."

"Why not Paris?" I asked.

"If it were a matter of erudition, the manuscript could have stayed in England, but if it required preservation, I don't believe the Vatican can be bested. My opinion is based on reputation, of course."

"But why would the Church of England give a manuscript to the Roman Catholic Church?"

"That's a good question, lad. Another is whether the purpose is to get it to Rome or simply to get it out of England. Drummond was chased here. There is bound to be political intrigue."

"I hate politics," I said.

"Courier work is not why I became an enquiry agent, either, but it is the only duty we have been offered today, and we must go where the work is available."

"The Jesuits! How did you know about the Jesuits?"

Barker put a booted foot on the corner of his desk and rested his hands on his stomach.

"For the most part," he answered, "the Jesuits are no longer the steel gauntlet of the Roman Catholic Church, but with work such as this on an international scale, the Vatican would choose a Jesuit."

Having no convenient response to that, I attempted to look wise.

"The Vatican, then," I repeated.

"Aye, lad. The Vatican."

CHAPTER FOUR

I hailed a cab and Barker told the cabman to take us to Soho and the Café Royal. From past experience, I knew that meant two things, both of which I approved: we were going to see an old friend, Pollock Forbes, who haunted the place, and we would have an excellent lunch. There was no better restaurant in all London save for Etienne's Le Toison d'Or.

The café was bustling when we entered and the eighteen waiters in their tuxedo jackets and floor-length white aprons were doing battle with a roomful of hungry souls, many of them celebrities. Oscar Wilde was no longer there, but the decadent artist Aubrey Beardsley sat at a table with his knees up, sketching the general chaos. I heard rather than saw the Irishman Bernard Shaw being disputative somewhere in the back of the room, and I waved at the bon vivant Max Beerbohm as we entered, his black hair as glossy as a billiard ball. If Cyrus Barker were not there to keep me in line, I was in danger of becoming one of the overly intellectual and underpaid writers who frequented the place. Thank heaven he came along when he did.

Barker looked about the room, such a dour fellow he could suck the very bonhomie from the place, but we dined here a few times a year. It was a storehouse of information and there was a Masonic temple in the back.

"Langer!" the Guv rumbled in that way he has that makes the floor shake. A man detached himself from a corner and came our way. He wore a double-breasted suit and had a mustache so thin it was like another eyebrow.

"Hello, Barker," the man said, looking about as if the restaurant were about to erupt in a brawl, which it might. Langer was the private detective, bailiff, and chucker-out for Nicholson, the owner of the Royal.

"Where is Forbes?" Barker asked.

"Hasn't been here in a fortnight."

"Why not?"

"Under the weather, I've heard."

"Is he still at the Albany?"

"Yes, he is, sir."

"What room?"

"Fourteen, I think."

"Thank you. Come, lad. Lunch will have to wait."

My stomach tried to disagree. A fellow near me was tucking into a dozen seasoned oysters and a woman across from him was spooning some sort of chocolate cake between her pouty lips. Barker's ham-sized hand had to pull me out the door by the arm.

The Guv had paid the driver to remain and we clambered aboard once more. My stomach groaned as we pulled away from the curb. There would be other lunches, I told myself. Someday.

"You're worried," I said, reading his face.

"I am," he replied. "It's not like Pollock to be absent for a day, let alone an entire fortnight. Where is the flow of information going? We need to speak to him if we are to stay ahead of what is happening."

Pollock Forbes was a Scottish laird's son who was expected to inherit the title. Unfortunately, he was tubercular. While giving the appearance of being another wastrel of the Royal, he collected information in droves from dozens of informants: political news, Continental news, town gossip, and even scandal. Everything was fodder for his ample brain. Forbes was the leader of the Knights Templar, an organization so secret that its members almost never met. All information was channeled through him.

We soon arrived at the Albany, a series of flats in Piccadilly for gentlemen of a certain class; that is, unmarried and wealthy. Forbes himself would have called it "toney." It was full of its own importance. The Albany was known for the names of certain bachelors who lived there, such as Forbes. Everyone there had their reputations lifted merely by belonging.

Barker crossed to a solid-looking concierge and they exchanged handshakes. It was the second one I'd seen him do that day. As I said, Barker does not care to shake hands. He expects to be attacked at any moment as a matter of course, and his hands must be free. However, this was not a mere handshake. It was a secret one, establishing identity. Without another word, we made our way up a stairwell and eventually to a door with the number 14 in gold upon it. Barker tapped, which is to say he practically knocked it down in one blow.

The door was opened by a harried-looking young man in a black waistcoat and shirtsleeves. The sleeves had been rolled to the elbow and he held a wicker dustbin in his hands. He scrutinized us as he ran the back of his hand across his damp forehead.

"May I help you, gentlemen?" he asked.

"I'm here to see Pollock," my employer said, proffering the business card he pulled from his waistcoat.

The young man glanced at it, then nodded.

"Come in. He should be awake. But pray, sirs, do not tax him. He is very ill."

We were led into the bedchamber. Pollock Forbes lay in the center of a large bed, bolstered with several pillows. He wore a white nightshirt and the scale of everything made it seem as if he were a mere child with a case of catarrh. Only it wasn't catarrh at all, it was consumption, and it was consuming Pollock inch by inch.

"Hello, Cyrus," he croaked. "Thomas. Thank you for coming to see me."

"Pollock," I said. "You didn't tell us."

Forbes shifted in his pillows. "Mustn't grumble."

The servant, or whatever he was, gave me a stern look and went to empty the bin. I saw it was full of pocket handkerchiefs, most of them spattered with blood. He's dying, I told myself.

"I've been offered a certain important case," Barker said. "By chance, did you make the suggestion?"

"I may have told a fellow, who told a fellow. You accepted the assignment, I take it?"

Barker did not answer. He appeared to be annoyed. "Whose idea was it to set up the Home Office as a ruse so that we could deliver the satchel ourselves?"

"Mine, I'm afraid," Forbes said. "I had intended to take it myself, but alas, I am undone. I suggested you go in my stead."

The young man returned with the emptied bin and Forbes immediately tossed another soiled handkerchief into it. The servant frowned at us. We were disturbing the patient.

"What can I do for you?" Forbes continued. "I assume you came for something."

"I need a list of people likely to go after the satchel, but you're in no fit state to give it, Pollock. We'll look elsewhere. There's no need to trouble yourself. Get well, and we'll see you at the Royal in a fortnight."

Pollock coughed and spat a gob of blood into a new handkerchief.

"I'm not going back, Cyrus. My doctor has ordered me to Aberdeen. If I'm not any better, soon it's the Sandwich Islands for me. Or Fiji. You know what that means, don't you?"

The Guv and I looked at each other, thinking the same thing. Was he referring to his death?

"You're being uncommonly thick, both of you. I thought you were private enquiry agents."

For once, I actually worked it out first.

"You're leaving," I said. "Who's going to take over the Knights Templar?"

"That is precisely the problem. Cyrus, I need you to take over the running of the society."

"You have said that to me on several occasions," Barker answered. "Why would you think me a proper candidate? Surely there are others more qualified."

"Qualifications do not necessarily make a good leader." Forbes coughed again, bringing the young man running, but he recovered. His voice grew weaker and weaker. "Cyrus, you must belong to a dozen secret societies, from the Heaven and Earth society in China to the Freemasons."

"Yes, but I don't attend meetings," he replied. "I belong neither to be a student of esoterica nor to do good for society. I do both of those already on my own. The last thing I want is to spend my precious evening hours raising a herd of solicitors and bankers from one degree to the next through an elaborate initiation rite, merely to impress their employers. I want to do things that matter with my life. You know I don't believe in rituals. If I did, I'd become Church of England."

"But think, Cyrus," Forbes went on. "Imagine a flood of secret information arriving from all London into your office; pertinent facts coming every hour!"

"But at what cost?" Barker asked. "I barely have enough time to teach my own antagonistics class as it is. How am I to run an agency and handle all of this information?"

Forbes settled back in his pillows. His wavy hair was damp, his face shiny. His lungs must have been saturated. It hurt to watch him struggle for breath. I didn't have a great number of friends on this earth, but I considered Forbes one of them. I didn't want to lose him.

"You can't."

Barker gave him a withering stare. "You expect me to shut down the agency?"

"No. I expect you to give it to Thomas. You put his name on the door. Congratulations, by the way."

"Thank you," I replied.

"You expect Thomas to look after the agency's cases while I do what, exactly? Sit at a desk every day reading memoranda? London already has a spymaster general."

"Not forever. I could put in a good word for you. My opinion is still respected in this town."

"Don't do so on my account. It isn't a situation I seek."

"Cyrus, let's face it. You're not twenty-five anymore. Or forty. Your leg is in a brace. I imagine you don't heal as quickly as you once did."

"I'm perfectly capable of doing my work, thank you! I get about as I have always done. A little slower for the moment, perhaps, but my bones will knit together again."

From his pillow, Forbes contrived to press him. "How would you like to be able to plan your life for a change, like other mortals? You could go home at a decent hour, and not work past midnight, as you so often do."

I shook my head at him. That wasn't the way to convince the Guv. He liked working past midnight. Pollock caught my signal and nodded. He tried a different tack.

"You'd be doing important work, as well, work you are uniquely suited for. It's the next logical step in your development. We need, our country needs, your expertise. There are important events occurring just now. Many of them concern Germany, which is quickly becoming England's chief rival. Do you really want me to hand such delicate information to another man, a less competent one, merely because he rose through the ranks and it is his turn? Don't make me do that!"

The young man came into the room again. He put his hands on his hips.

"Pollock," he said.

Forbes waved him away. "I'm all right, Charles. Let me alone. This is important."

"So is your health."

"You need not be chained to a desk, if that is what concerns you," he said, turning back to my employer. "You may make your own rules. I chose the Café Royal because I liked it. It became my workplace. You could work out of your antagonistics class, if you wish."

Pollock kept glancing at me, hoping I would encourage Barker to accept, but he did not know what he was asking. Helping Forbes in this endeavor would be tantamount to treachery in the Guv's mind. It was difficult enough that I might have opinions of my own, but to try to change his was unthinkable. I shook my head. Pollock would have to convince him alone.

"The work is not as onerous as it sounds," he continued. "Thomas here can help."

"He's not a Templar," Barker countered. "He's not even a Mason."

"Then make him one."

"I'm sorry, Pollock," I said, "but I have to agree with the Guv. I'm a married man now and too busy to attend meetings or be initiated into arcane secret societies with all-seeing eyes."

"We can work that out," Forbes croaked. He was almost panting. "Actually, you can work it out yourselves. I don't care. Whatever works for you will suit me. Or rather, us."

"You say 'us,'" Barker said. "How many is 'us'?"

Forbes mopped his forehead with a clean handkerchief. There was a great stack of them on his night table, as well as the bloodied wicker basket to drop them into.

"We have a hundred members in Her Majesty's army, at least. More from the navy. I suppose we could muster an army of our own. There are politicians, MPs, clerks, barristers, bankers. We've even got a Yeoman Warder or two. We both know you could never be in an organization with a leader you do not respect. Neither would most of the other members. You have a reputation in this town."

"Pollock, do not exert yourself," Barker told him.

"I do not ask you to say yes today. Just promise me you will not say no until you have time to consider the matter. I leave in a few days. Surely you can decide by then."

Barker grunted to himself and then finally spoke. "Very well. I would not consider it for anyone else in the world, but you are a friend."

"Charles!" Forbes cried, tossing pillows off the side of the bed.

"Yes?" the man said, returning to the room.

"I'm going to take a kip. Show the gentlemen out."

Charles waved a hand toward the entrance. We followed him. Then the door was shut in our faces.

"What have I got myself into?" Barker muttered to the door.

"No," I said, staring at the brass number. "What have we gotten ourselves into?"

The cabman was still waiting when we returned. There was snow on his hat and greatcoat, and on the back of the piebald gelding in front of him. Such conditions would send most jarveys back to their stables quickly. It helped that Barker had a reputation for being a generous customer.

"Where to, Push?" he asked.

"Carlisle Place, Westminster!" the Guv bellowed in my ear.

I would not ask. I promised myself I would not ask.

"What's in Carlisle Place?"

"The archbishop's house."

"What archbishop?"

"Keep up, Thomas! There are only two archbishops in England and we are not in Canterbury."

CHAPTER FIVE

I don't want Pollock to die," I said to my employer as we climbed
into the hansom. "He's always been a good friend. He never
got married and never traveled far. He only ran an organization that no one has ever heard of."

"There is a reason it is unheard of. The Templars are necessary, Thomas. There is a flow of information that moves about
London that needs to be sieved through the minds of certain individuals, to make correct decisions, to speak with the right members of Parliament, to take action."

"But not Pollock anymore."

"None of us are promised our full threescore and ten. It is a
hostile world in which we live."

"It isn't fair."

"No, it isn't. Fair is a concept that has no meaning here. There
is no system of checks and balances here."

"Thank you. I think I prefer comfort to common sense."

"Do not we all, lad?"

We sat with our own thoughts for the rest of the journey. Carlisle Place looked as if someone had broken off a piece of Westminster Abbey and set it down a few streets away. It could have been ancient, or it could have been finished last week and carefully aged. That happened these days.

We alighted from the cab and a no-nonsense cleric met us at the front door, inspected our card, and led us from the entrance. We walked past statues of unidentifiable apostles and gold filigree crosses. The Guv looked askance at such lavish adornment. The cleric was too sedate, and I missed the winged feet of Swithen from Downing Street again. Finally, we came to a pair of ornate doors and he stopped us. He stepped inside with the door slightly ajar and I heard the murmur of low conversation. Then we were led in.

The man sitting in the center of the room was recognizable to anyone in the world who ever read a newspaper. He was draped in a caped robe and a skullcap, both in a shade of scarlet so bright that it picked up light from the window behind him until it almost glowed. It was Manning, Cardinal Manning, the Archbishop of Westminster, the highest-ranked Roman Catholic leader in all Britain. Everyone had heard his story, how he'd graduated from Balliol College and quickly begun to climb the rungs of Anglican ecclesiastical success. He would certainly have been Archbishop of Canterbury by now if he hadn't gotten into a quibble with the Church of England over some matter and suddenly cast off not only his position but the Church entirely, causing a public sensation when he joined the Roman Catholic Church. His career rose as swiftly among the Roman clergy from position to position until he became the Archbishop of Westminster. The same rank, but a different church entirely.

Of course, I'd seen etchings and photographs of him, but I was not prepared for the man himself. He looked like every sketch of Virgil I'd ever seen. His brow and crown were huge, as if he were carrying about the largest brain in Christendom. His eyes were steel blue, his face so ascetic as to make one imagine him living in a monkish cell, subsisting on a single cup of gruel per day.

"Come, gentlemen," he said in a reedy voice. "Sit, sit, by all means. I have a busy schedule today, but nothing is more important than this. Have you taken possession of the satchel?"

"I have," the Guv replied.

The archbishop placed an arthritic hand on the edge of his chair. "I trust the Prime Minister has not revealed to you what is inside."

"He has not."

"I should prefer that it stay that way."

Barker nodded and then tilted his head back in thought and shook it instead. "Nay, sir, you cannot ask that of me. I will be sending my partner and myself into mortal danger. I might risk it myself, but I would not ask it of him, who might leave his young bride a widow."

"I'm sorry, Mr. Barker, that is private information that belongs solely to the Roman Catholic Church."

"Then I would have to decline the request to convey the satchel to its destination."

The archbishop gave a wan smile. "It was worth the attempt. You must understand, this valise contains something that has historical and religious significance of the highest order. It is vital that it reach Rome quickly. I was awake all night discussing matters with the Archbishop of Canterbury. At first we considered keeping it at the Bodleian, but they have neither the security nor the knowledge of how to care for such a treasure."

"But the Vatican does," Barker murmured.

My mind tried to conjure what kind of manuscript could have such significance. Letters from Martin Luther perhaps? The original Book of Kells? More likely anti-popish doggerel. That was the kind of thing coming out of Eastern Europe these days.

"You are correct, sir. The precise ownership is in question at the moment, but Her Majesty's government is lending it on a near permanent basis to the Vatican archives."

"That is very wise, I'm sure," Barker said. "I will still need to know what it is."

The archbishop raised a hand.

"In good time. You should know, if you don't already, that there has arisen a certain national pride in countries to the east of here. Take Germany, for example, or Austria-Hungary, those states that once erroneously called themselves the 'Holy Roman Empire' until the Habsburgs lost power. Along with this growing conservative patriotism has arisen anti-Catholic sentiment. Children are teased in the schoolyard by both teachers and students. Young men are beaten and women assaulted. Openly wearing a rosary can get an old woman spat upon in the street, even by people she had known for decades. Parishioners are told to go home when in fact their ancestors have lived in the same village for hundreds of years, often longer than their neighbors."

"I have heard something of this, Your Eminence," Barker said. "Pray continue."

I had my notebook in my lap and had been scribbling notes. The archbishop looked quizzically at the page.

"Pitman shorthand," I explained, a trifle embarrassed.

"Ah. Yes. Where was I? The Germans want to expel Jews, gypsies, and other refugees from their borders, as well. Politicians pound podiums and curry favor with the common people, while preachers spew vitriol from the pulpit in order to stir the crowd against their old enemy, the Roman Catholic Church. Our buildings are being vandalized and our numbers dwindle.

"You must understand, Mr. Barker. England has its Rosetta Stone with its pride of place in the British Museum. Paris has its Moabite Stone in the Louvre. Berlin? Vienna? Their museums are still empty. They have made exorbitant purchases that proved to be fake. They have sent expeditions that found mere trinkets and pottery shards. A major find would justify their positions as premier countries in the world. Not to have one is an embarrassment. This, gentlemen, this was their major find. Somehow, Mr. Drummond snatched it from their hands and ran. Whoever lost it must be near mad with frustration. Not only was it taken, but by an Englishman. That must rankle most of all."

Barker had listened patiently to the archbishop's story. Old men are often long-winded. Now he leaned forward eagerly, and perhaps with a little annoyance.

"Your Eminence, what am I guarding?"

"Must you know, sir?"

"I fear I must."

"For the last time," Manning said. "Can it not be prevented? In its way, it is a terrible secret."

Barker stood. "Sir, I fear we are not the men for this assignment. I cannot work under such circumstances. Come, Thomas."

We were halfway to the door when we were called back.

"Gentlemen, wait," the archbishop said.

"You must either trust us, sir, or not trust us," the Guv said, with his hand on the door. "You cannot do both."

"Yes, yes. You are correct, Mr. Barker. Trust you, I must. Very well. It is a manuscript. A very old one. It is held in the satchel between plates of glass."

"How old?" the Guv asked.

"As near as we can ascertain, the first century."

Barker's brows rose above the rims of his black-lensed spectacles. He was surprised, and not much surprises him.

"The first century? Not the second?"

"Yes."

"Is it a gospel?" Barker continued.

"It is."

My partner resettled himself in the chair. "Which one?"

"It is a fifth gospel," the archbishop replied.

Cyrus Barker grunted in frustration. "Apocrypha, then."

"Actually, no. For the last fifty years, German scholars have speculated that Luke and Matthew drew events from both Mark and an unknown source, one as old as Mark, which many consider the first written gospel."

"To whom is it attributed?"

"There is no name implied in the text. The Archbishop and I simply called it the 'Alpha Gospel.'"

"That would make it the Epsilon Gospel," I said. "The name implies that this is actually the first gospel."

"Historically, it may be so."

Barker grunted again. "So this is what the Foreign Office agent was carrying that got him killed."

"Yes, it was. The young fellow was very rash, stealing the manuscript and bringing it here at the cost of his own life. Brave, perhaps, but rash. He had a family."

"Who is trying to retrieve the manuscript? Is it the Germans, then?"

"We don't know," Manning replied. "Mr. Drummond was quite a traveler. Moscow to Bern was his territory, or so I've been told. It could be any one of a half-dozen countries, and in those countries are dozens of states that were countries themselves in recent memory. It would be more difficult to work out how this satchel arrived here than to deliver it safely to the Continent."

"Your Excellency," Barker said. "I hardly think the gospel would be any safer there, though I admit the Vatican archives have a fine reputation for security."

"Mr. Barker, I must disagree. A man was killed yesterday trying to safeguard the manuscript. I fear he will not be the last. You were chosen because the size of your agency is small. You might slip through a net spread wide enough to catch the Home Office. At Calais, the Jesuits will take possession of the satchel."

"How many Jesuits will it take to replace us?"

The Archbishop of Westminster actually chuckled.

"Ten or so, I should imagine. You will meet Monsignor Bello in Calais."

"I look forward to that," the Guv replied. "Will the manuscript be studied or merely hidden away?"

The old man took the edge of his chair and pulled himself forward.

"That," he said, "is a very canny question. I wish I could give you an equally canny answer. Only time will tell."

"Is it possible that the manuscript is a forgery?" the Guv continued, not willing to be put off.

"There is always that possibility. We deal in forgeries every year. However, why create an unknown and controversial manuscript if a copy of one of the four gospels could earn more money?"

"It might not be about money," Barker said. "However, I am just speculating. One can speculate all day."

"You are correct, Mr. Barker. I do it often."

"Your Eminence, may I ask what you think? I am a humble layman. I know the Good Book, but I cannot parse it in Greek or Aramaic. What say you? I assume you read it yourself. Do you believe it is real?"

"I have not made up my mind, I'm afraid. I wish I could. The Alpha Gospel does indeed have verses quoted in both Matthew and Luke, as well as one or the other. You understand, Matthew was writing to the Jews and Luke to the Gentiles. Yet both borrowed from this unknown author. It is maddening. Suppose it is genuine—just suppose. Who wrote it? One cannot say Matthew, Mark, Luke, John, and an unknown author. If this information is released, and I'm not quite sure it ever shall be, there will be consternation among the clergy. Was it John? The Apostle, that is, not John of Patmos. Was it Thomas or Peter? James, the brother of Jesus, is a likely candidate. I've heard references to a lost Gospel of Lazarus. The problem is there is nothing obvious in the manuscript to show who wrote it. It could be Mary Magdalene! That would turn a few bishops I know red-faced."

"What else was in the manuscript?" Barker asked. "Besides the quotes by Matthew and Luke?"

The archbishop settled back. His feet were too far from a footstool nearby, so I pushed it closer.

"Thank you, young man. Let me see. There were not many miracles in the book, which was no more than eighteen pages in length. There were no terms like 'Son of Man,' but Christ proclaimed himself the Son of God and made reference to prophecies in the Old Testament. If there was anything evident in the text it was that Jesus knew what kind of changes he was bringing to the world."

Barker nodded, clearly enthralled.

"I will say this to the manuscript's detriment," the archbishop continued. "It does not change one's view of the Lord. One does not come away feeling one has had a profound experience. Matthew and Luke lifted the best of the sayings. There was some overlapping with Mark, as well as some Gnostic gospels. One could theorize that this was one of the books considered in Nicaea that was not accepted into the New Testament, and it then fell out of favor until it was forgotten. It is good, but it will not win souls in the far reaches of Assam or Amazonia. Not by itself, anyway."

"A pity," the Guv said.

"For the Christian actively seeking the face of God, however, there is a turn of phrase or two and some new verses that make one feel that the anonymous author actually knew Jesus."

"How old would you say the manuscript is? I know you said it was first century, but how late? The nineties? The seventies? Earlier?"

"It is certainly very old, but we have had only a day to examine it. We are as frustrated as you seem to be, Mr. Barker. Were I to guess, and really, it is no more than a guess, I would say either late eighties to mid-nineties, possibly even earlier. The Archbishop of Canterbury agrees."

"Very early, indeed," I said.

"Quite."

The Guv looked grave, even moved.

"Take the case, Mr. Barker. It's kept an old man awake forty hours. Let the Holy Fathers in Rome puzzle over it for a while."

Barker started to rise, but His Eminence's hand came down upon his and he prayed over us in Latin. It took a few minutes. In the middle of leaning forward, the Guv found himself in a difficult position, literally. He dared not move during the prayer, so he sat with one hand on the back of the chair and the other clasping the archbishop's. The old man eventually wound down and we were able to depart.

"Protect it, Mr. Barker," the old man said. "Protect it with your life. I prayed for courage and wisdom for you. I suspect you may need both."

CHAPTER SIX

After we returned to our chambers, Barker spent a good part of an hour on the telephone set arguing loudly with someone in Cantonese or Mandarin. It might have been a full-blown dispute, or not. For a nonspeaker, it is difficult to tell.

Six o'clock arrived. We gathered our sticks and hats and went home. All I could think of was seeing Rebecca's face again. Her smile was everything. A downcast look would make me do whatever was necessary to lift it again. I still pinched myself that this woman, this prize, had decided against common sense and most of the Jewish East End to become my wife.

It wouldn't do to be seen giving her a resounding kiss in the front hall, and anyway, she was in the kitchen with Mac. He was teaching her the process whereby the meal begun by Etienne Dummolard in the morning reached our table hot and freshly prepared at dinner. Some of the food was kept in the icebox ready to cook, some simmered for hours on a low flame, while salads were prepared with fresh ingredients from a small greenhouse and the kitchen garden behind the house. I told Rebecca she need not go to the trouble, that Mac had done everything for years, but she said she wanted to learn herself. She said it was "wifely," whatever that means.

"Hello!" I said, putting my head into the kitchen.

That smile bloomed immediately. Mac evaporated in that way he has. He is very sensitive to moods. I gave her the kiss I promised myself and hugged her.

"I missed you," she murmured, brushing back a black curl that had escaped her knot of hair. "Did you miss me?"

"My dear, you have no idea."

Barker took himself off as soon as he entered, muttering a word under his breath: "Mensurites." I wondered if we would take the satchel to Calais tomorrow. He did not seem to be in much of a hurry. After several years, I have learned both to not ask questions and to act as if I knew all along when he decides to reveal a plan.

Dinner was served, beef Wellington with roasted potatoes and cauliflower. Barker did not speak of the case at all, as if nothing of interest had occurred that day. He ate and rarely spoke. Rebecca was still studying my employer's foibles, and one was that he rarely compliments or complains about a meal unless pressed. In her presence, I could not speak of the case, either, which gave us little to talk about.

"Are you going to class tonight?" she asked me.

I had been taking a fencing class while waiting for the Guv to be well enough to resume his antagonistics. It was one way to stay in fit form.

"I had intended to, if it isn't inconvenient."

At this, I looked at the Guv and not my wife, but she was the one who answered.

"Of course not. I was planning to do some sewing."

"Good, then," I said, when Barker did not change expression.

After dinner, Mac shooed us out of the kitchen and I went upstairs to change. In turn, I told Rebecca about my day, which alternately alarmed and interested her. Then she told me about helping Etienne, which was in many ways more alarming still. He is like a dragon in its lair. I tucked my uniform into my bag and prepared to go. I could be back home after eight and we would have a few hours to ourselves.

The antagonistics school the Guv owned in Soho had been temporarily closed due to his injury. Not long after, a man by the name of Alfred Hutton came to see us, asking to lease it on the nights when it was empty. He and a coterie he brought with him wanted to use the building for fencing. The rooms were well appointed for it; there was a long row of mirrors on one side of the room, padded floors on the other, a locker room, and a water closet. Since I was in charge of all business aspects of the school, I readily agreed and had him sign a contract on the spot. Before I knew it, I was attending the class myself. I'd had a fencing lesson or two at university and as far as I was concerned, it was the next logical step in my training.

When I arrived a quarter hour later, most of the group was assembled.

"Come, gentlemen!" the captain called. "Class starts in two minutes!"

Captain Hutton looked like a musketeer. He had an impressive imperial mustache, a military bearing, and an encyclopedic knowledge of European blood sport going back to Roman times. His class was a ragtag group of men, many of them writers, so I felt myself at home.

We went through the footwork at first: advance, retreat, lunge, and recover. Hutton discussed distances, the short, the middle and long, and the need for a thorough knowledge of each, as well as how to use it against an opponent. Then we retired for a rest. There was a large pitcher of sparkling water studded with lemon slices on a table, alongside several tumblers. Hutton pretended not to notice that some of the class generally carried a flask of gin among their effects.

"Captain," I asked, since Hutton was once an officer of the

King's Dragoon Guards, "Are you familiar with something called 'Mensurites'?"

The corners of his waxed imperial quivered like the antennas of an ant. "Mensurites! Where did you hear such a word?"

"I heard it in passing recently," I answered, unwilling to tell him it came from Barker or in what context I had heard it.

Hutton cleared his throat. "It's a style of fencing in Eastern Europe, taught mostly in universities and schools. It's also known as 'academic fencing.' Gentlemen, come here!"

He's an excitable chap, our captain, and there is a bit of the scholar in him. I had noticed before that he can be easily thrown off track by the proper question.

"Thomas," he said, "bring your *épée*."

He pulled me into the center of the room. I hate it when I'm called into a demonstration and I don't know what is about to happen. I always feel and look a fool. Unfortunately, I had brought this on myself.

"*En garde!*" he cried, and I stepped into position, sword in front of me, held loosely in my right hand, the left floating behind my head, balanced mostly on the back leg, but ready to step forward with the right.

"Mr. Llewelyn has asked me to demonstrate what is known as academic fencing. Here he stands in the classic fencing position. Step forward, please."

I did so and our blades touched. We fenced for a moment. Naturally, he was the better man.

"Classic," he said, stopping. "But actually, not classic at all. It is from the modern French School. Now, Mr. Llewelyn, will you demonstrate the La Canne position taught in your own antagonistics class?"

"Yes, sir."

I stepped back so that my left foot was in front and the *épée* was in my right hand behind me, raised over my head so the blade hung down in front of my eyes. My left arm was flung forward, bent at the elbow.

"Very well. That looks a trifle awkward, does it not? The left arm floats unprotected, almost asking to be slashed, while the sword hovers about the head from behind. How was such an odd position created, Mr. Llewelyn?"

"I scarce can say, sir," I answered.

A student behind me raised a hand.

"Yes, Mr. Barrie?"

"Sir, it was meant to be worn with armor! The left hand would be holding a shield or buckler."

"Excellent. Now, Mr. Llewelyn, let us fence for a moment from this position."

We put on our masks and began. It was awkward, as he said, but I was used to it by now. The sword circles one's head, then whips across in front of the face. He lunged and I jumped back. I lunged and he stepped to the side. I had never seen him in our La Canne class before, but the skills must have been the same as the medieval form of swordplay. I nearly caught him once, but he jumped nimbly away at the last moment.

"You've got the gist, gentlemen. We have the modern fencing position, right foot forward, and we have the older Medieval style, with the left foot forward. Do you see?"

We all agreed that we did.

"Is this how Mensurites fight, Captain?" I asked.

"That is another good question. Come, Mr. Llewelyn, let us take positions again. Let me move a little closer. Begin!"

I stepped back and raised my sword arm high.

"Stop!"

I pulled off my mask. "What's wrong?"

"You stepped back."

"Of course I did."

"Mensurites never step back. They fight toe-to-toe."

It took everyone in the class a moment to understand what he was saying.

"You could get yourself killed, sir!" I cried.

"They sometimes do, more often than they might admit. Oh,

and their swords, the Korbschläger and the Glockenschläger, they have no button and one edge is sharp. I'd even say razor sharp."

We all considered that for a moment.

"Oh," the captain added, "and the general target is the head."

"How does one keep from getting cut?" another student asked, aghast.

"One doesn't, Mr. Hope. The duel ends when one of the fencers bleeds. One often sees men from that part of the world wearing dueling scars. The *smite* shows everyone this man is a Mensurite. It is a badge of honor. Students bleed like slaughtered pigs in the ring. Some do battle dozens of times, getting one scar after another. It becomes a form of fascination for them. I have seen some truly hideous dueling scars during my visits to Heidelberg and Berlin, men with missing noses and twisted faces sitting in cafés as if the disfigurement were commonplace, which in a way, I suppose it is."

I looked about. There were perhaps a dozen of us, each of our faces frozen in a rictus of disgust.

"Now," Captain Hutton went on. "I believe we shall spend the rest of the class practicing academic fencing and how to defend against a Mensurite. Fortunately, all of your blades have buttons and you are not using sabers, so there are no sharp edges to concern you. You also have masks. All the same, have a care. I have had more than one metal splinter in my neck and do not recommend them."

There are plenty of battered canes about our school. Hutton placed one on the mat closely behind each of us. We faced each other, adjusted our masks and began. What happened after was sheer panic. We were completely unaccustomed to fighting an opponent at such close quarters. It was ungainly. It was unnatural. It was difficult to thrust, to parry, or to riposte. I longed to step back over the stick to more comfortable ground, but I dared not.

I noticed immediately how a clash of swords, with so little room to maneuver, ended with the button of the sword rasping along the wire grillwork of the mask. I shuddered to imagine such a duel without it, facing a naked blade. It seemed all too easy to be cut to ribbons. Fencing requires space. Oh, I suppose a man can endure a minute or two, but nothing beyond that. The thought that one might do this sort of thing voluntarily and even pay for the privilege was beyond all reckoning.

Then I faced Alfred Hutton himself. The man had no trouble at all with close quarters, or long quarters, or any sort of quarters. He was so skillful, I suspected he'd teethed on a sword as an infant. No longer a soldier in uniform, he needed something to slake his bloodlust, and at the moment, I was that something. Against all odds, I survived the encounter. My mask, however, was dented in several places, and required some pushing from the inside later to return it to its original shape.

By the time we finished, we were all damp and exhausted. All, that is, save the captain, who looked exhilarated. It occurred to me that an Englishman does not learn such things from a book. A man wishing to resurrect an archaic art might go to great lengths, such as fencing with real blades without a mask. Come to think of it, did I see part of a scar on his chin, nearly covered by that imposing imperial? It made me pause.

Afterward, a couple of students suggested a drink at the Royal, which was only a street away. I would have readily agreed had I not a beautiful bride awaiting me. Fencing is a fine pastime, but after all, there are priorities. I bade them all adieu for the night and endured some chaffing from the lot. They knew where I was going and why.

I left them and went in search of a cab. When I saw one, I raised an arm, the one not holding the bag with my change of clothes. The next I knew, I was tackled from behind. There was a brief struggle. Three men stood over me in long blue coats and billed caps. They attempted a kick or two, but as it happened, I was a better fighter than all of them. After a minute, the assailants turned and fled, laughing as they disappeared into the night. As I sat up and looked about, I realized their intent. They had taken the Gladstone in which I carried my fencing uniform, which they must have thought was the satchel.

There was little harm done. One of my hands was skinned a bit, and my waistcoat had lost a button. I would have to purchase a new uniform and replace my bag. I realized how desperate someone was to lay hands on the manuscript. Climbing into the cab, I realized something more: the Prime Minister had failed. The Mensurites, whoever they were, knew we had been hired, possibly even before we began. Perhaps we should be released from our duties. That led me to consider something else: somewhere among Her Majesty's Government, the Roman Catholic Church, and the Home Office, there was a spy. Our possession of the ancient text put us in grave danger.

I arrived in Newington a quarter hour later, tired and bruised, anxious to talk to Barker. I went into the house and encountered Mac in the hall. He jumped from his butler's pantry by the front door like a cuckoo clock.

"Is the Guv in?" I asked.

"He is, but he is leaving soon."

"Leaving? Why?"

"He did not confide in me."

That was the extent to which he would answer my questions. In the library, Rebecca stood from the settee and greeted me.

"How was your evening?" I asked.

"It was fine. How was yours?"

I shrugged. "The usual. Nothing to speak of."

There was no use alarming her over so trivial a matter, I had decided. Such an incident, involving being tackled by a trio of young men bigger than me in order to lay hands upon a manuscript that could very well change the face of Christianity would only frighten her. I would tell the Guv as soon as I could speak to him.

Cyrus Barker entered the room with a businesslike, almost

grim expression. He came to where Rebecca was sitting and bowed to her.

"Mrs. Llewelyn, I have a favor to ask."

"Certainly, Mr. Barker. What is it?"

"I should like to borrow your husband for the night. All night, if convenient."

CHAPTER SEVEN

I s what you are doing dangerous?" Rebecca asked. "Is it illegal?"

"What we shall be about is not illegal," Cyrus Barker assured her. "However, the government would not be well disposed
toward what we shall be doing."

"We're breaking into the satchel!" I cried.

"We are."

"But it's in the vault at Cox and Co."

"Oh, lad, pray give me some credit. Ma'am?"

Rebecca leaned back in her chair and crossed her arms. She had
more sangfroid than I, willing to challenge the Guv, but then she
did not feel the need to win his approval.

"Does this happen often?" she asked.

"Which, Mrs. Llewelyn? Working all night or involving ourselves in questionable activities?"

"Both."

"It does not happen often, but it happens."

"Take him, then, but bring him back in the same condition."

"Agreed." The Guv turned to me. "Thomas, go to this address. You are looking for Professor Alan Wessel. Ask him to come for the night, and be persuasive."

"How persuasive?"

"Offer him a financial inducement. Professors are never well paid."

"Yes, sir."

"Oh, and don't bring him here. Go to Limehouse."

"Ho's?"

"Precisely."

Twenty minutes later, I was at the University of London, where I found the professor was giving a late tutorial. I waited outside in the hall for him. Eventually, the door opened and he ushered the student out. Wessel was perhaps fifty, with thick spectacles and a short beard. He was still wearing his robes. After the student had gone, he looked at me, trying to decide if I were a student myself. I stood.

"Professor Wessel?" I enquired. "Barker sent me."

The man stiffened. "Cyrus Barker?"

"The same."

"What does he want?"

"Your services, sir. I suspect they shall be required all night."

"All night?" Wessel exclaimed. "Are you mad? I have a wife. I cannot go off to who-knows-where without a word to her."

"Then write a message. I'll see it's delivered."

"Look, this is deuced inconvenient," he said. "What does he want with me?"

"I don't know the particulars," I admitted. "What is your field of research?"

"Ancient languages."

"Ah," I said, the light dawning. "I suspect you will find this an interesting night. Very interesting, but then it generally is when Barker is about."

He frowned, looking at me doubtfully. "See here, this had better not be some sort of undergraduate prank!"

"No, sir, it's no prank. Mr. Barker says I am to pay you fifteen pounds for your work tonight."

"He did? Fifteen pounds?"

"Did I say fifteen? I meant twenty."

He nearly ripped his gown pulling it off. He stepped into an office, donned a heavy coat, a hat with furred flaps, and a pair of stout leather gloves. He wound an absurdly long scarf about his neck. I led him through the drafty quadrangle and hailed a hansom.

Cabs are dear when one wants to be delivered to one of the more disreputable parts of the East End on a moment's notice, but I'd already cracked open Barker's coin purse, so to speak, so what is a few extra pounds, I say. I paid, Wessel complained about the inconvenience, the cabman snapped his whip, and the gelding dug in his hoofs and pulled. We all had our expertise to contribute.

Eventually we came to a narrow lane in Limehouse, dark and neglected. It ended in the ruins of an old church that I suspect was Roman Catholic, due to a small, dilapidated door in the very back. I was well acquainted with that bolt-hole. It ran under the river, bisecting Limehouse Reach, and fetched up in a restaurant of sorts.

"Where are we?" Wessel asked as I opened the derelict door and moved to light a naphtha lantern. I could see the concern growing in his face. "What is this place?"

"Ho's," I replied. "It's an Asian restaurant. Of course, it's after hours."

As I spoke, I saw a man staggering along in the snow toward us under an armload of packages. I looked twice before I realized who it was.

"Jeremy!" I cried, holding the lamp higher. "What are you doing here?"

"I'd like to know that myself," our clerk replied. "Mr. B. gave me orders before he left. He said it will be a long night."

"God help us," Wessel muttered behind me.

"We're being watched," Jenkins said. "Or so Mr. B. claims."

"Youths in blue uniforms?"

"No, Home Office johnnies, I reckon, or Vatican assassins. Take your pick."

"I hope they enjoy standing all night in the cold while we're snug in Ho's restaurant," I said, trying to ease Wessel's mind.

"I hope this isn't a waste of my time," the professor replied.

In lieu of a reply, I walked down the steps into the narrow tunnel. It always made my heart race. Wessel and Jenkins followed behind. Jeremy seemed familiar with the place, although I had never seen him there before.

"Mr. L.," Jenkins said. "Could you take one of these sacks? My arm is cramping."

"Certainly," I replied, lifting one. It seemed uncommonly heavy. "My word, it's the satchel! How did you get it?"

"Hand delivered by a messenger boy as you see it now."

We could hear the water coursing above the tunnel. It takes some nerve to get used to walking under the Thames and I could sense Wessel's discomfort.

"Are you sure this is safe?" the professor asked, his voice echoing off the walls. "Perhaps you can find someone else in London to help you. I could make you a list!"

"No, Professor," I insisted. "You are here, and now you must see this through. Remember those twenty-five pounds."

"You said . . . never mind."

At the far end of the tunnel, Barker was talking to the owner, Ho, arguably his closest friend in the world. Ho is short, stout, bandy-legged, ill-tempered, and argumentative. He was proving the latter with Barker even at that moment. He must have been the one the Guv was arguing with over the telephone. He turned away, muttering to himself, while Barker addressed my companion.

"Professor Wessel, it's good to see you again. I believe I've got something here that will interest you. It may even astound you."

"Why bring me to this blighted spot, then? Why cannot this be done at the university?"

"I found it necessary to guard all entrances to a building and this place is the most secure in all London. We shall also need food."

"No food!" Ho called down the tunnel, and they argued again. Or perhaps they were just haggling. It was difficult to tell.

I helped divest the professor of his things and led him into the restaurant. He was at least a trifle mollified. An aroma came from the kitchen despite Ho's threats and the spacious room was warm from a large fireplace. It would be churlish to require more.

Barker turned to the professor. "It was good of you to come on such short notice."

"Very well, Mr. Barker. Anything for a fellow Templar. I am at your service, but let me send a note to my wife before we begin."

I didn't want to leave and miss anything, but there was the note to be delivered. Muttering to myself, I threw on my coat again and ran out the door. There was a public house nearby called the Cod and Winkle, and there was certain to be a messenger there, despite the cold. I skittered along, heedless of the weather, alternating between stepping into deep snow and slipping on bare ice. I found a boy inside the pub so skinny and cold that I tripled the amount I would normally pay him, enough for a meal and a fire for all his family that night. Then I ran back, falling only once, and reached the door again within a few minutes.

When I entered the restaurant again, the Guv and Jenkins were carefully laying out the manuscript on a long table. Dark strips of something that resembled a decayed banana peel were sealed between small sheets of glass. There was writing on both sides of each one. Immediately, Wessel crossed to the table and bent over it. He shuffled sideways until he came to the first and moved closer until both his elbows rested on the table and his nose was an insignificant distance from the glass, close enough to fog it.

"Oh, my word," he murmured. "It's a Greek copy of Matthew. Here are the genealogies. The book of the generations of Jesus Christ, the son of David, the son of Abraham."

He stopped and looked up at us. "Is this manuscript authentic?"

"That is what we have brought you here to ascertain," Barker replied. "That, and translating it for us."

"Where did it come from?"

"Best not to ask."

Wessel bent over the manuscript again. "Look here! It's suddenly lapsed into the beginning of Mark. What is this, some sort of apocrypha?"

"Again, that is for you to determine."

He looked up. "Do you think I might have a cup of tea? Any kind will do."

He was instantly absorbed into the manuscript again. At a nearby table, Jenkins lifted various items out of a hamper basket: paper and leather, ink pens and rulers, paintbrushes and watercolor sets. Our humble clerk was the son of the best forger of the nineteenth century, and Jeremy had learned everything at his father's knee.

"It lapses into Mark, with the coming of John the Baptist," Wessel continued. "Then it skips over to Luke with the virgin birth. But look here, some of the verses are new. John's birth is recorded, while other verses have been discarded."

"What are your initial thoughts on the manuscript other than the words scribed upon them?" the Guv asked.

Professor Wessel cleared his throat and smoothed his beard.

"I'm only a linguist, but it appears to be made of leather. Originally it was one long strip, a scroll, then later cut into pieces and bound. There are holes along the side here. You see how the bottom is cut at a slight angle. The beginning of the next portion begins with the same angle cut. It's very small, but then one could not carry a pocket-sized manuscript about if one were a first- or second-century Christian convert. Even owning such a thing could get one crucified."

Jeremy brought a chair beside the professor, and began sharpening a pencil with a jackknife. Normally he had more sail than ballast by now, but he knew how important the work was, and he'd brought his own ale in case a catastrophe occurred and there was no ready cask.

"There are nine plates here with two sheets for each, making eighteen pieces of glass," the professor said. "Each contains three lengths of manuscript. The writing is very small. The author was trying to cram as much onto the scroll as he could. Some are longer than others, because whoever cut them tried to do so at the end of a chapter whenever he could."

"Why is it so dark?" I asked.

"Age. It's nineteen hundred years old, or thereabouts."

"A.D. 100?" Barker asked.

Wessel raised a finger.

"You mustn't hold me to that. It's old, I can tell you that much. I see nothing wrong so far with the syntax. The language is not as elegant as Luke or Paul, but more so than Mark. The author was probably not a fisherman like the others. Unfortunately, his name is not in the manuscript, at least not in the portion I've read. Let me get back to it now."

By then, Wessel was in the thrall of the manuscript. He was no longer a fish caught on a hook, fighting. He was now complicit in his own capture.

"What is it?" he said in hushed tones, as if to himself.

"What does it appear to be?" the Guv asked.

"A new gospel."

"Or a very old one."

Wessel sat back in his chair and ripped his eyes away from the ancient pages. "How old? Are you implying that this came before all of them?"

Barker shrugged his huge shoulders. "I'm not as knowledgeable as you on such matters. This was given me by a person of great authority. I am to deliver it to a place of safety soon."

Wessel frowned as he realized what Jeremy Jenkins was there to do.

"You are making a copy?" he exclaimed. "You intend to switch the two?"

"No," Cyrus Barker replied, "but I am making a facsimile. It may be necessary to do so."

"I believe this to be genuine, linguistically, at least. You wish me to translate it for you?" he asked, as Jenkins began to stain a strip of leather with watercolor.

"Can you do it?" the Guv asked. "It need not be perfect; I understand there is little time."

The professor ran a hand across his beard. "I'd like a copy. A photographic copy."

Barker shook his head. "I can allow a copy of the copy, but not of the original. You cannot publish anything without genuine proof."

"I don't need it. A copy is fine. I only want the words."

"No more than I," said the Guv.

I got out my notebook and sat back. It would be a few busy hours.

"Shall we begin?" I asked.

Wessel held up a finger. "One more question, first, Mr. Barker. Do you yourself believe this to be genuine?"

"Who can say? The individual—individuals, actually—who hired me thought it important enough to be sent abroad. Post-haste."

Our guest sat back and crossed his arms. One could almost see the thoughts streaming through his skull.

"I understand the need for secrecy. It has not been proven to be authentic, or even more than apocrypha. One could not announce to the world that it had been found until it has been studied and tested. Can you at least tell me where it came from?"

"It appeared in Germany. I cannot be more specific yet. I know not how it got there to begin with, but it was brought here. Beyond that, I cannot say."

"What do you intend to do with the translation?"

"To read it and keep it locked away. It will not be published. And you?"

"The same."

Barker reached out his hand. Wessel took it. There was that Templar handshake again. "If word ever surfaces, we'll both know who did it."

"What of these fellows here?"

"They are with me and are my responsibility. I have known them for years. Shall we begin? Time is fleeting."

The professor leaned forward eagerly. I have a bond with Cyrus Barker, going back years now. I would not betray his trust any more than I would Rebecca's. He asked me on that wintry evening never to reveal a word of the manuscript. Therefore, I shall not.

Wessel began translating then, slow and fast, and slow again. Translation is a difficult task, even for an expert, which I believe the professor was. He spoke without reference works or aids. I didn't exactly warm to him, but I appreciated him more.

"What are you doing there?" he asked at one point, glimpsing my writing.

"Shorthand," I replied.

"But I cannot read it."

"I assumed you would want a more detailed and exact copy yourself," Barker said.

"I would, but I don't know this fellow from Adam. How do I know that he can copy every jot and tittle?"

He was referring to Jenkins.

"He can," I told him, aware that our clerk's appearance is not prepossessing. "There isn't another man in Europe who can do what he does. He is a master forger."

Jenkins looked at me out of the corner of his eye. His lips pulled back into a subtle smile and returned as before.

"Can he make another copy for me? I'd pay him."

"Jeremy?" Barker asked.

"I'll do it tomorrow night, Mr. B., but I won't take any money for it."

Wessel looked thwarted for a moment. I would not give him a copy of my notes and Jeremy would not give him a copy of the manuscript to take away with him. He wanted something in his hands to prove to himself this Arabian Nights dream was real.

"This is most irregular!" he cried.

"Shall we continue?" Barker asked. It was more an order than a question.

We set to in earnest. In places, the Greek letters were nearly illegible and the professor had to guess. In others, he nearly strangled himself in syntax, trying to draw every meaning out of a word in order to speculate what the unnamed author intended. With each passing sentence, he grew more and more excited.

"Remarkable, sirs! Amazing. Forgive my annoyance before. I did not know what honor you were bestowing upon me."

"Fortunately for us, you are a Templar."

"Not much of one, I'm afraid. I'm too busy to attend many meetings."

"Your industry does you credit."

Wessel returned to translating. "Some of this is mildly heretical. Jesus appears as more of a radical. Not politically, I mean. Money should be given generously to the poor, elders should be revered for their wisdom. He wanted to do more than change society. He wanted to change men's souls."

"Was this manuscript intended for Jews or Gentiles?" I asked.

"Both, I think," Wessel said. "I believe that it was used to write both the book of Matthew, written for the Jews, and Luke, written for the Gentiles."

It was nearly dawn before we finished our work. By then, we all had stiff necks and sick headaches. Jenkins would work until breakfast while we had a few hours' kip.

At last, we saw Wessel out of the tunnel. The snow fell silently, save when a gust of wind pushed the crystals across the frozen crust. I walked him to Mile End Road and hailed a passing cab. The professor said he needed to get away to think alone. He shook my hand and climbed aboard, and I promised to send him my typed notes. When I returned, Barker stood in front of the battered door, the shoulders of his coat as white as mine.

"What now?" I asked.

"Ho has offered us a pallet for a few hours. You take it. I need to read the manuscript a few times. Then we shall take a cab home and go into the office late."

"Did Ho actually offer a place to sleep of his own volition?"

Barker brushed the snow from his shoulders

"Very well, he was persuaded."

Ma Dong, Ho's chief cook, passed us and went into the restaurant. We followed after. A minute or two later, Ho came down with his arms full. He had a chair, a contraption I recognized as a water pipe, an incense burner, an offering bowl, and a bell. He set the chair in the middle of the passage, spread out the articles on the floor around him and sat, knees spread wide, his burly arms crossed, his face as hard and masklike as a stone idol.

"Go," he said. "Study your silly Christian text. I must purify my tearoom with proper Buddhist prayers."

CHAPTER EIGHT

It was half past eight when we reached Craig's Court. My employer sat down at his desk immediately and began a letter. He writes slowly and deliberately, but he makes up for these shortcomings by being illegible. When I first saw his handwriting, I wondered why he made the effort of sending messages and letters at all, yet somehow he manages to receive a response for all his efforts.

The Guv tapped the end of the pen on his lower lip, drew a few scribbles, inspected what he had written and added a few more lines. If that wasn't enough, he began humming to himself. At a turtle's pace, he blotted the letter, folded it, slid it into an envelope, and wrote an address on it. Then I'm blowed if he didn't take out another sheet and begin a second letter. Thankfully, it was shorter, and when he was done, he folded it into a square. This he handed to me.

"Send this along, will you, Thomas?"

"Of course, sir."

I stepped out into the court and then into Whitehall Street, looking for blue coats. It was one of those brilliant days, hard and shiny as a skillet, the kind that reminded me that we were on a ball hurtling through space, wrapped in the thinnest layer of warmth.

I was about to study the letters when a boy cut through the crowd and I stopped him just long enough to push both letters and a sixpence into his hand. We didn't speak; in fact, we did not even acknowledge each other. My hand was suddenly empty while his was suddenly full. My duty done, I went back to our chambers.

A few minutes later, the outer door opened and I tensed. My hand went immediately to the shelf in my rolltop desk where I kept my short-barreled Webley. Barker made no noticeable movement, but I knew a pistol holster was attached to the inside of his desk by his leg. The Guv and I had discussed having a small window installed over my desk, in order to give me time to react. However, windows work both ways.

We needn't have bothered. Another tyke rushed in, deposited an envelope, caught a coin Jenkins flipped to him, and rushed out again. Jenkins brought it to us and my employer opened it.

"Ah," he said. "Pierce's list."

"You really intend to investigate Drummond's death, then?" I asked.

"I would have no need for the list otherwise."

"Do you intend to give the satchel to the Home Office, then?"

"Let us say I have considered it. Let me look at this list."

I rose to come round, but he raised a hand. He drew out a small black leather-bound notebook and copied them down in his unreadable scrawl and then handed the latter to me. My eyebrows rose at the first on the list.

"The German government?" I asked. "What, all of it?"

"Let us hope it is not that one, Thomas. I fear we don't have the resources to handle it. However, I would imagine they would send agents more experienced than youths in blue coats. If that is the best they possess we have little to worry over."

"There is nothing but a question mark afterward."

"We shall see if we can change this into facts. Next?"

"Count Valentine von Arnstein, broker of antiquities. Austrian citizen of Graz, Styria."

Barker rose and studied a map of Europe that was framed by the bow window.

"Styria is in the southernmost part of Austria. Graz is the capital."

"It doesn't sound like a spot rich in antiquities."

"True, lad, but it isn't very far from Trieste. One could take a steamer to Palestine."

"The manuscript certainly qualifies as an antiquity of great value."

"How valuable, I wonder," the Guv said. "I dislike the word 'priceless,' but it is possible that wars could be waged over it. Germany is not feeling amiable toward England at the moment. It's possible, the manuscript was stolen by a German nationalist and given to Drummond to foment a war."

"What kind of nationalist?" I asked.

He pointed to Germany on the map with a thick index finger.

"In your lifetime, these were seperate countries: Bavaria, Prussia, Hesse, Hanover, and a dozen others. Bismarck unified them twenty years ago. The unification was not popular for all. Now that he is dead, some may want to have their independence."

I stood and stepped behind him, looking at the image of unified Germany. "Now his successor, Kaiser Wilhelm, is a nationalist of another sort. He wants Germany to be a colonial power to rival England."

"Wouldn't a holy manuscript be a fine prize for either party?" my employer asked. "Who is next on the list, Thomas?"

"Karl Heinlich. It says he is an American speaker, a proponent of atheism."

"Atheism," the Guv murmured.

I expected some critical remark, but he made no comment.

"What would an atheist want with a biblical manuscript, the oldest gospel known to man?"

"To ridicule it, perhaps," Barker replied, returning to his desk. He settled his encased limb on the corner of the desk with a wince. "Or to burn it."

"Is there a chance that is political, as well? He could be a spy. America wants colonies as much as Germany."

"You've been reading *The Times*," he said, with some degree of approval. "However, that doesn't make Heinlich a spy. Not yet, anyway. Who is next?"

"Daniel Cochran, another American. Some sort of evangelist it says. Obviously, having a holy manuscript would win him thousands of followers. Not to mention funding."

Cyrus Barker wagged his head and tsked. "Such a cynic, and at your age."

"Yes, well, eight months in prison will do that to a fellow."

"Nevertheless, you are correct. Cochran belongs on this list. Is there another candidate?"

"One more. A collector of antiquities named Lord Grayle. He lives in Hampshire, but has a pied-à-terre in London. Ha! Pierce calls him a fanatic. He must have plenty of money to have that sort of hobby."

"Aye, no doubt."

"Five names," I said. "And all are in London. We'd better hurry if we're going to question all of them and still make the late express to Dover."

"There is plenty of time."

"My word. Why do I even bother?"

Barker rose from his seat and donned his heavy overcoat. He took a blackthorn from the rack. I suspected this cold weather was settling in his injured knee. Without a word, I gave him way.

"Let us stop and see if the German ambassador will see us. He's probably busy, but it is worth the attempt."

The German embassy was near Belgrave Square. Even in winter, it was neat, precise, well tended, and somehow alien to the British way of life. It isn't that we're lazy, we simply like things to be comfortable. As we stepped inside, every chair was arranged precisely on the tiles beneath and the books in their shelves were neatly aligned. Even the fronds in their pots were a uniform length.

We met a receptionist who led us to a clerk, who led us to a secretary, who informed us the ambassador was able to see us. Before I fully grasped that fact, we were seated in front of a large desk, staring at the representative of Kaiser Wilhelm's government in the British Isles. He was smoking some kind of strong cigarette in a green holder, with one hand, and holding our card in the other.

"Gentlemen, come in," he said, waving us to seats.

"Thank you for seeing us without notice," Barker said.

Paul von Hatzfeldt had a bulbous head and very little chin. He was thin, fastidiously dressed, and in his long tails he reminded me of a stork. He had a small mustache and I suspect his thinning hair was dyed. He was relaxed in the presence of two enquiry agents and did not consider it below his station to speak to us. He was the first German I had spoken to who had no trace of an accent.

"How may I be of service to you?" he asked.

How indeed? I wondered. I didn't expect the Guv to spout that we had the satchel for which his countrymen were searching all over London. But then, he was not the sort to announce his intentions.

"Sir," my employer said. "Mr. Llewelyn and I have been hired by the family of the late Mr. Hillary Drummond to look into the manner of his death. His body was found in Whitehall Street. At the time of his death he had just arrived from Germany. I say just; it was no more than a quarter hour since his arrival."

"I see," von Hatzfeldt said, nodding. "Pray continue."

"I spoke to a government official at Charing Cross Station who said there was a bag of some sort that was recovered. He would not say more than that. He was vague about his facts, was he not, Mr. Llewelyn?"

"He was," I said. "Very vague."

I tried not to raise a brow at the Guv's remarks. We had no idea if Drummond even had living parents, much less hiring us to work on their behalf.

Barker leaned forward in his seat. "We wondered if perhaps you might help us discover what was in the satchel and why he brought it from Germany."

The ambassador crossed his long limbs after smashing the end of his cigarette in a tray. "This is the first I've heard of this. As far as I'm concerned, the family should have the right to look inside a man's satchel. If it contains something that does not belong to the German government or an individual of my country, they are welcome to it. I feel that countries, mine included, should not take what does not belong to them. It makes for bad relations."

"I agree," Barker said. "I merely wish to be able to give Drummond's effects to his mother."

"What was Mr. Drummond's occupation?" the ambassador asked.

"His parents could not say. He had worked in various fields while here in England and the only information his mother received in his letters was that he had retained a situation. I suspect he was the adventurous type, floating around Europe."

Leisurely, Hatzfeldt picked up a pencil and began to set down notes. He was almost the antithesis of the grunting, irritable Salisbury.

"What was Mr. Drummond's given name?"

"Hillary."

"I haven't heard of this before now, but that is not rare. If he died two days ago, it would take one more day for news to arrive from Berlin. If it were important we would have received a telegram by now. I cannot think what Mr. Drummond carried in his bag, but if his family hopes it is full of marks, I fear they shall be disappointed. They seem to have little to go on. I do not envy you your assignment."

"This is typical of the work we do, sir," the Guv said.

"Then you are brave fellows. I have not had the pleasure of meeting an enquiry agent before. It seems to be an unusual occupation."

"It has its moments," I said.

"This appears to warrant a telegram to Berlin, I think. How did Drummond die again?"

"He was stabbed in the back with a sword and then run over by a cab."

"For such a phlegmatic society, you do have more than your share of murder and intrigue."

"If we did not, Mr. Llewelyn and I would be selling vegetables at a stall in Tottenham Court Road."

"Sir, I doubt very much that you would sell vegetables."

"Tell me, Ambassador, have you heard of academic fencing or Mensur? Oh, but of course you have. I see the scar upon your chin."

"I am the Count of Düsseldorf, where I attended university. Of course I know academic fencing. My chief memory of Mensur is being afraid during my first bout. I assumed I would be disfigured for life. I was not very good, you see. When I was cut, they packed salt in the wound to make the scar more prominent."

"Why do it, then?" I asked.

"One must play the game. A man is nobody and nothing in Germany without the scar. Mensurites get the best positions, the prettiest girls, and the most aristocratic friends."

"I see," Barker said, although I'm sure von Hatzfeldt had not said anything the Guv didn't know already.

"I would like to talk about this further, but I have an appointment. Should you discover anything, please come and see me again. I am as interested in Drummond's time in Germany as you."

Barker stood. "We thank you. Perhaps we shall solve this case quickly with your help."

"I hope so."

Both of them nodded and we left the embassy. We found an omnibus and climbed aboard. Inside, it was marginally warmer than out. Barker looked pleased with his efforts.

"What have we accomplished?" I asked. "Besides alerting the Germans we are connected to the satchel, that is."

"They already know, Thomas, or they would not have stolen your linens last night."

"They were not linens. It was a fencing uniform. A good one that I now have to replace."

"We needed to make a show of strength to prove to Berlin that we are not afraid to step into the lion's den."

"And?"

"The ambassador is an old warhorse. He's been here for a decade or two and he will not leave until he is carried out. He's not above diplomacy and even espionage from time to time. That is an essential part of an ambassador's training, receiving word that something has occurred, concealing any knowledge of it, and awaiting a response from their government."

"Do you believe he knows something, then?"

Cyrus Barker looked out the window at people passing by, hunched into their scarves and collars. "Not necessarily, but he should by end of day."

"Sir," I asked him straight-out. "Are we going to Calais today or not?"

"Let us allow the day to play out, shall we?"

I suspected Barker was formulating a plan for going forward but was not yet ready to tell me. As an assistant, it had been irritating, but as a partner, it was maddening. Cyrus Barker and I were involving ourselves in the highest levels of government intrigue and the reputation of our agency hung in the balance.

We arrived in our chambers. I was about to throw some coal on the fire and make a remark about Bob Cratchit, but it would have been unintelligible to my employer. He rarely reads anything from our century on the assertion that civilization is falling about our ears. However, I was stopped in my plans by the expression on Jeremy Jenkins's face, and by a pile of folded papers and small envelopes on the silver salver on his desk. Unwinding the scarf from my neck, I tried to puzzle out what they were and the answer came immediately to my lips.

"You've accepted Pollock's request to lead the Templars."

"I have, lad," he said. "We have not discussed the details, but I think we can accommodate his wishes."

"Can we? How many messages have come in during the last hour?"

"Twelve," Jenkins supplied, no more overjoyed at the news than I.

"They will have to be transcribed, and some answered," I said. "After that, they must be destroyed. This is important information and the notebook must be kept secret. It cannot fall into anyone's hands, even the government's."

"Agreed," Barker rumbled.

"Who shall undertake the work?" I asked. "I can't do it. I'm with you most of the time, unless you intend to start investigating without me. We would receive over a hundred per day if we had this same number every hour. I cannot do it."

"Nor can I," Jenkins stated. "I've got so much to do here, my other duties would suffer!"

We all knew that Jeremy had few other duties. The first half of the day he sits and glares at the *Police News*, his back teeth aching from the amount of alcohol he'd consumed the night before. Fortified by a strong cup of tea and a light meal, he generally came to life in the afternoon. By two o'clock he was fully functional, for him, at least. He dusted, swept, kept files, and conveyed visitors' cards to Barker's desk. At five thirty, he was set free like a schoolboy on the final day of term, to go to the Rising Sun public house.

From time to time he helped us actively on a case, and his skills as a forger were unrivaled, as the night before would attest, but that was not often. What reason would an employer have for a clerk who did little or nothing? I assumed it had to do with how he was first hired. I know that the Guv greatly respected Jeremy's father, whose exploits were legendary. There were forgeries of his in private collections whose owners knew were painted by Jenkins *père*. There were also countless copies in museums all over the world whose curators were unaware of the deception. He was equally skilled in art and lettering. Jenkins was nearly as good as his father. Obviously, Barker kept him around for his skill with a pen, even though his clerking skills were minimal at best, but I doubted Barker expected him to handle the Templar correspondence. One might as well give a quill to Voltaire and ask him to write a shopping list.

For once the Guv looked stumped, glaring first at me and then Jenkins to solve the problem. One can imagine how surprised I was when I found the solution.

"Sir, last year, you agreed we would need Mac here in the future. He's helped with enquiries on several occasions and is highly competent. He's also very precise. I believe he would enjoy the challenge."

"Thomas, we need him at home! Who will cook the meals?"

"We don't need him the entire day, sir. He can work a few hours here or help as needed. The rest of the day he can be at home, polishing silver to his heart's content."

Barker crossed his arms and sat back in his chair. "You sound as though you have considered this."

"You know he's always wanted to be an enquiry agent."

"I prefer him at home. Everything runs smoothly when he is there."

"Consider this: offer him the position, allow him to set the proper number of hours, and ask him to hire his own replacement at his convenience."

"Which would be never," he said.

I smiled. "Precisely."

He mulled over the proposition. "Do you believe him willing to become a Templar?"

"Is it necessary to be a Templar to do the work?"

"I would prefer it, since some of the missives will be about the society itself. Others are copies of notes meant for other agencies. Yet more are notes by Templars informing me—or rather Pollock—since my acceptance is not yet known, of something they believe I need to know."

"Such as?" I asked. "Could you be more specific?"

"Unrest in the north of India, perhaps. The British Army buying rifles from a particular company. Russia eyeing the Crimea, that sort of thing."

"But all of that is in *The Times*."

"Most of it. Two days later. A good deal can change in two days."

"I hope Mac will be up to the challenge," I said.

"Should he wish, I suppose he could go back to his own duties."

I shook my head. "I wonder if the *agency* is up to the challenge."

As we spoke, a boy hurried in, dropped a letter on top of the stack, and took a tuppence for his trouble.

"Thomas, go round to Cox and Co. and procure a sack of sixpences. I suspect we shall need them."

CHAPTER NINE

W hat are your thoughts, lad?" Cyrus Barker asked a short while after lunch. He was looking out our bow window at the occasional snowflake.

"About the case," I answered. "I must admit that I cannot fathom why you do not take the satchel to Calais and have done with it. It was an honor to be chosen for the assignment. I should think you'd wish to impress the Prime Minister with your abilities."

"I doubt the Marquess of Salisbury would be impressed by anything or anyone."

"Why do you think Pollock Forbes recommended us for the work?"

"Wheels within wheels," he rumbled. "Sometimes I doubt that moving into Craig's Court was a wise decision, being so close to the seat of government."

"Oh, surely you don't mean that. You love these old rooms as much as I or you would not have had them rebuilt and repaired as you have."

"I am being manipulated, and I refuse to be manipulated," he said, ignoring my last remark.

"The Prime Minister waves the flag at us and claims that England is ill-used, but I think otherwise. Drummond would not have been free to wander about Europe as his mood took him, sending occasional letters back home. He was one of England's prime agents. No, he was sent into Germany for one purpose: to get the satchel and bring it here. He stole it, plain and simple. Spying is dirty work. Oh, perhaps Drummond told himself that he was serving his country, but why? England had nothing to gain from the theft, other than to humiliate Germany. If that is the objective, it is a foolish one. The Kaiser is a scoundrel who wants to own an imperial power exceeding our own."

"But he can't," I said. "The Kaiser is late to the table. Most of the globe has been divided already. Germany owns Alsace-Lorraine and a few bits of arid land in Africa. They would have to go to war to get what they want."

"Don't think the Kaiser hasn't considered it. I hope his advisors can talk sense into him. He can rattle his saber as much as he wants, but he must not draw his blade or there will be bloodshed. A blade always cuts both ways."

"I was not aware that Germany was so fond of cold steel. It is an old-fashioned weapon."

"The Mensurite academies represent the more nationalist and traditional families of Germany, harking back to before Bismarck's unification. Old families, old money. I'm sure Wilhelm will call any liberal or unionist activities plots designed by Jews and Roman Catholics, both of whom are below contempt in his eyes."

"I suppose handing their manuscript over to the Vatican would be considered adding insult to injury, then."

"Without doubt, Thomas. Regardless of his personal politics, the Kaiser will do anything to appease his patrons. They are the backbone of his supporters."

"You are certain, then, that it is the Germans?"

"I am not. There are nationalists and university fencing traditions all over Eastern Europe. There are old families with too much money who give it to men that tickle their ears. However, it is Germany alone that longs for a relic or icon on which they can legitimize their claims. We should move forward on the assumption that Germany is behind Drummond's death, but maintain the ability to change our minds should further information contradict it."

"Agreed."

Returning to my desk, I took a sheet of paper and began to set down what the ambassador had said precisely, while I still had it in my mind. The work took perhaps ten minutes. It had been a discouraging meeting. Once I was done I took the Hammond typewriting machine and prepared to put a piece of paper into it.

"B'lay that, confound it!" the Guv cried. "Out. Take Jenkins along. Buy him an early pint or two. I must think and I cannot do so with that racket!"

There was a gasp of wonder from our outer office. A pint in the afternoon? And possibly another after? Jenkins could hardly believe his luck.

"If you wish," I said, feeling ill-used.

I donned my coat and hat, my gloves and muffler, and ushered Jenkins out the door. We headed south on Whitehall Street. The sun was shining, but generating little warmth. It takes some work to get the Guv in such a mood, although it is not unheard of. Under normal circumstances he counsels patience. Physician, heal thyself, I thought.

We turned in at the former gates of Scotland Yard, then left into the Rising Sun, Jenkins's sanctum. I bought each of us a pint of stout. Everyone knew Jenkins there and no one knew me, so he slipped away and left me to myself. Brooding is contagious, and I had definitely caught whatever Barker had. Seeing him up against it was disheartening.

The Guv needed an hour or two, I reckoned, making it the

perfect day for book hunting. I had money in my pocket and time to waste, so why spend time in a public house? I left Jenkins in his element and stepped out into the cold, my mind buoyed. Yes, a book was just the thing.

Then a boy ran headlong into me, asked if I was Thomas Llewelyn, and on being told I was, pushed a note into my hand. Blast, I thought. Reaching into my pocket, I flicked a sixpence in his direction. He caught it and evaporated.

The note read:

Red Lion. Come if you can. Urgent.

The Red Lion was a public house at the foot of Whitehall, not far from Westminster Bridge. I debated whether to return to our chambers and deliver the note to the Guv. The urchin had placed it in my hand, however, and addressed me by name. Was it a trap? Possibly. However, it was the "Come if you can" that puzzled me. It implied that the sender knew me. There was no order, no threat. Should I go, Barker would simply note that I was overlong in returning.

My sword cane was in my hand. It was midday and I would be fully visible in Whitehall Street for most of the way. I read the note again. It was harmless enough, I decided. I would risk it. The thoroughfare was free of blue coats or suspicious persons as I walked along, swinging my stick. No satchel at all, chaps, I thought, just a man out for a stroll. I reached the pub without so much as a scratch and stepped inside.

A chair squeaked. I turned my head and saw one turned away from the door. I looked about, seeing if there was a more promising lead forthcoming, but there wasn't. I ordered and took my pint of nut-brown ale to the table where a man sat in the chair that was turned away.

"Terry," I murmured in greeting.

Detective Inspector Terence Poole nodded. He was an old friend of ours, but that friendship had come to him at a cost. We had grown too friendly and that familiarity with a pair of enquiry agents had damaged his career. In theory, there was an invisible line separating private agents such as ourselves from the Met. We were not to congregate, to have a pint together as we were, or to socialize during the evening. His promotion from inspector to detective inspector moved him out of our kin, but from time to time we'd receive a surreptitious card or a message from him. Seeing him face-to-face now, I realized what a risk he was taking. Should anyone who knew us both walk through the door, Poole might find himself in a spot of trouble. Another spot, that is.

I looked away and sipped my ale. Two unacquainted men jammed into the corner of a busy London public house.

"I hear congratulations are in order," he said in a low voice. "On your marriage and promotion, I mean."

"Thank you," I replied. "However, I assume this subterfuge is not merely to pat me on the back."

He smiled. When I first met Poole back in 1884, he wore long Dundreary whiskers of a ginger color. Now they were gone, replaced with a regulation mustache. I understand the need to have officers look clean scrubbed and neat in their uniforms. It breeds solidarity and a sense of trust in the middle classes. It also made it more difficult to distinguish between officers. Gone were the homely black beards of the rural constabularies. The younger men who had joined the Met clean shaven had begun to grow mustaches either to appear older, to achieve positions, or to look like one of their fellows. One could sell mustache wax by the pint at the Yard these days.

"What have you done now?" Poole asked, glancing about.

"What do you mean?"

"The commissioner is in a lather. Barker's done something to tread on his bunions."

"That's not difficult," I said. "The man is a bunion himself."

Poole buried a smile in his pewter mug. "There must be something."

"No, I don't think so. We've been busy, but I wasn't aware we were treading on anyone's toes."

"What about now? Anything stirring?"

"I can't discuss our current case."

"Ahhh," he purred.

"Ah, yourself."

"Animal, vegetable, or mineral?"

"I said I can't discuss it and I mean it."

Poole nodded as if it were a foregone conclusion that I would break the silence and lay it all before him. I might have at some time, but now I was part of an agency, not a mere hireling. Like Poole himself, I had to toe the line.

"We are . . . working for the government."

"Same here," he said. "The pay is rubbish, isn't it?"

"Scotland Yard is out of it, I understand."

Poole nodded. "Probably best, then," he said. "We're not begging for work. My caseload would choke a draft horse."

"Good," I answered.

Poole took a gulp of his pint and waved for another. "It's almost comical, isn't it? Munro and Barker. The two of them are stubborn Scotsmen obsessed with their work. The same work. And yet the two despise each other."

"I wondered what caused such hostility," I said.

Pool gave me a strange look. "You're joking, aren't you?"

"No," I said. "Why?"

"You don't know, then?"

"What are you on about?"

"Oh, this is too rich. I could barter with this for all the information you possess."

"Look," I told him. "If you're going to tell me, then tell me. If not, don't leave me dangling on the hook."

"Oh, it is tempting," he said, trying not to chuckle. "I'd make you promise to keep me informed, but it was difficult and dangerous enough for me to meet you here. If the commissioner knew I was still Cyrus's friend, I'd be sacked."

"Look, Terry, I cannot reveal anything on this case. Sworn to secrecy and all that. If I could, you'd be the first to know."

Poole nodded and began his second pint. "I understand. It was just too good a fly to drop in front of you."

He took a long, slow sip. I don't know which he savored more, the ale or keeping me waiting.

"Well?"

"Oh, very well. Munro was the johnnie who turned down Barker's request to become a constable years ago when he first came from China. He didn't care for your Guv's curriculum vitae, since it was not provable without traveling to Peking and questioning the Imperial government. Then there was the matter of Cyrus's spectacles. I believe Munro actually demanded that he remove them, which, of course, he refused."

"I see."

"Things rolled downhill from there, I hear. The commissioner is known for his temper and your guv'nor is not known for his amiability. There was an argument, which became a shouting match, and either Cyrus marched out or was thrown out. Which it was depends on who tells the story."

"I'd like to have been there."

"I, as well. I was a newly minted inspector at the time, relegated to far-off Wimbledon. I only heard about it later. You know how policemen will talk. No one knew Barker from Adam, of course, but there was no love wasted on Munro among the men. He never had that knack for making himself well liked. Too much of the bully in him. He never remembers your name, unless you are on his list of the Great Unfavored. I should know, I've been on that list for years. He's put me on every rotten duty in London, but I won't quit. I've got a wife and a pension to consider."

"How is Mrs. Poole these days?"

"Cracking."

"So, is that all? Between Barker and Munro, I mean."

Poole smiled again and took another long pull at his pint. "From what I've been able to piece together, Barker left in a towering rage. Munro had been, well, Munro, I suppose. Cyrus was walking north when he came to Craig's Court and noticed the private detective signs fluttering in the breeze. One of the offices was to let."

"Number 7."

"Precisely. He purchased the building on the spot. It took him less than two hours to track the estate agent and fill out the proper forms. It took less than two weeks to furbish and furnish the place, hire Jeremy, and open his doors. With no experience whatsoever, beyond some story about keeping the Empress Dowager from getting poisoned. Have you heard that one?"

"I have."

"Can you imagine it? Most of the detectives in Craig's Court are former police officers. This fellow swans in with no experience but plenty of money, buying the prime office in the street. They were inclined to hate him, naturally, which they did until they heard about his row with Munro. Then they became sympathetic. Some even helped him along a little. They—we—even suggested he place a large hoarding over the entrance, THE BARKER AGENCY, so that every time Munro took a hansom north in Whitehall he had to pass that blasted sign and recall that he was responsible for it."

"If you had been in Munro's shoes, would you have given him the situation?"

"Good Lord, no. He was unsuitable in every way. He doesn't take orders, he never does anything the same way twice, he tends to ride roughshod one minute and forgive like a saint the next. Your Guv is one of the most nonconformist men in London, and I don't mean his faith. He'd have been sacked within a week."

"So, Munro was right about him."

"Yes, but he needn't have been so shirty about it. The man has no tact."

"How did he come to be commissioner, then?"

"James Munro is relentless and tenacious. When the Irish Special Branch was created, it wasn't very popular. He begged for it, wheedled, connived, if you will. The Met learned early that it is best to let him have his way. He'll find a man's weaknesses and exploit them. He's actually a good judge of men, which is necessary in his work, and to be truthful, he's not a bad administrator. He knows how to deal with government agencies and can genuflect to both donors and aristocrats. Everyone above him admires him. Every man below him despises him. But then, I've never worked under a commissioner I'd care to have a pint with."

"So when did you first meet the Guv?"

"There was a murder in Wimbledon. A multiple murder. I was investigating it when I found him questioning a witness. Who was this bizarre fellow in his long leather coat and dark spectacles? As I said, we at the Yard have no love for private agents. Anyway, I sent him off with a flea in his ear. Afterward, every witness I spoke to admitted they'd spoken to him already, generally the day before, which I took to mean that he was a day ahead of me. He has a particular camaraderie with the lower classes. You know, buy the man a pint, ask him about his family, and commiserate about his worthless job. Barker's the opposite of Munro. Everyone below him respects him, and he feels no need to impress his superiors because, frankly speaking, he doesn't find them particularly superior."

He took another pull of his pint. I wondered if he was going to have a third and what kind of work he'd be fit for after three drinks.

"I ran into Cyrus again in much the same manner as I did the first time. The thought to give him an earful occurred to me, but instead we began talking. He explained that he'd been hired by the family of one of the deceased women. The murders occurred at a small dinner party. Two couples, both young, butchered like pigs, they were. Blood everywhere, knife marks in the table, broken crockery.

"There was an escaped murderer in London at the time who was known to have been born and bred in Wimbledon. He still had family there. Tracking him down was my priority, but as I spoke with Barker, he revealed what he had learned: one of the murdered women had recently had a baby. Apparently, the other had been trying for some time to conceive, but had miscarried. Not once; three times, it was. Cyrus talked to me about the emotional, nearly physical need of some women to have a child. They might do anything to have one. How can a gruff fellow like him have such insight into the mind of a woman?"

"I've wondered that myself," I said.

"Without even seeing inside the house, or having permission to visit the bodies, he put forth a theory. Mrs. Pangley had snapped during the dinner, possibly after the other, Mrs. Lee, had gushed about her child. She'd stabbed Mr. Lee with a dinner knife, then Mrs. Lee, but in the struggle with her, she had been stabbed, as well. A mother will do anything to protect her child, which at that moment was upstairs in the nursery. Mr. Pangley, who must have been completely astonished, tried to get his wife to leave, but she wasn't about to go anywhere without that infant. So, it was goodbye to her husband.

"After that, it would have been a simple matter for her to climb the stairs, take the baby, and leave. It was a young family with no servants, and the nanny had left for the night. Mrs. Pangley made it to the stairway, but was bleeding heavily from her wound. We found a trail of blood to the stairs. She never reached the top step. Nobody knew what happened until neighbors heard the baby crying, the only being alive in the house.

"The wounds and the story matched the truth. Cyrus gave all the credit to me. He hadn't been hired, he said, to solve the case for the general public, but merely to satisfy Mrs. Lee's family. They were horror-struck at the tale, of course, but defending her child while she herself was dying was just the sort of thing the young Mrs. Lee would do, they said. Can you imagine two young ladies in their finery, stabbing each other with knives over the best china?"

I absorbed that thought for the next minute, or tried to. It wasn't easy. "And you and Barker became friends after that?"

"Of a sort, I suppose. I was loath to open myself more fully to him, but as we began to know each other, I trusted him. We helped each other on at least three more cases and were partially in competition on five others. He invited me to dinner at his home, and before I knew it, we were mates."

"Until you were caught."

"Right. Stopping by at his offices too often was my fault. I'd been moved to 'A' Division and he was just round the corner. It was noted by the other inspectors, your chambers being so close to Whitehall Street. They peached on me to my superiors. They might not have cared a whit, but Munro did. He threatened to sack me, instead demoting me and transferring me to Ipswich. Ipswich, can you believe it? Nothing happens in Ipswich. People die naturally in their beds there. When a string of burglaries led to a murder, I used Barker's methods and, to my astonishment, solved the case. As luck would have it, the victim was the son of an MP. I was made a detective inspector on the condition that I did not make use of a certain private enquiry agent again."

"You haven't spoken to him, then?"

He laughed. "Of course I have. I'm merely more devious about it now, like speaking to his assistant streets away from Scotland Yard."

"Not his assistant. His partner."

"Yes. You do realize how fortunate you are, don't you? You were a former felon without a situation six years ago. You've done well for yourself."

"No," I said. "Mr. Barker has done well by me. I've improved, but not to the level of being a partner in the agency. Look, let us change the subject. Do you believe Munro is involved in this matter?"

"How should I know, since you will not tell me of it?"

"Sorry."

"Just tell your employer—your partner—to be extremely circumspect. The commissioner is an old rascal and he has all of the Metropolitan Police behind him. Expect a visit. Thanks for the drinks."

"Drinks?"

"You're the new partner. I'm but a lowly working man."

He was off. It had been good to talk with Poole again. I'd missed him and I'm sure the Guv felt it even more keenly than I. I paid the publican and left.

There were four empty glasses on the table at Jeremy Jenkins's elbow when I returned to the Rising Sun. However, I realized that he could drink twice that in two hours and that this was him being abstemious. I bumped him on the elbow and nodded my head toward the door. He readily rose from his chair. I tossed some coins on the bar and we left.

"The Guv is keeping a tight lip these days, Mr. L.," he said. "What's a-going on?"

I filled him in, believing he needed to know.

"Is this gonna change how we work?" he asked.

"I wish I knew."

When we arrived in our chambers, Barker was sitting as he was before, still resting his leg on the corner of his desk, still staring out the window, though the snow had stopped. I was doffing my coat and hanging my muffler on a peg when I saw the blood. There was only a splash, a little more than mere drops. It was in front of his desk, having missed his Persian rug by half an inch.

I looked at the Guv. There was a cut in the sleeve of his coat, near the shoulder. No obvious bloodstain was visible. I turned my head. Beside Barker's faded coat of arms, one of his claymores was missing. No, not missing, I realized; it was on the table below it, streaked with blood.

"Gave as well as got?" I asked. That was a question he often asked me after a bout.

He smiled. He rarely smiles and when he does he looks like a wolf baring his teeth.

Turning my chair to the desk in the middle of the room, I sat and faced him.

"Why do I think getting Jenkins and me out of the building was a ploy to flush someone out of the bushes?"

"I am not responsible for what you think."

"By the way, greetings from Terry Poole."

"Ah!" he said, removing the injured limb from the desk. "Terry. What is he about these days?"

"He brought a warning. Apparently, Commissioner Munro is after your scalp."

Barker glared at me, or I assumed he did. Behind those black spectacles, it's hard to tell.

"Well," he replied at length. "The man's welcome to try."

CHAPTER TEN

An hour or so later, the Guv sent me to get the latest edition of *The Times*. So far, nothing had been printed about Drummond's death. Barker wanted to know when the funeral would take place so he could see who would attend. We frequent a newsstand in Charing Cross Road. I purchased a copy and returned, clutching my bowler in the chill wind. No one has ever accused me of having second sight, but something told me I was being followed.

"'Ello, Gormless," a voice said in my ear.

I jumped away and glared. There was a thin fellow beside me, rather young, in a top hat and suit, but no overcoat. I was wary of young men, thinking them Drummond's pursuers. This one lifted his head enough for me to see under the brim of his hat, and when I did, he tipped me a wink.

"Oh, no," I said. "Tell me it isn't so. Vic, you old muck snipe, I hoped you were dead."

Soho Vic was one of the earlier banes of my existence. He was an errand boy, or an organizer of errand boys, who arrived at odd moments, always managing to insult me, go through my pockets, and steal Barker's guest cigars. I hadn't seen him in a year or two at least. He'd not only grown like the proverbial weed, he'd somehow acquired a reputable suit and hat. When I last saw him, he was barefoot in all kinds of weather, and wore loose trousers held up with rope.

"Foozler," he countered.

"Rat bag."

"Gibface."

"Lackwit."

He waggled his eyebrows. "Like old times, init? Fancy running into you. I'm on the way to your Guv's chambers."

"Where have you been all this time?" I asked.

"Push sent me to a tutor. Taught me to read and write proper enough to become a clerk for a solicitor in Cheapside."

"You mean there is someone on earth stupid enough to hire you?"

"Half days," he said, ignoring the insult. "I still run me messenger lads. Your master said he wants ter see me."

"It must be a mistake, Stashu. No one wants to see you."

Soho Vic was not his actual name. Stanislieu Sohovic was born in Poland and brought to London as an infant. What happened to his parents I never heard, but when I first met him he was a kind of half-pint Fagin, watching over a warren of dirty mud larks who kept things together by delivering messages, picking pockets, and whatever else was necessary to survive. I would have warned Barker about having a soft spot for hard-lucks if in fact I was not one of them. Stashu was the diminutive of Stanisleiu. He loathed it, therefore I used it.

Vic opened the door to our chambers and removed his hat with a grand gesture, then closed the door against me when I entered. I struggled in.

"As I live and breathe," Jenkins said. "If it isn't the tyke! Good to see you, Vic."

"Mister Jenkins, you are a sight! Haven't aged a day since we last met."

I gauged Soho Vic was about seventeen now. His hair was combed, his face washed, and someone had actually wiped his pug nose.

"Vic!" Barker boomed.

Soho Vic liberated a cigar from a box on Barker's desk and threw himself into a chair.

"So, what's the situation, Push?" he asked the Guv.

"I wondered if you would like to make some money, Vic."

"I'm not averse. What do I has to do?"

"Due to matters I cannot discuss, I shall be sending and receiving a good deal of information here in Craig's Court for a time. I need some reliable couriers. How many of your lads are up to such work?"

"Ten or fifteen, I'd say."

"What would be necessary in order to make someone choose one of your lads over any others to deliver messages in Whitehall?"

"A clean suit and shoes for each of them. No gloves or overcoats. We'd have to fight to keep them."

"Done. What else?" Barker asked from the recesses of his wing-backed chair.

"A place to stay. P'rhaps with piped water. Suits don't go with dirty faces."

The last I saw Vic's face it was none too clean. How a few years can change a person. Or Vic, for that matter.

"Done again."

"'Ere now, this is too easy. You want summat in return."

Barker nodded. "I do."

"Spit it out, then!"

"Very well. I want you to give up your other endeavors for a little while. No more dipping. No more snaking."

Dipping was picking pockets, of course, and snaking was climbing in through windows and chimneys in order to unlock doors for a professional thief. These were criminal activities, of course, but when you're cold and starving, you're not exactly particular.

Soho Vic shook his head. "That would put us too much in your debt. We'd be dependent on you. Go all soft. You've already got us reading and writing. There's plenty of work here, but a like number of boys doing it. What's to stop us from getting our hats handed to us?"

Vic bit into the end of the cigar, then lit it from a striker on the desk.

"Organization," my employer said. "Fifteen boys delivering messages regularly, impressing the clerks in Whitehall, ready to stand together if one of you is threatened."

"I get it."

"I'll act as a reference."

"No, thanks, Push," Vic said, holding up a hand. "Your name is not exactly what it once was."

"We're going to change that, you and me."

"You're up to something," Soho Vic said.

"Up to my neck," Barker admitted. "And it's barely started."

"And I imagine you're keeping Witless here in the dark."

He grinned at me. Someday I was going to stuff his throat with those teeth. All the same, he was probably right.

Soho Vic swiveled his head in my direction. "Is this on the level?"

"If it's Cyrus Barker, you know it is," I said, shrugging my shoulders.

"I'll think about it," he answered.

"Don't think too long," my employer said. "There are other boys who would jump at the chance. I offered this to you first because we've had a business arrangement in the past."

"Right. I'll let you know. Lots to think about. Some of these messenger boys in Whitehall have scrabbled hard to get where they are and won't take kindly to having the likes of me waltzing in and taking over."

"I didn't promise it would be easy," Barker said. "I need someone with determination."

"A 'lean and hungry look,'" I supplied.

"I forgot what a prat you are," Vic told me.

"Dung beetle."

"Lick-spittle."

"Guttersnipe."

"Enough!" Barker growled. "Mr. Jenkins, will you come here
a moment?"

I heard the chair squeak in the next room. Presently Jenkins
tottered in, looking mildly suspicious. We are called by our last
names either when we are in trouble, or when we are about to be
asked to do something we don't wish to do. Neither is a happy
prospect.

"Sir?"

"I need you to arrange for food and lodging for Vic and his boys
for a few days."

"Naw," Soho Vic said, his voice scornful. "We can feed ourselves right enough."

Jenkins pinched his lips together in worry. "How far away shall
they be?"

"I want them in Lambeth, near Waterloo Bridge," Barker said.
"Find a reliable land agent on the south side of the river. A temporary property for a dozen, mind. Near a pump."

"When, sir?" Jenkins asked.

"Now."

"I'm off, then," he said, and he was.

Soho Vic knocked on Barker's desk. "Here, I didn't say I'd accept the offer."

"You'll accept it. The tips here would be double those in the
East End."

"We'd have to knock some heads, show people we won't take
nothin' off no one."

Vic looked at me, as if I could help him make such an important decision. He was but seventeen in spite of his bravado. I nodded. We both knew the Guv was a man of his word.

"Gotta go," he said. "Things to see, people to do. Ta, Push. See yer later, Fopdoddle!"

"Not if I see you first," I called.

When he was gone, I crushed the end of his cigar in an ashtray.

"This is getting expensive," I noted casually, though I knew Barker could purchase a half-dozen such residences.

"Along with the information the Knights Templar receives, there is a substantial amount of money provided by wealthier members of the organization, and a certain amount of speculation. Only for sanctioned use, of course."

"Are we up to this, sir?" I asked. "This sounds like a large endeavor, even for you."

"Mr. Humphrey next door might be willing to deal with the financial matters."

"You mean the president of Cox and Co. Bank? He's a member of the Knights Templar?"

"Yes, of course."

"I thought so. How large is this organization exactly?"

"I cannot say," the Guv replied.

"You're helming an organization and you don't even know how many members you have?"

"Oh, I know how many, lad, but I cannot say. You are not one of us."

CHAPTER ELEVEN

I genuinely believe that those we question should have the courtesy to wait patiently for our arrival. True, we had not set an appointment, and also true that they did not know us from Adam, but that was mere negligence on their part. They should have known, or so I explained to the Guv. He merely sighed from deep within his broad chest.

"'Landgraf Johann Valentine von Arnstein,'" I read from the Home Office's list of suspects. "'Austrian citizen with no clear purpose.' *Was ist ein Landgraf?*"

A wheel of our hansom cab dipped into a pothole, and Barker seized the leather-covered door in front of us.

"You are the scholar, lad, not I."

"Let's see . . . *Graf* is some kind of noble. A count, I think. So a *Landgraf* would be a count who owns lands. Extensive lands, perhaps, or borderlands. In either case, he is an aristocrat. It's an odd thing about aristocrats—"

"They feel little need to answer questions put to them by mere private enquiry agents."

"Precisely," I said.

Count Arnstein was not at the Austrian embassy, neither was he at Brown's Hotel in Mayfair. The desk clerk would not tell us where he was, but a concierge, with two of my guineas snug in his pocket, informed us that the fellow was riding in Hyde Park. It seemed unreasonable to be riding in such weather. It just solidified my opinion that most aristocrats are inbred. Eventually, we tracked the suspect to his lair in an indoor pen that was part of the famous stables. I was going to speak to him but I was distracted by the absolutely gorgeous bit of horseflesh he was putting through his paces.

"My word," I said, coming to the gate. "Is that an actual Lipizzaner?"

The count nodded to me. He wore a dark coat and a low helmet of black velvet.

"I never thought I'd live to see one. Is he Spanish Riding School trained?"

"He is," Arnstein said in a low voice, as he had the horse actually walk sideways, hoof over hoof.

"The Habsburgs owned Austria and Spain four hundred years ago," I replied. "As I recall, the Spaniards brought six Moorish horses to Vienna and those six eventually sired the entire strain."

"They did."

He removed his helmet as he spoke. The man was perhaps forty, with short curling hair and side whiskers, and a lean face. His lower lip protruded from under his upper; it was the famous, or infamous Habsburg lip, common to many of that ancient and powerful line. Europe was littered with paintings of his ancestors. I was trying to recall if any of the Holy Roman emperors had been seen on a white charger when I was stopped as the man struggled to get off the horse. The count had only one arm, the sleeve pinned to the shoulder. Bad luck, I thought.

"Can I help you, gentlemen?" he asked. His accent was far

stiffer than the German ambassador's. I tried to picture a bloodthirsty monarch, but this fellow did not measure up.

"Count Arnstein," said Barker. "We are enquiry agents."

"Detectives, you mean?"

"Indeed. We have been hired to search for a missing manuscript and your name has been mentioned. Have you heard of such
a thing?"

"Thin strips of dark leather, written in Greek?"

"You know them?" I asked.

"I should say so," he told me. "I found them."

"Found them?"

"Discovered them, rather. I own a curio shop in Palestine.
Often I purchase items from the residents: coins and relics, potshards, that sort of thing. I also dig for them myself. It does not
require sound limbs to do the work, if one has the money to hire
workers."

"Do you work for your government?" the Guv asked.

"Franz Joseph is my cousin, but I am not employed by them
otherwise."

We stepped into a locker room where the man laboriously
began to change. I wanted to help him but it would have been an
assault on his dignity, I think. Luckily, there was one of those
wooden frames that remove boots to help him get them off. We
backed away to give him his privacy. He came out ten minutes
later, looking dapper.

"We appreciate your speaking to us, sir," Barker said.

"I have a meeting in three hours and nothing else to occupy
my time. Also, I have never spoken to a detective before, let alone
two. It is cold here, however. Perhaps we can meet at my hotel for
some sherry." He turned and called to a man waiting nearby.
"Boy!"

The man came running but he was not less than sixty.

"Rub the horse down for me. Feed him the hay we brought and
half a sack of oats, no more. Then blanket him and put him in his
stall. With fresh water, mind."

"Yes, sir."

"We have a hansom waiting, if you will share it," the Guv said.

As if by some miracle, the sun had reclaimed the heavens when we came out. One felt safe removing one's gloves. Hyde Park was glittering in the sunshine, and one would not wish to be anywhere else. As if by mutual agreement, the Guv and I turned away while Arnstein climbed slowly into the cab.

"You need not accommodate me, sirs," he said. "I get where I need to go, if a trifle more slowly."

"As do I, sir," Barker replied, indicating his brace.

Within fifteen minutes, we were ensconced in a lounge at Brown's, three stuffed leather chairs facing a generous fire. A few minutes later, our sherries arrived. Neither Cyrus Barker nor I like sherry, but sharing a drink with someone can open channels between you.

"For whom do you work, Mr. Barker?" Arnstein asked.

"I'm afraid my client prefers to remain anonymous."

The count smiled. "That does not seem quite fair if I am to answer your questions."

"True," my employer admitted. "Let me put it this way. Part of my search is to answer my own curiosity. I have not been officially retained to track down your manuscript."

"Ah, but you see, it is my manuscript no longer. I sold it to the German government and have been duly paid. If they lost it that is not my concern."

"You delivered the manuscript to Berlin?" the Guv asked.

"No, to Vienna. An envoy of the Kaiser met me along with a scholar who verified the authenticity of the material. Then we traveled to my bank and placed the amount in my account."

"How much were they willing to pay?" I asked.

"I would rather not say, but it was a princely sum. I anticipate the German government will attempt to retrieve the payment, but my solicitor assures me that I am in the right, legally. Nevertheless, I am here."

Barker pulled himself deeper into the overstuffed chair, and I watched as the fire flickered in his reflective lenses. He managed to sip the sherry without making a face.

"Why are you here, Count Arnstein, if you have no need of the manuscript any longer?"

The count leaned forward as if we were coconspirators.

"I am buying a dam, gentlemen. Or rather, commissioning one. My homeland may not be known to you. It is Styria, in Southern Austria. During the spring thaw each year there is flooding, some of it quite severe. My little country is not as prosperous as when my family ruled Europe. It was fortunate that I made my discovery when I did. It may be our only chance to build the dam at all."

"Surely you could find engineers in your own country."

"Not on this scale. The ones I met were very much immured in the eighteenth century. The Germans refused me for obvious reasons and my people have no wish to be beholden to the Swiss. You English have a reputation for dams and earthworks. I thought I would try here with the famous Major Pennycuick. His dam in Madras is a marvel, I'm told."

I raised my shoulder a little to let the Guv know I'd never heard of the chap. In my defense, engineering marvels are not the first thing I hunt for in *The Times*. I prefer *The Idler,* anyway.

"How came you by the manuscript, Count?" Barker asked.

Arnstein moved forward, more animated than I had seen him before.

"I have been consumed with biblical excavation since I was first taken to Palestine by my father when I was a youth. He, too, was interested in Old Testament sites. There is so much still to be found! There is Solomon's tomb, for example, or some sign that his father, David, once lived. An undistinguished building in Jerusalem might contain the Upper Room where Christ dined with his disciples. Palestine is a treasure trove!"

"Surely your health must make your work difficult," I said.

"I am a different man under a hot Palestinian sun," he replied.

Set me down in a dig and I shall climb about like a monkey. Perhaps if I had lost this limb I might have missed it, but I was born without it and I make do to accomplish anything."

"The manuscript, sir," Barker repeated from the depths of his chair. "How did you come by it?"

"My curio shop is in the Old City. There we clean and authenticate what we find. Meanwhile, the shop also purchases discoveries and items sold by locals. This may include tomb robbers. Sometimes it is difficult to tell them from the general population. I should like to tell you I made the discovery of the manuscript myself, but I'm afraid it came in the front door. Two boys, no more than seventeen, found a cave while searching for a leather ball. The manuscript was in the bottom of a pot that was cracked but still sealed. I quickly saw how important the slips—that's what we called them, slips—might be."

"How do you know it is not a forgery?" I asked. "I mean, if anyone could spot one, I'm sure it's you, but how do you know?"

"Three ways, Mr. Llewelyn. First, one painstakingly studies the words in the text. Then one examines the fragments under a microscope. We had the boys lead us to the actual cave where we found shards, but no other slips. Then we consulted a translator from the University of Athens, under secrecy, of course."

"You said three ways. What is the third?"

"It is by understanding how forgers work. A letter wrong and our Greek friend would pounce upon it like a cat on a mouse. Any attempt to use oil paint or India ink would be revealed under my microscope. One must be scrupulous or lose one's reputation. There are others clawing for my position, you see."

"You say the Germans pay well," Barker rumbled.

"Oh, yes. The manuscript would legitimize their claim as a modern imperialist nation. Everyone in Jerusalem knew of it. Old fragments and fakes were brought out like an old whore in a new dress, hoping to impress the Berliners. The Kaiser himself wants something to prove his own fitness to rule, a sign from on high, if you will. He wants a new bauble to impress everyone. He is a child in adult's clothing."

"What of Franz Joseph?" I asked. "Does he have no need for such a manuscript?"

"He would rather drink champagne and be cosseted by Viennese society than concern himself with religious scholarship. However, we are cousins and good Catholics, so I will not quarrel."

"Ah," Barker mused, looking into the fire.

"Do you think you will find it?" Arnstein asked.

The Guv shrugged his brawny shoulders. "Who can say? It is somewhere. People are looking for it. I might as well follow the herd. Perhaps fortune will shine upon me."

"I believe it might."

The count finished his thimbleful of sherry and poured another.

"I miss the food from home," he said.

"Viennese food?" I asked. "Weiner schnitzel and sauerkraut? Sacher torte?"

He shook his head. "Too rich for me. I prefer a humble *Beuschel* myself, and perhaps a *Kolatsche*."

"Is the dam vital to your country?" Barker asked.

"A town was destroyed last spring after the thaw. A church that stood for a millennium was gone in a day. It is already too late for this year, but perhaps it will be finished for next year."

Barker nodded.

"My father was banished, you know. To be sent to Styria was to be an exile from Vienna and the Court. It would not do to have close relatives intriguing about you. However, my father came to love Styria. I was born there and know little else. Vienna glitters, but the stars over Graz sparkle like diamonds."

"Very poetic," the Guv replied.

"You are a practical man, Mr. Barker."

The count moved to pour more sherry into my employer's delicate glass, but Barker put a rough hand over the rim.

"Where do you suppose the manuscript is now?"

"I have no idea and I don't especially care. My only concern is that the Germans are not successful in their suit and that they don't blame the Catholics."

He stood and nodded before walking away.

"Conclusions?" Barker growled in my ear, a bass note.

"I don't know," I admitted. "I cannot understand aristocrats. When a fellow tells me Franz Joseph is his cousin, I don't know how to respond. He's just a chap as I am, I suppose, but I can no more understand a man coming to London to buy a dam than he can a convict becoming a private enquiry agent."

"You were never really a convict."

"Oh, no? There are scars on my fingertips from picking oakum."

"I'll trade your scars for mine, laddie," Barker said, smiling.

"I'll keep mine, thank you. Why did he bother speaking to us at all? Is he that well mannered? We've been given an airing once or twice by a duke who doesn't like us meddling in his private affairs."

"More than twice. There is nothing to force them to even answer Scotland Yard's questions."

"Count Arnstein was forthcoming about how the manuscript came into his possession," I noted. "Unfortunately, there is no way to corroborate any of his statements."

"Aye," said the Guv.

"He may never have even been to Jerusalem. I did see curio shops near the bazaar during my honeymoon, but he could just as easily find a map in the British Museum or a guidebook to Palestine and pretend to know what he's talking about."

Barker pushed the tiny glass of sherry farther away on the table as if he would be contaminated by it.

"I envy you your recent visit, Thomas. I was there once, on my way to England, but could only stay half a day. I could have spent a month there. I suppose excavating ancient treasures is like enquiry work in some ways. A man can get caught up in the work and never leave. To possibly unearth one important find in a lifetime, a scroll, a carving, an ancient village, would be enough to make the heat, the flies, and the solitude all worthwhile."

He was staring deeply into the fire now, but he was far away. There it was again. He'd been cast out by his own church for supporting Charles Haddon Spurgeon in his disgrace. Now Barker was adrift, unable to find a church that followed his tenets and envious of those who found spiritual refuge.

"Let's be on, Thomas, before you fall asleep."

Irascible, that's what he was. I was awake, for the most part.

"Yes, sir," I said.

We stepped out into the thaw again. There were patches of dead grass pushing up through the melting snow. I could no longer see my breath.

I would take Rebecca to the zoological gardens in Regent's Park, I decided, if the weather turned fair in a few days. Our marriage was still new, and I felt I needed to entertain and impress her. I wondered how she was, sitting in her house, taking visitations from her crowd of Jewish brides, young and old.

"Let us walk, Thomas."

We strolled through Hyde Park, one hand on our sticks, the other in our pockets, as if there were not a manuscript hidden somewhere, as if it were a Sunday afternoon and we had nothing better to do than take the air.

"So, when, sir?" I asked, jumping puddles to reach an omnibus in front of the palace gates.

"When what, Thomas?" he asked.

"The manuscript, sir. When are we taking it to Calais?"

"Whenever it suits me," he said, as he stepped onto the omnibus. "Stop asking."

CHAPTER TWELVE

W e were not long in our chambers when a man entered with a constable. Then another constable, and another, and another. By the time they had all arrived, there were six of them. The Guv sat back in his chair and regarded our visitors.

"So many?" he asked.

"Barker, you're under arrest," said Commissioner James Munro of the London Metropolitan Police.

"You're going to need a few more men, I think," I said.

He scowled. "You, too, Llewelyn."

"Then you definitely need more men."

"Of what are we accused?" Barker asked.

"Never you mind. You'll answer questions in the investigation room."

"I could answer them here as easily as there."

Munro stepped back, ready to wave the constables to take us. He was a stocky fellow in his mid-fifties, with a dark mustache and graying hair cut short on a bullet-shaped head. He frowned. He always frowned, every time I've ever seen him.

Barker sighed and rose from his chair. Of the six constables, three looked ready to attack, while three others seemed more likely to retreat.

"There is no need for that. Come, Thomas. May we be allowed to take our coats?"

The men watched us carefully, as if we would pull pistols from our pockets. I drew it out, wrapping my scarf carefully into my coat, then donned my rabbit-lined gloves, merely to irritate Scotland Yard.

A constable came forward and took the Guv's arm. Cyrus Barker seemed to swell, then, the menace of him, the protean danger that he could cause. Everything around him became a weapon, from the hat rack to a book on Jenkins's desk. I'm not sure if one could kill someone with a book, but if it were possible, the Guv could do it. Then just as easily, he diminished, and became just a man, a normal man, if one did not know better.

"Shall we go?" the Guv asked. "Jeremy, inform our solicitor."

"Righto," Jenkins said from behind his desk. I'm certain Munro's entrance had woken him from his chair. On one hand, he'd had no sleep; on the other, his waiting room had just been invaded, and there was nothing he could do about it.

A pair of constables held my arms on each side, but I still managed to stop at our waiting-room desk.

"Quite the watchdog," I said.

Our clerk smiled, with a hint of mischief in his eyes.

My concern was that the commissioner would make a public spectacle of dragging us to Great Scotland Yard Street, but for once, he did not take advantage of the situation. We were escorted past the old offices with which we were so familiar, to the gleaming new buildings that reminded me of a wedding cake. Once inside the front doors, I called over my head to a man behind the front desk.

"Morning, Sergeant Kirkwood!"

"Bless my soul," he replied to my back. "If it isn't the Guv and his nibs!"

We did not tarry. In the time it would take for Barker to light a pipe, we were marched to a holding cell and locked in.

That was standard procedure for hardened criminals such as Barker and myself. Even the most famous or infamous suspect must share a cell with the other dregs of humanity: the drunks, the pickpockets, the wife beaters and rampsmen, who make Scotland Yard such a colorful and interesting place. They cleared a bench for us and we sat.

"I wondered if you were going to fight your way out of our predicament," I said to the Guv.

"I considered it, lad, but I cannot think that anything we have done warrants an arrest. Therefore, I suspect there has been some new development."

A half hour crawled by. The Yard hopes that its very reputation shall break down a man's resolve and he would be only too glad to confess, given enough time. Believe it or not, it actually worked now and again.

Eventually, I began to wonder what time it was, when the turnkey arrived and took us to the interviewing room. Munro was awaiting us.

"Such treatment, sir," the Guv said, as if it were a compliment. "Interviewing us yourself. I'm certain you have many matters that require your attention."

"Barker, where were you last night?"

"We went to see a friend in Limehouse."

"Who was with you?"

"Thomas, here, my clerk, Jeremy Jenkins, and a professor of classics, Dr. Wessel of the University of London."

"And what were you doing there all night? I am informed that you didn't return until this morning."

"That's an interesting piece of information to have at one's fingertips," Barker said. "It's almost as if we were being deliberately observed."

The interrogation rooms are small and cramped. The Guv and I had been thrust onto one tiny bench. He got most of it. Across from us, Munro laced his fingers over his waistcoat, which the benefits of too many social and governmental functions had distended. A constable took notes beside him.

"Answer the question."

Barker shrugged, as if it were a small matter. "Professor Wessel and I come together about twice a year to discuss eschatology."

"E-s-c-h—" I began, for the benefit of the constable.

"Shut it, Llewelyn," Munro said. "Barker, are you telling me you debated the Revelation until dawn?"

"Almost," the Guv said, nodding. "He availed himself of a cot for the last few hours."

"You are telling me that you were not using the professor to decipher an ancient manuscript in your possession?"

"To what manuscript do you refer?" Barker asked.

"Do you have several? I'm referring to the one you have been entrusted with by Her Majesty's government!"

"I believe you will find that the manuscript to which you refer is locked in the vault of the Cox and Co. Bank."

Munro pounced in anger.

"Barker, I don't know what sort of cheap conjuror's trick you used to spirit the Gladstone bag to Limehouse, but you cannot fool me. Suspect you are and suspect you have always been. You are a man with no provable past, and you are locked in cells like these every couple of months."

My employer raised his hands, palm up. "My past can be proven if one can read Mandarin, which is perhaps the most widely spoken language on earth. Should you wish my record to be free of arrests, you might consider not arresting me so often."

Munro closed his eyes, reining in his temper. He exhaled slowly, then opened them again.

"You were hired to take a bag to Calais, not mess about in Chinatown."

"How did you know that?" I asked. "Were you spying on Downing Street as well as Limehouse?"

My hands were prone on the table between us. Munro brought down a fist upon one of them and thumped it as if it were a cockroach.

"Ow!" I shouted in the confined space. One or two words might have slipped from my lips that I would not use on the Sabbath. For once, Barker did not look as long-suffering as usual when an untoward word was spoken by his assistant or even his partner.

"That hurt!" I said, rubbing my injured hand with the other.

Munro shook a finger at me. "Let that be a lesson to you, Prisoner 7502."

There it was: 7502, my number as an inmate in Oxford Prison. He would never accept that I had served my sentence, that the theft I had supposedly done had, in fact, never occurred, or that I had been framed by an earl's son, for whom I worked as a batsman.

I was about to give Scotland Yard's favorite son my opinions about his manner, his knowledge, his disposition, his morals, and his piglike features, but at that moment, Barker kicked me under the table, nearly fracturing my ankle.

"Ow!" I cried.

"We digress," the commissioner said. "Mr. Barker, why have you not delivered the bag to Calais?"

"Because I did not wish to," he said. "I did not find the time to be propitious. Thomas was attacked last night by three youths who believed a bag in his hand was the one they were seeking."

Munro rounded on me, me with the crushed hand and near broken ankle.

"Is this so?"

"It is," I said, while wiggling my fingers to see if they still functioned. They did, but just barely.

"Describe these youths."

"Three of them, university age, I'd say. Couldn't really describe their faces because they were running away, but I'll not forget their uniforms."

Munro raised an eyebrow. "Uniforms?"

"Yes, sir. The coats were a blue wool, with a collar and no lapels. They were double-breasted and the apron came to a point in the middle. That is, the coat hung to their knees, but it was six inches lower in the middle."

"Are you getting this all down, PC Gaines? What else did they wear?"

"Highly polished black boots. I believe their trousers were tucked inside them. Oh, and they wore matching caps with black patent-leather peaks in front."

"Clean shaven?"

"I have no idea. The closest one was. They snatched my bag and ran off with it, throwing it back and forth as if they were in a rugby match."

"And where were you?"

"On the ground. They tackled me."

Munro gave a terse laugh.

"They took your bag after all your training?" he asked. He turned to Barker. "This is your prize student?"

The Guv did not rise to the bait.

"And what was in the bag, Mr. Llewelyn?"

"Clothes, sir. A fencing uniform, to be precise."

"Was there a sword?"

"No, that is back at the school."

"That is good news," Munro said. "Whoever has been stabbing people this week does not need another weapon."

Barker nodded, agreeing. Then he stopped and looked up at him.

"Did you say 'people'? Has there been a second stabbing?"

"There has. Come, follow me."

We followed him down the narrow halls, with PC Gaines trotting along behind. The commissioner led us down a set of steps to the lower floor. If I were not already familiar with the building, I would have known where I was by the heavy odor of carbolic.

"The Body Room."

For some reason known only to the architect, this was what it was called rather than "the Morgue."

Munro threw the door open, and without preamble, warning, or preparation, he pulled the sheet from the corpse's face.

"Wessel," I muttered.

"Yes, Wessel. He met his fate in the Commercial Road. Did he have the bag, Barker? Did you give him the bag? Is it in fact gone?"

My employer wasn't listening. He was staring at the supine body of the professor.

"No," Barker murmured.

"You maintain that the satchel is still in the vault in Cox and Co.?"

"It is there. Sound as a pound sterling."

"The thought occurred to me that I might hold you over for a day or two, until the deadline for delivery to Calais is passed."

Barker nodded, a polite bow. "That is at your discretion."

"When is the deadline?"

"That is at mine."

"Are you taking this seriously, Barker?"

"I am standing in front of the body of an acquaintance of mine. I assure you this case has my full attention. May I examine the body?"

Gently, he uncovered the torso. It was almost as white as the sheet, save for livid spots of purple.

"Two stab wounds."

"Three," Munro said. "There is one in the small of his back. Bad form. Only a coward stabs a man in the back."

I thought it likely that the ambitious commissioner of the Met had stabbed many men in the back during his career, but for once I held my tongue.

"A dray cart man named John Hackett came running into 'H'

Division early this morning," Munro said. "He'd been parked at a curb, delivering his first load of hay at a livery in the Commercial Road. He was inside for a few minutes, talking with the stable owner and settling accounts. When he returned, there was a hansom parked behind him. The cab was mostly in the street and had stopped because the horse was eating his new hay. There were men and women talking in loud voices and gesticulating, and Hackett tried to pull on the horse's bridle, asking for some help. They were able to draw the horse away with the offer of an apple, but when they looked inside the cab they found both the cabman and the passenger inside, dead, run through with swords. Inspector Meadows of 'H' Division theorizes that more than one man boarded and killed the two of them. At some point, the driver slipped off his perch into the front of the cab below. The horse, who had paced this route every day since she was a filly, came down the Commercial Road more than a mile before she saw the tempting hay, and since there was no driver to stop her, she wandered over and began to graze."

Munro moved to another sheeted form and exposed the head and shoulders.

"Horace Quincy, fifty-four, cab badge number 672, lived nearby in Bethnal Green. Married, three children, one grandchild."

It was a jowled, heavy face, stubbly and lined, yet I could still picture the man cooing over his new grandchild. He might have driven Barker or me in the East End or the City. We went there often.

Then I pictured a cab horse meandering down Commercial Road pulling a spectral cab full of bloody corpses. That included the body of Professor Wessel, who had quite possibly had the best evening of his distinguished career, and afterward was run through with two swords simultaneously. It was my fault. Not the running-through part, of course, but I had drawn him there with offers of money he never received or spent. I had convinced him to stay when the location had been unsafe. Then I had sent him off in a cab, knowing how dangerous it might have been to be associated in any way with the Barker and Llewelyn Agency. Come to think of it, perhaps I had run him through myself, at least metaphorically speaking. He wasn't the first I had drawn to his death, nor would he be the last. Somehow, at Barker's behest, I had become a sort of Grim Reaper.

A constable put his head in the door, and whispered in Munro's ear.

"Ah," he said after the constable was gone. "Your expensive solicitor stands in the front entrance, threatening mischief."

"You're not keeping us, then?" I asked.

He opened the door into the hall again and waved a hand toward the stairs at the distant end.

"I don't need to," he said. "You run roughshod all over everything. You don't need my help to get yourselves in trouble."

CHAPTER THIRTEEN

It felt as if all the air had been sucked from the room. Barker paced about the office, staring at the floor.

"We couldn't know," I said.

"We should have known."

My employer does not believe in chance. Somehow everything is in our hands, and if the worst happens he blames himself. One cannot talk him out of it, or reason with him, or even try to calm his soul. Perhaps the worst is that he will never talk about it. He bottles everything inside and stores it. How many bottles are in there? I wondered.

For some reason, when Barker is wretched, he paces with his head down and his hands behind his back. I believe it is a hold-over from his days as a ship's captain.

"Oi!" a boy cried, dashing in. "'Scold out there!"

He slipped a note onto Jenkins's desk and hopped about shivering while he waited for our clerk to open his drawer and give him sixpence. The tyke was underdressed in a thin jacket, but he owned shoes, so he was doing better than some who went about this time of year in rags wound round their ankles. After studying the coin he received to make sure it was genuine, he tugged at his cap and spirited himself out into the cold.

I crossed to the door and closed it. Jenkins had securely locked the money box and was entering the room with the envelope presented on a silver tray. The latter was secondhand, probably purchased in Covent Garden. Were it sentient, I'm sure it would have wondered how it went from a mansion in Surrey to an enquiry agent's office hard by Scotland Yard.

We all met in the middle, Barker from his perambulations, I from the door, and Jenkins from his desk. Our employer snatched the letter from the salver and we all went our way without comment, save for a small grunt in the back of his throat.

Snick.

I liked that sound, a sharp, well-honed Italian dagger slicing through an envelope of expensive vellum. I raised my eyebrows.

"Pollock Forbes," Barker said. "His list of suspects."

"Shall I collate the two lists and type it for you?"

"Aye, do," he replied. "It will keep you from underfoot."

Somehow our near collision in the center of the room had become my fault. I sat, compared the lists, both of which had some of the same culprits in common, and began to type.

Halfway through the newly revised list I fell into a blue funk and stared off into space, but soon got back to work. I pulled the paper from the Hammond, placed the battered typewriting machine under my desk, where I would batter it further, and then relayed the sheet to Barker's desk.

"Sir, I shall require an hour or two off."

The Guv's brows sank like the evening sun behind his dark quartz spectacles, but it was more curiosity than pique. Reaching over the desk, I pointed to the final name of the list of suspects.

"Rabbi Mocatta?" he demanded, as if I were having him on.

"Apparently."

"You intend to confront your wife?"

"I don't know if 'confront' is the proper word, but her father is on a list of spies and murderers, and it is possible she knows why."

"I've known the man for years," Barker rumbled. "He is a member of the Board of Deputies. I find it difficult to believe he could be involved in such matters."

"No less than I, sir. But as you yourself say, the human heart is capable of all sorts of wickedness."

"When did I say that?" he demanded.

"Sunday, I should think. You are at your most Old Testament then."

"Very well, but please instruct your wife not to speak to her father concerning this matter."

"What about the manuscript, sir?" I asked.

"I shall think and plan. Pray, make it obvious as you hail a cab that you are unencumbered by a satchel."

"Yes, sir."

"And armed! Shall you return?"

"I cannot promise what will happen after the next hour."

"Then I shall speak to you later, lad."

I nodded and left. Raising my stick, I attracted a cab and clambered aboard, making it obvious to anyone who might notice me that there was nothing in my hand, no bulge in my coat, nothing peering from under my bowler hat. That accomplished, I sat back in the cab and thought.

How could Rebecca's father, that bookish little rabbi, get himself on a list of spies and assassins? Surely it must be some kind of mistake. I intended to ask Rebecca. She had been spending a good deal of time with him lately.

When I arrived in Newington, Rebecca was still not at home. Mac was curious about my early arrival, but I put him off. She returned in half an hour. Harm, Barker's Pekingese, scurried to the door, but when he recognized her, he wandered away. Like Barker, he found her vaguely suspicious. At the moment, I did, as well.

"Thomas, you're home early!" she said, breaking out in a smile as if my arrival were an unexpected gift. She saw my face, however, and it faded like a morning glory.

"What's wrong?" she asked.

"Let's go upstairs and talk about it, dear."

The look of confusion and concern on her face made me feel cruel for even bringing the matter to her attention. I led her through into our sitting room, where she immediately threw her arms around me in fear. Her slight body was trembling.

"What is it?" she asked.

"Probably nothing," I said. "Sit down. I'm sure it is a mistake. We have been gathering a list of suspects in the case we are enquiring after and for some reason your father's name appeared on the list."

"My father? How could his name be on some sort of criminal list? It is absurd! It is, isn't it? What sort of case are you investigating?"

"Spy work, really. An agent was killed. We are to deliver a package to France. Actually, we are overdue, but the Guv works by his own times table."

"I wish I could think of some way to help you."

"Has your father been acting out of character lately? Is he less talkative? More secretive? Does anything appear to have unsettled him?"

Then my wife did the last thing I expected her to do. She lowered her head and began to cry. She didn't sob. It isn't her way. She cries silently, and the tears seem to pour out of her, falling from her long lashes to the floor without trickling down her face. It was so unsettling to see that I would have climbed the Pennines just to make her stop. Of course, I leaped up and gave her my handkerchief and held her as the tears came and waited for her to stop.

"I've been lying to you, Thomas."

Those were the worst words I could have possibly imagined her to say. I am pessimistic by nature even in the best of times, but still, it was a shock. Was it another man? Was she leaving me and visiting her parents for support? My life began to fray about the edges.

"What's wrong?" I asked, a trifle huskily.

"I haven't been seeing my family while you are working. I've been helping out at Le Toisin d'Or."

"What?" I asked. "You've been working? Rebecca, I promise that I make enough money to keep us both. There's no need for you to work."

"I wanted to surprise you. You should have a wife who can cook for you."

"I don't expect you to cook, though I'm flattered you think it so important. I'm sorry if I spoiled your surprise. I merely asked about your father."

The tears began again. I gave her my handkerchief and held her. It wasn't about the cooking, I realized. Her misery was about her father. Perhaps my concerns about him were not unknown to her.

"What is happening with him?" I asked.

She rested her forehead against my shoulder and wiped her eyes.

"He won't see me anymore. I've been cut off for marrying you."

"What?" I asked, astonished.

"My mother won't see me, either," she continued. "My sister informed me and that is the last I have seen of her. Most of my friends have stopped coming to call, and are distant when I visit them. I am being shunned."

"Because you married me?"

"Yes."

"But you told me a widow can marry whomever she wants."

"That's true, but her family is not obliged to like it. Or her circle of friends."

I sat back and tried to take it all in.

"Am I that objectionable?"

"Of course not. You've been very polite to everyone. You've even participated in the holy days. You studied everything, tried to be friendly, and never put a foot wrong."

"What's wrong, then?" I asked. "Your family struck me as nice people. A little distant, perhaps. Does the fact that I'm a Gentile concern them so much?"

"Not a Gentile, Thomas. A Christian."

"You're not making sense, Rebecca," I told her.

"If I were to convert from the True Faith to Christianity, it would be a great insult for my papa, both as a rabbi and as a father. It would be a blemish on his life's work. It might be suggested that he resign from the Board of Deputies. You know his work is itinerant, that he leads synagogues that have no permanent rabbi or fills the position temporarily if another is sick or traveling. I fear he is not being requested or even made welcome now."

"Look, Rebecca, I said we'd decide what we would believe together. I certainly didn't intend to push Christianity onto you. In fact, I offered to convert. The Lord knows my heart. I believe He'll accept me in a synagogue as well as a church."

She patted my hand.

"It's not that simple, Thomas. It never is in Judaism. The worst thing I could do is convert, but even if you converted, it wouldn't make much of a difference. Christians who convert are not made particularly welcome. In theory, perhaps, but not in practice. You are not of the Chosen People, you see. Oh, men like Mac or your friend Israel Zangwill would defend you no matter what, but others will never fully trust a Gentile, no matter what the situation. Our people have been mistreated by Christians so much over the centuries that one who willingly comes among us must be a wolf stalking the sheep."

"But we joined Brother Malachi's Judeo-Christian church in order to please everyone."

"I know, but in doing so, we've pleased no one. If there were a gulf separating our religions, my relatives might feel safe, but they see Brother Malachi's church as a kind of bridge between them.

Not a welcome bridge, but a snare for gullible Jews. In short, a trap."

I put a hand to my forehead. "I never meant to do this. I'm sorry. It wasn't my intent to drive a wedge between you and your family. We could reconsider a synagogue—"

"No, Thomas!" Rebecca said, looking fierce. "The decision will be ours, no matter the consequences. I won't be dictated to by my family."

"I'm sorry you've been going through this," I said. "You should have told me."

She lowered her head again.

"I was ashamed. Not of you in front of them, but of them in front of you. It is so small-minded. My sister would call it provincial. I suspect my parents have been warning her off. She and her husband are more dependent financially than I, you see."

"Is that all?"

"Isn't that enough?"

"You've been sneaking away to slave in an ogre's kitchen because your parents are too stupid to appreciate what a fabulous daughter they have?"

She laughed through her tears. "Etienne is not an ogre."

"Have you looked closely, lately?"

"Stop it," she said, slapping my hand.

"Tempest in a teapot, dear girl," I told her. "We haven't begun to fight back. We'll go door-to-door until every Jew in London appreciates you as much as I."

"I wish it were possible."

"You just wait."

She sighed. "I will."

"But how is your father on this list?"

"I have no idea, but I know this: he has a temper, as gentle as he may appear, and when it shows he is prone to make rash decisions. Then, rather than correcting them, he defends them to the death. I'm afraid that was how he lost a permanent position as a rabbi before."

"How do you think we should handle this?" I asked.

"I don't know," she admitted. "Perhaps my parents have had things their own way for a while."

"They'd have to be barmy to toss away so beautiful a daughter."

"How you talk, sir. Perhaps they need to have their perch shaken a bit, if that isn't too mean-spirited. I have done nothing to warrant censure. My parents would have defended me against anything when I was married to Asher."

"Leave it to me, then, my employer and me. Between us, we're awfully good at shaking birds from perches."

"It cuts, I must confess. He's my papa. Protecting me or my reputation should not stop merely because I married a Gentile."

"No, it shouldn't," I said.

"Do you forgive me for keeping a secret from you?"

"Rebecca, I'd forgive you anything."

She dabbed her eyes, folded my handkerchief and gave it back to me with a sniff. Her eyes were red from crying.

"Do you feel better?" I asked.

"I do. I've been carrying that burden around for months."

"You should have told me the moment you knew. We must have no secrets between us."

"No secrets," she promised.

"Just trust me."

"But you're so different from Asher, you see," she said, sitting down on the settee. "He didn't care what mattered to me or what I thought as long as I kept a proper house and invited the right people to tea. You don't care a fig about those things."

"I don't have a high regard for our species as a whole. If I have to live according to someone else's expectations, then already he has not lived up to mine. Your father is so concerned that this group shouldn't associate with that group, and yet if he were treated that way, I'm sure he would consider himself ill-used."

"That's Papa. He always worries about supporting his family. Mama loves her house and servants and nice china, and he must be on good terms with everyone and work hard to meet our needs."

"Not your needs," I said. "I'm taking care of those myself now."

"Yes," she said, touching my sleeve.

My mind wandered for a moment. "I'm not the ideal son-in-law, but he might trouble to get to know me before he condemns me. That's how it works for most people I know."

She laughed again. "You're terrible, you know. You always make yourself out to be a fool. Everyone underestimates you."

"I prefer it that way. Some of my East End associates need not know that I quote Keats and Shelley, and some of my West End associates need not know that I carry a sword cane. Not everyone is entitled to know everything about me. Or us."

"That sounds like hard won advice. Did you acquire that philosophy in prison?"

"Rebecca, until you came along, the entire earth was my prison."

She took my hand in hers and held it tight, running a finger along the lines in my palm.

"You will do your best to keep safe, won't you?"

"I'll take precautions, such as they are," I replied. "You haven't reconciled yourself to my work yet, have you?"

"You can't change. I understand that. The occupation has overtaken you and now you can't quit. It's true, I'd rather you were a stockbroker. It's much easier than telling my friends you are an enquiry agent. But then, as you said, you're not here to meet their expectations, are you?"

"Precisely."

"You know, I'm starting to agree with you. People can be so petty. Perhaps I'm taking their opinions too much to heart. I have you. What else do I need?"

"At last, we agree on something," I said.

CHAPTER FOURTEEN

I returned to Whitehall so quickly that even Barker looked surprised. He was standing by the coatrack and had begun to don his heavy overcoat when I entered.

"Is the matter with Mrs. Llewelyn concluded?" he asked.

"Not yet, but it shall be soon. Where are we going?"

"Finbury Park."

I snapped my fingers. "The American evangelist, Cochran."

"Precisely."

When we reached Finbury, we found the tent fully assembled and people making preparation for the evening event. However, there was no sign of Cochran himself. We began asking one man after another where he could be found. Finally, we were directed to a small public house nearby, where we found Cochran in a corner drinking nothing stronger than lemonade. He was a little over thirty and he reminded me of a matinee idol, with good features and hair neatly parted and pomaded behind each ear. However, he was a spindly fellow beneath that theatrical chin. At some point, perhaps, his body would mature and he would become the sort of fellow women follow with their eyes, if not their hearts.

"Sir," Barker said, bowing.

Cochran looked up from what I presumed were the notes for his sermon. He rose while trying to turn over in his mind just who these two men were, the taller one especially. I'd seen that look on a thousand faces by then and would see a few thousand more.

"May I help you, gentlemen?"

I stepped around the Guv and put our business card in his hand. Barker sat, in spite of the protest of the captain's chair beneath him. Going to a table nearby, I pulled a chair closer to them. Meanwhile the evangelist ingested the novel term "private enquiry agent" and tried to make sense of it.

"Are you gentlemen with Scotland Yard?"

"No, sir," Barker said. "Not in this matter. However, we have cooperated with them in the past. Our offices are but one street apart. We are working for a family who has just lost their son. Hillary Drummond was his name. He had arrived in Charing Cross from Germany mere minutes before his death a couple of days ago.

"Who is this Drummond fellow?"

"He was working for the government."

"How did he die?"

"He was trampled by a horse and carriage after he had been run through with a sword."

Cochran raised a brow. "What did he do to deserve such a fate?"

"That is what we have been hired to determine. We have been questioning anyone who had recently arrived from Germany. The government has been kind enough to give us a list. We understand you came here from Berlin."

"Yes, I did," Cochran said, leaning forward and clasping his pale and bony hands. "We had a very successful tour: Hamburg, Berlin, Leipzig, Nuremberg, and Heidelberg. Many souls were saved. The country is ripe for the Lord's work."

"No doubt," Barker said. "Did you acquire any new workers or assistants during your tour who might have followed you here?"

"You suspect someone in my camp following?"

"Everyone on the list must be questioned. It is my profession. No one bears you or your followers any ill will."

"I wish that were so. Europe has become decadent. The cities I have spoken in have been sophisticated and prosperous. They have also teemed with vice the way a ghetto teems with rodents. They are a far cry from my home in Albany. I hope England shall prove to be a more pious nation, sir."

"Are there any Germans with you?" the Guv asked.

"None."

I stopped taking notes and looked over my notebook at Cochran.

"Who translated your sermons while you were in Berlin?" I asked.

"No one. I speak German. My parents immigrated to New York from Bavaria. My brother and I were raised in a community among hundreds of Germans."

"Are you sympathetic to the German cause, rather than the English one?"

"I'm not unsympathetic. After all, I have German blood, and not a drop of English." Cochran frowned and looked down at his feet. I could almost hear the wheels and cogs turning in his head. "What do you want, Mr. Barker? I have a sermon to finish."

"As I said, I am investigating a murder."

"Am I a suspect?"

"Mr. Cochran—"

"Reverend Cochran."

"Reverend Cochran, your name appears on a list provided by the government. My work, as I see it, is to eliminate suspects from that list until I am down to one. Provide me with a proper explanation of your business here and we shall be on our way to question someone else. When did you arrive in London?"

"Three nights ago."

"The night before Drummond's death," my employer said. "Where are you staying?"

"The Savoy."

I coughed. He was staying in the grandest, newest, and best-appointed hotel in London, if not all the British Isles. Cochran looked at me as if I accused him of something, which I hadn't. That is, not yet.

"I was exhausted from the trip," he answered. "I slept until nearly nine, then ate my breakfast late."

Barker nodded, as if this were natural, which I suppose it was; the clergy keeps irregular hours.

"Did you break your fast with your colleagues?" I asked. "They may be able to vouch for your presence."

Cochran's cheeks turned pink. "I saw them around noon. They were staying at a hotel nearby."

"Oh, really?" I asked. "What hotel is that?"

"The Metropole."

The hotel was in a bystreet not far from the Savoy. I'd been there a time or two on a case. It did not quite have an unsavory reputation, but I would not put a group of religious followers there.

"So, you were not seen," I said.

"Ah, but the staff at the Savoy will remember me."

"Aye," Barker said, "but the staff is very discreet there. I'll wager they would say you were not there if you were, but I'm not certain they would corroborate a guest has been there."

I glanced at my employer. One corner of his mustache was higher than the other. He was enjoying this exchange.

"I was there!" Cochran continued. He was clearly nettled.

"We'll go to the hotel later, Reverend. You did say 'Reverend,' did you not? What denomination is that?"

"It is no denomination. We are the One True Church!"

"The One True Church? You mean there was none until you started your crusade?"

Cochran frowned. "No, that is the name of our church, the One True Church."

"So, yours is not the real One True Church. That is merely the name you have chosen."

"That is correct."

"Then what happened between the Lord's death and resurrection and a few years ago when you began this church?"

"There is an unbroken line of martyrs in their fight against the Whore of Babylon!" he replied.

"These martyrs, are they a continuous procession of saints or did they come along piecemeal?"

"It does not matter, sir. It was the ideas they brought with them and developed, one concept upon another."

"I see."

Cochran frowned. "Anyway, this discussion has nothing to do with whatever you have come for."

"That is so, sir," my employer remarked. "We have gone off on a tangent. Tell me, have you heard of the words 'Mensur' or 'Mensurites'?"

"No, sir, I have not," Cochran said, showing signs of impatience.

"Did you notice any group of men, especially young men in uniforms, while you were preaching in Germany?"

"A few, as I recall. Military outfits, you know, frogged jackets and the like. Caps. Not the same each time. Green, blue, black. Rather smart-looking uniforms. I didn't know why they had come or who they were."

"Did you preach a particular message while you were there?" the Guv asked.

Cochran shifted in his chair. It was hard wood, and uncomfortable, not unlike a pew, in fact.

"I preached the same message I'm preaching tonight: The Downfall of the Whore of Babylon and the Return of Christ."

"Do you mean the downfall of the Roman Catholic Church?" Barker asked, his hands folded over the head of his stick.

"I do."

"And who then shall rise?"

"The Teutonic race, of course."

My employer glanced at me, as if a theory had been confirmed.

"You have found a topic of interest to the public, I am sure."

"We've filled the tent every night. Two services, in fact. I hope we'll have three on both Saturday and Sunday."

"Have you noted any suspicious persons about during your tent meetings here?"

"A few protesters. Catholics. A few Jews."

"Why Jews?" I asked. "I mean, what concern would they have with your preaching there?"

"We marched through the City and the East End," he replied. "A procession of sorts, to drum up interest."

"Did it work?" I asked.

"It did. Our camp meeting is free. It is good for the soul. It is uplifting and pure. We even hired an omnibus to ferry people here."

Free entertainment with transportation? What East Ender would refuse? Of course, many of them—the bricklayers, dock-workers, matchmakers, and sugar refiners—would be glad to discover they were Teutonic, the pure race who would eventually inherit the earth. A man who works sixty or seventy hours a week would be glad to hear that.

"That is reassuring," Barker said. It was as close as I'd seen him come to sarcasm.

"You should attend!" Cochran said.

"Thank you, Reverend. We should be glad to."

Cochran shot me a glance as if to say "I dare you." Not to Barker; but to me, personally. I did not think I had been particularly rude to him. In fact, I had bitten my lips a half-dozen times.

"Well, sir," my employer said, rising from his seat. "Thank you for your time and your invitation. Your answers were honest and forthright. We shall let you finish your sermon. Come, Thomas."

We turned and left. Barker shook his head.

"Let me get this right," I said. "The Teutonic races, that is, the Germans, the Baltic States, the English and the Americans, shall take over the earth, civilize it, create a utopia, then present it to a grateful Christ, who will say, 'Well done, good and faithful servant.'"

"I hate to see Scripture twisted in order to prove a theory."

"Mensurites," I remarked. "He saw Mensurites in Europe."

"He would. They are in the open there. Speaking of which, I assume Cochran's camp meetings for the poor are subsidized by meetings for the rich and curious. It is not only the deprived who want entertainment, and an American revival meeting might be diverting to some."

"Perhaps Cochran bought or stole the manuscript and hoped to use it as a talking point in his sermon. Drummond stole it or acquired it somehow, and took it to England. Cochran came to get it back and brought some youths with him from Heidelberg. They killed Drummond here, in London and now they are stowed away in a hotel nearby, hunting for the manuscript, and waiting to either depart or to join the ranks, so to speak. Perhaps Cochran has even promised to take them to America and resettle them."

"Perhaps," Barker conceded. "But you are speculating."

"It was just a theory. I wish we could find one of those Mensurites and make him explain why he is here and who brought him."

"How is your German?" the Guv asked.

"Rudimentary," I answered. "It was necessary to read at Oxford. I studied it from a copy of *Popular Educator*. Afterward, I lost most of it. There was no one to practice with, you see. If one doesn't use it, one forgets."

"A pity."

"That doesn't mean I can't work out a simple conversation. It will merely take a while." I glanced at the Guv. "What about these blue coats? They have to be somewhere in London. Shall I start with the Metropole?"

"There are a number of hotels in London, let alone inns. For all we know, whoever funded these lads has a house, in which case it would be a waste of time."

"But, sir, we've got to do something," I argued. "We can't sit here all day."

"Perhaps we can sell the satchel to the highest bidder."

"What?" I practically yelled.

He chuckled. "Your face. It was worth the remark to see it."

"This is serious," I said. "We could get in a lot of trouble."

"I don't see why, since we are not charging the government a farthing."

We were near Finbury Park itself, flanking a row of shops, the kind that offer basic services such as barbering and fish and chips. Barker consulted his watch.

"We have three-quarters of an hour. Do you know what I require?"

"What?" I asked.

"Cocoa," he said, and walked into a small and quaint-looking neighborhood tearoom.

"Cocoa," I muttered under my breath, and followed after him.

CHAPTER FIFTEEN

Once Barker had his fill of cocoa, we started walking, I with my hands in my pockets, he carrying his stick in a pair of black leather gloves stretched across his farthing-sized knuckles. I found myself thinking of Forbes again. There would be no more chatting over mochas and dominoes in the Royal, no secret talks in the Freemason's hall behind the restaurant. All the flavor of the establishment would be gone without his presence. How could I visit it anymore without hearing his sparkling wit, as barbed as Wilde's or Whistler's. Who would relate pertinent information that had come to his hand from an urchin just minutes before? Death, our shadow, an ever-present menace.

"I am not pleased with this day so far," I said.

"What did Pollock Forbes say?" he replied, as if reading my mind. "Mustn't grumble?"

"I'm good at it."

"You have certainly grasped the essentials. Tell me, do you

believe Mrs. Llewelyn would find the idea of your joining an organization such as the Knights Templar objectionable?"

It still gave me pause that the Guv referred to Rebecca in such a manner. Sometimes he can be as frosty as the weather. Certainly, I did not expect him to call her by her given name. Knowing him as I did then I realized he is slow to accept changes, such as a married assistant and his bride. It would come in time, if we were patient. But as he said, things were about to change in more ways than one.

"I don't believe she will object as long as it did not take me often from the house. Rather, it is the other Mrs. Llewelyn who would object. My mother taught me not to make vows save in a church and not to be aligned with organizations whose motivations cannot be described in one sentence."

Barker grunted, not breaking his stride.

"A wise woman, your mother," he said. "Under normal circumstances, I would agree with her. If we were bankers, say, or barristers. However, we are enquiry agents and information is our stock-in-trade. Also, I am already one of the highest-ranking members, and though I am not inclined toward the work of the leader, preferring to go my own way, the opportunity to gain a treasure trove of information should be seriously considered."

"You make a valid point for why you yourself should accept the position," I said. "However, you have not proven why I should join."

"Let us suppose that a note arrived addressed to me. If it concerned a present case it would be vitally important to you, but if it concerns Templar business, you should not read it. How would you know? I cannot expect my correspondents to stamp a red cross on an envelope merely so you will know it is for my eyes alone. Such an obvious message might never reach Craig's Court."

"Even so, sir, I am loath to do it. However, if there is no other way, I shall give it much thought. Would I have to attend a ceremony in which I am blindfolded and made to answer questions, promising never to reveal something under pain of death using methods from the Spanish Inquisition? Come, you are a plain man, the plainest that I know. What have you to do with capes and costumes, secret rituals and such?"

"As little as possible. We both have much to consider. I shall not press you. We will discuss the matter when necessary. Do you find that acceptable?"

"I suppose."

"Agreed. Excellent."

I nodded, thinking that there was another reason why his moniker among the London underworld was "Push."

"What precisely is a tent revival?" I asked him.

"It is an evangelistic service, often held in a large tent. They are very popular in America. One rededicates one's life to the Lord after hearing a rousing sermon and contemplates the coming of Jesus."

"I assume one pays for the privilege," I said.

"Cynic!" he cried, then rumbled a laugh. "Traveling is expensive and a preacher cannot be expected to pitch his own tent, especially if it holds over a hundred people."

"Surely one cannot hold a revival in a tent in mid-January?"

"*The Times* says the service shall be held in a former equestrian stable, now a pedestrian course."

"I hope they scrub the place and lay fresh wood shavings."

"While we are there, I shall pray for your soul."

"Let us not forget who attends service regularly and who does not," I replied.

He harrumphed and marched ahead.

The tent of the evangelical camp meeting was in the middle of an arena, erected exactly as it would have been outside. The shelter was large, like a circus tent though plain, the ground covered in fresh wood shavings, with both risers and chairs to pack as many seats as possible into the space. I had no feeling about the meeting one way or the other; that is, I had no prejudice of which

I was aware. Now that I saw how it was arranged, it was very like the Methodist meetings I had attended as a child, based upon the example set by John Wesley. I looked at the program, where I gleaned that the One True Church was based out of a town in the state of New York.

"Schen-ec-tity," I sounded out.

"New York, so I have read in newspapers, is rife with various small sects," Barker said.

The nomadic church began to fill. I saw both the poor and the wealthy present, looking more as if they were looking for entertainment than spiritual sustenance. There was a clergyman or two in the audience, come to view the competition. The service began with hymns both recognizable and not; somehow they had conjured an organ, though most of the sound was muted by the vastness of the arena. There was a reading from the Book of Revelation and the inevitable collect. Finally, Cochran rose to address the crowd.

He could not speak without the use of his hands, waving, thrusting, and pointing, in a way that Barker's hero, Charles Haddon Spurgeon, would find unseemly. I noticed a few aristocrats tittering at the American.

"Ladies and gentlemen, I thank you for allowing a Colonial to come to your grand city, the greatest in the world. Even London, however, has become complacent, no longer hoping for the second return of our Lord Jesus Christ."

I had sat through enough religious movements to understand the process: the purpose was to draw the audience members back over a few nights. The first was relatively calm, filled with the hope of livelier preaching the following night. During the second, often on a Saturday, with many attendees having enjoyed a half day off, the preacher would swoop down upon the unsuspecting spectators, calling them sinners with a great need for salvation. The final day, the Sabbath, all music and sermonizing, was to draw the sinner to cast off his sinful nature and prepare his soul for what was to come. Often there were conversions by the hundreds, accompanied by crying, healing, gyrations, and other forms of hysteria, while promising that Cochran and his flock would prepare the earth for Jesus Christ and His coming.

"Bosh," Barker growled, as if reading my thoughts. "We cannot prepare for His coming. We are sinful, imperfect beings. The Scripture says he must come to us."

Cochran veered from his sermon to preach about the dangers of atheism. In particular, he spoke of another suspect in our case, Karl Heinlich. He claimed the man had been following in his wake, attempting to sway the new converts. Heinlich had confronted him after unbelievers had picketed outside their camp meetings. Cochran said he expected persecution, and Heinlich was simply a manifestation of it. All the same, he chose to avoid at all costs this man and his filthy humanist doctrine.

So far there was little I had not heard before. Why the Foreign Office would list the very Reverend Cochran was a mystery. That is, until his sermon took an unexpected turn.

"Recently," the preacher cried, mist rising from his mouth in the cold tent. "Recently, we have come from a triumphant harvest of souls in Berlin and Heidelberg. I am pleased to see this race of hearty Saxons preparing for the work before us. The Teutonic race came from the east of Europe, spreading across the west to England's shores, intermarrying with the native people to produce strong and intelligent men and women, the apple of God's eye. We in America are fortunate that so many of your people have migrated to our shores and populated a once wild land, peopled by savages. We must join together, the Germans, the English, and what you so quaintly call 'the Colonies.' Why, even your queen and her late husband set the example to produce a perfect race!"

I shook my head, but noticed many nodding in agreement. It was eugenics. Everyone likes to be told they are in fact superior to their neighbors. They already considered it likely, and now they had proof.

"I have brought a specimen of the best of our kind, a modern

Viking, a student at Westphalian University. May I present to all of you Mr. Gunther Voss!"

A young man came to the stage, a brawny and handsome fellow, clean shaven, clear eyed, and strong jawed. His hair was flaxen, his scanty side whiskers ginger, and his eyes a blue so deep that I could see them from fifty feet away.

"Young Mr. Voss, how do you find your hosts here in London?"

"They are a fine people," he said, with only a trace of an accent. "I am pleased to be related to all of you. Your women are especially handsome."

The men laughed and the women blushed and tittered. Voss looked disconcerted, as if he didn't understand what he'd said. I ventured to the Guv that the Viking did not appear to possess a sense of humor.

"It has been said," Cochran continued, "and I believe it true, that England has been tainted by a wave of refugees, producing a race of smaller and feebler young men. Once we were Vikings, now we are weak versions of our former selves. You, sir! You in the third row. Will you please stand and come to the platform?"

"Me?" I asked, feeling as if a pail of cold water were poured down my collar.

"Yes, you. Come, good people. Encourage this timid fellow to come forward, for if he does not come now, how shall he come and join our band of believers?"

I was pushed forward against my will and stumbled a bit as I stepped up to the platform. Both the preacher and young Voss came to join me, Voss towering over me.

"What is your name, sir?" Cochran asked me.

"Thomas Llewelyn."

"Ah, a Welshman, from the race conquered by our Saxon brothers. It was only natural that such an event should happen. And what is it that you do, Mr. Llewelyn?"

"I am an enquiry agent," I said.

"An enquiry agent," he boomed. "No doubt you work in an office, totaling figures."

"Something like that," I said. He knew my occupation.

"You are not a large man, sir. Do you have any brothers?"

"Yes, I have six."

"Six! Soon we shall be outnumbered. And are some of them larger than you?"

"A few. Most are my size."

"No doubt. If I may observe, you have what is called a scholar's stoop. Do you read a great deal?"

"I read at Oxford."

"Do you get much exercise out of doors?"

"Out of doors? No, sir," I answered. "A little riding."

"Ah," Cochran said. "Now, Mr. Llewelyn, would you do me a great favor? Will you strip to the waist?"

I looked at him in consternation. Strip to the waist? It was unheard of. Out of the corner of my eye I saw Voss beginning to remove his tie. Light dawned in the old Llewelyn noggin. I was to be compared physically to the young Goliath. With a sheepish look the Guv's way, I reluctantly removed my jacket.

"Ladies and gentlemen, I direct your attention to the back of the stage. You notice these drapes here? Bingham, will you pull the rope?"

The velvet curtains fell to the floor to reveal, well, nothing much, merely a frame consisting of two vertical pipes supporting a horizontal bar. By now Voss had removed his shirt, drawing admiration from the room. He was built like a rugby three quarter: thick chested, muscled, and clean of limb. His singlet was cut like a wrestler's or a weight lifter's. As I pulled my braces up over my singlet, I felt my face burn.

Voss bowed to the audience in a theatrical way that proved he had rehearsed this a hundred times and in many cities. Going to the frame, he leaped up and grasped the horizontal bar. Then he pulled himself up and rested his chin on it. Down and up, down and up, faster and faster, as if it were nothing. I crossed to the bar beside him and stared balefully up at the metal bar.

"What is wrong, Mr. Llewelyn?" Cochran asked gleefully.

"I cannot reach the bar, sir."

The room erupted into laughter at my expense. I told myself to inhale and exhale and try not to look a fool in front of my business partner. And everyone else, for that matter. A box was brought and I almost needed two. I jumped and caught the bar and slowly pulled myself up to it.

"Bravo, Mr. Llewelyn. Good show!"

Two, three, four, five. My arms ached, and I stopped. I hung in there for thirty seconds.

"There's no need—" Cochran began.

I pulled myself up again. Six, seven, eight, nine, ten. Of course, the German was tossing them off like they were nothing. Eleven, twelve, thirteen?

When I first came to be hired by Cyrus Barker, he informed me that I had no strength in my chest. Up to that moment there seemed no reason why I should. There is a chinning bar in our basement. I had never gone beyond five sets of ten, but I had never tried. This seemed a fine time to find out.

Young Mr. Voss was doing one after the other, but there was a sheen on his upper lip. He had never faced a fellow who knew what he was doing. As he chinned himself, I realized something else: I need not do the same number of chins as he. I merely needed the endurance to be the last one on the bar.

Around thirty-five, we both felt the weight of gravity. I needed something to take my mind off what I was doing. Sucking in a deep breath, I began to sing.

"God—save—our—gracious—Queen. Long—live—our—noble—Queen. God save the Queen!"

There was a whistle from the poor seats. In an instant, I had turned the camp meeting into a music hall. It was natural at the first refrain, at the very first notes, to join in. It was every Englishman's duty. Even a Welshman or two has been known to sing it.

Gunther Voss was starting to slow. His singlet was soaked with perspiration. Mine was, as well, but that had been expected. I do not enjoy shaming a stranger to our shores. On the other hand, for all I knew, this very lad may have stabbed Hillary Drummond to death, and stood over his body as he expired. He could have killed Wessel or that poor cabman I had seen in the Body Room that very day. I'm not the sort to clothe myself in the Union flag, but just then my arms were burning and my chest felt as if my heart were about to burst and I didn't want to disappoint a tent full of people singing in praise of Her Majesty. I would not.

The bar went slack for a moment and then there was the recoil as Gunther Voss of Westphalia fell to the ground. By then I was merely muttering the words between gasps, but more than two hundred voices were singing lustily enough that no one noticed. As Voss fell, there was a cheer from everyone, rich and poor alike. I wondered if a few of the gentlemen had placed wagers inside the holy tent. I had bested the German. So much for Teutonic unity.

The moment he fell, all the energy drained out of my body. One more, Tommy Boy, I told myself. One more. One more for the Queen. No. One more for the late Hillary Drummond, and his wife and son. Especially for his son. One more for Wessell and Horace Quincy, whose grandchild would never see him again.

My arms were like rubber and barely usable. I had done over fifty, maybe approaching sixty-five. I strained and pulled and gritted my teeth. Salty sweat was rolling into my eyes. One more! One bloody more!

I felt the cold bar on my chin and I let go. I felt myself plummet, landing not on my feet, but my side. A blanket of wood shavings broke my fall. My ears heard the roomful of cheers, like sweet music.

Someone bent over me and lifted me up. It was Cyrus Barker, of course. He began brushing the shavings off my bare limbs and sodden shirt. Someone brought a towel and three or four people brushed me down like a horse. Another shook my hand and it felt like it belonged to somebody else. I was thumped on the back, patted on the shoulder. A woman kissed my cheek, I think. Someone took my hand and raised it in the air, as if I were a boxing champion.

Barker threw my coat over my shoulders and led me outside to the arena, then out into the street. Many people were walking out of the building with us. Not everyone, of course. There was still a service to complete. I heard a fellow say he was going back in to get his money from the collection plate.

The feeling of exhaustion and lethargy cannot be described. I was half conscious. I rested my cheek on the chill circular window of the cab when it arrived and the cold air felt marvelous.

"Nice work, lad," the Guv said.

I was a married man now and a partner in the agency, but the words still meant a great deal to me.

"Thank you, sir."

That wasn't the sweetest thing, however. The sweetest was the thought that back there in Finbury Park, Reverend Cochran must be seething.

CHAPTER SIXTEEN

The garden behind Barker's home in Newington was dormant, giving a very good impression of being dead. The twisted Japanese maples were naked and shivering in the chill breeze and the many structures therein, the bathhouse, gazebo, potting shed, and porch that skirted the koi pond, were covered in snow. The pond itself was not frozen, being fed from an underground spring, but a necklace of ice encircled the edges. If the koi fish therein were still alive they did not rise to the surface. Barker did not wander his personal half acre in the mornings as he did the rest of the year. Everything had been prepared for spring by his Chinese gardeners, and there was little to do. He wandered his expansive garret over our heads, and looked down upon the garden from his dormer windows, planning the new year's growth. There was a stoic beauty, but I wouldn't go out in it on a dare. Even Harm, the little Cerberus that considers the garden his private domain, had spent the days since Christmas curled in a ball on a pillow in the front room.

"Lad!"

I stepped out of the kitchen into the hall, still clutching my tea-cup. It was the morning after the tent revival and I was still sore from my efforts.

"Sir?" I called to the stair.

"We're going to the funeral of Major Drummond this morning." The rough voice carried down two sets of stairs. "Dress appropriately."

"Yes, sir."

I finished the tea, crossed to the front hall, and knocked upon Mac's door. It opened and he wordlessly handed me a black arm-band and a top hat freshly wrapped in crepe. He prides himself on being one step ahead of everyone. I let him because it means he does most of the work. I carried the articles into the kitchen.

With some trepidation, Rebecca set a plate in front of me, with a fresh hot *pain au chocolat* on it. Behind her, our chef Etienne Dummolard glowered, not that this was anything new. He is a growling bear and a tyrant to work for, but she did not protest. She is made of sterner stuff than most people realize.

I took a bite. The bread was a golden brown, hot and steaming from the oven. The chocolate squares inside were partially melted, the way I like them. It was delicious. However, it was not perfect. When one has been fed for six years by a culinary genius, one grows to expect certain things. The top was perfect, but the bottom was overcooked and chewy.

"Delicious!" I said.

Rebecca's face fell.

"You see?" Etienne said in triumph. "Overcooked!"

I shot him a gimlet eye. If he wanted to insult my wife, I would give him his choice of sword or pistol. He glanced at the window, imagining the need to step outside, and became more polite.

"No, no, no, *mon petit chou*, we shall try again. You have the talent, now you must study and work hard in the craft. We shall try again later."

"It's really, really good," I said, finishing the last of the roll.

My bride looked deflated. She wiped a bit of flour from her forehead with the back of her hand.

"I'm to attend a funeral this morning," I told her, indicating the hat.

"Fine," she said, taking my hand. "Let us go, then."

Upstairs I changed quickly as she draped collars, ties, and hose over the side of the changing screen, until there was nothing more to add. She adjusted my tie. She had told me that two-thirds of the men in London need their ties straightened. I told her she alone was allowed to adjust mine.

Ten minutes later, I stood at the front door sweltering. Rebecca had given me a heavy coat, a woolen muffler, my rabbit fur–lined gloves, and my thickest boots. She doesn't do things by halves, my Rebecca.

Barker came down the stairs, acknowledged that I was present and favorably dressed with a grunt.

"Sir, you're carrying a satchel," I told him.

"I am."

"Are you taking it to the funeral?"

"Presumably. I want to gauge the mourners' reactions."

"Where is the ceremony to be held?"

"Brookwood."

"Ah," I said. "The LNR, then."

Waterloo Station is the London terminus of the London and South West Railway, but if one goes down to a private entrance at the lower level, one discovers that in fact there is a second railway wrapping around the first the way a morning glory circles around a rosebush. This is the London Necropolis Railway. Its purpose is to carry mourners and the deceased to burial at Brookwood Cemetery in the Surrey countryside, the largest graveyard in Europe.

At some time it was decided to write a Burial Act, discouraging any more urban burials and building more remote cemeteries after two millennia. This railway, with its private entrance and high walls that offered privacy from any gawkers on the LSWR line, was built to handle any exigency, from bodies arriving by boat to those spirited discreetly from nearby hotels. The terminus contained two mausoleums, first- and second-class funeral services, a choice of Church of England and Nonconformist services, and one room containing hundreds of what one wag in a journal called "wooden overcoats." It was all very professional and English, but that didn't matter. It still gave one a chill. The public called it the "Cemetery Station." Even when I traveled on the LSWR I was aware that on the next platform a mechanical lift was just then hoisting a casket from below to a waiting train. Let's face it, by its very name, it is a railway for dead people, and as often as Death stalks us, we still don't want to think of it.

I paid two fares and spoke to a porter about which funeral we would attend before the trip to Brookwood. Drummond was an Anglican and there was to be a service in the LNR station itself. It was not the first time I had attended a funeral of someone we didn't know and it would not be the last. It is part of our duties as enquiry agents, but I would argue with the Prime Minister's assertion that all our cases end in bloodshed. We gave any client what he desired, like any other member of our profession.

We sat near the back so as to leave quickly if necessary. The Guv took a seat on the aisle, with the satchel on one knee, and we watched the crowd for anyone who noticed it. He was taking an awful risk, but then he often did. I believe he was uncomfortable being in an Anglican service itself, though he joined in on the hymns he recognized, dragging everyone nearby off-key.

I was looking for blue coats, but I supposed that would have appeared too obvious now that they had been in the country at least a few days. They would disappear into the fabric of London life, or at least attempt to do so. That was what I would do in their shoes.

No one obviously looked at Barker's bag, though I searched every man's face in the chapel. Some looked solemn, others bored. It depended upon how well one knew the departed. It gave me an excuse for looking at other people. I thought it certain that whoever killed Drummond would be there at his funeral. Apparently, Cyrus Barker did, as well.

"No one, sir."

"Keep looking."

I did. It took me nearly twenty minutes of eulogy to spot him behind a pillar, an earnest-looking young fellow in a new coat and hat. Very new. He seemed to glance about as if the speaker were using a language he didn't understand, though perhaps I was being imaginative. He seemed the only person there out of place.

"Three o'clock," I said. We both knew it was not time I was mentioning, but degrees. My employer turned his head slightly to catch a glimpse. Meanwhile, I memorized his face: young, the beginnings of a mustache, a mere smudge on his lip, a few red spots on his face, the youth's complaint. Brown hair. He was observing as I was and it was inevitable our eyes should meet. When they did we both looked away.

"He is too young to be a spy," I said. "But he seems to be alone and he is not sitting, though there are many seats available. He does not appear to be an usher, and the days are long over when a youth leads a funeral procession."

"Agreed."

"I don't like having my back exposed in this manner," I said. "It makes me think of swords. I don't want the next funeral I attend to be my own."

The Guv raised his eyebrows and nodded.

"Here he comes," I murmured.

The youth sat on the aisle end across from us. He glanced coolly at the satchel and then ignored us, listening to family members tell recollections of Drummond. Who paid for him to come to London? More important, why? The service over, we boarded the train to Brookwood.

The service had been no different than any other. It was not the gothic affair the mourners expected, and perhaps even wanted. When we arrived the sky was hammered steel and it was so cold I saw pickaxes and a stone hammer alongside the shovel behind a tree nearby. I did not envy someone that duty. Drummond's remains were covered, a prayer was said, and those of us not of the family began to disperse. We did not say who we were and no one asked.

Brookwood was neat and new-looking. Rows of identical snowy white gravestones stood achingly perpendicular in ground laced with frost. Mausoleums crouched in corners covered in snow, not as uniform as the teethlike slabs. The cemetery might have looked more hospitable in the spring with manicured lawns and trees. Now the lawn was dead and the trees stunted.

Everyone began to board the train once again to London. I had done my best to keep the youth in sight, but it was impossible. When the train reached Waterloo, he had vanished like a wraith. One does one's best, but one doesn't bat people about in a funeral train to keep a suspect in sight.

The train returning us to London was an identical engine to the LSWR line. There were no skulls affixed to it. Only the morbid name gave the old Necropolis its reputation. We left the terminus, Barker still flaunting the Gladstone bag in his hand, daring anyone to take it.

Back in Westminster, we walked across the bridge and along Whitehall Street to our offices.

I take it Barker wanted to display the satchel a little longer. It was a bright morning, though still cold; our breath plumed from our chests. The tip of my nose was cold. The woolen muffler around my throat itched, but my hands and feet were warm and that is what matters when the weather hovers around freezing.

We reached our offices, and I began hanging items on the coat-rack in the waiting room. My nose began to run, as it always did in such weather. There was a coal fire in the grate. If I were not careful, I would fall asleep in my chair.

Barker set the blasted bag on his desk. It contained glass, was very important as far as the government was concerned, and yet he carried it about cavalierly, even disdainfully. He lifted the handle, and suddenly pulled at the small padlock. It came off immediately. I sat up in my chair, no longer tired.

My employer opened the Gladstone, and peered inside, rummaging around in the interior with his oversized hand. Then he removed an irregularly shaped block of wood and put it on the desk.

"It was a decoy," I said.

He nodded, distracted. He reached into the satchel again and removed a small wooden box. When he opened it, I saw various small tools: files, rulers, a jackknife, and a few pencils.

"A boat!" I cried. "You're carving a model of a boat!"

I'd never seen him do that before, but as he was after all the former captain of a merchant vessel, it did not stretch credulity that he would model a miniature boat. He lifted a pencil, and began to draw a rough shape on one edge.

"What boat will you model?" I asked.

"The *Arrow*," he replied.

"Ah."

The *Arrow* was a Chinese vessel that had caused the Second Opium War. The Chinese government had boarded and confiscated it, arresting the crew on a charge of piracy. Unfortunately, the boat was flying the Union Jack at the time, and when the governmental sailors took it down and the crew was arrested, it spurred an international incident. Diplomatic messages were exchanged. There was a good deal of saber rattling for a while. By the time the Q'ing government was ready to release the sailors, Her Majesty's government had created a list of demands. When they were not met, England began shelling Canton. It was a diplomatic nightmare, and China got the worst of it. Afterward, foreigners were free to enter the ports of Canton, and China lost face again.

"I'm surprised you aren't building your own boat, the *Osprey*."

Barker's ship was a Chinese vessel, about a hundred feet long. It had the customary junk sails, but at some point it had been gutted and a steam boiler installed. He'd had her for fifteen years or more. She was currently dry-docked on the South Coast.

He made no answer, but then he seldom did. Still, he got the old Llewelyn noggin going for once.

"I wonder what became of the old *Arrow*," I said.

Barker took up a jeweler's file and began filing a small part of the deck.

"I imagine the owners would have trouble selling it, given its history."

He stood, crossed to a table for an oil lamp, and set it on his desk.

"Didn't you tell me you won the *Osprey* in a game of fan-tan?"

He gave me an abstract grunt, as if caught between answering me and getting this particular plank perfectly smooth.

"As I recall, your boat is a lorcha, like the *Arrow*," I went on. "An Asian approximation of a European vessel, but with junk sails. Yours has had a steam boiler and propellers installed. Did you add those yourself?"

The Guv shook his head. "The owner added it himself, inexpertly. The entire boat was a ruin. It took me three years and all the money I had to make it seaworthy."

"She was the *Arrow*, but you renamed her the *Osprey*. An osprey dives into the water to seize its prey, just as you used the boat to search for salvage."

My employer took the block into his lap and began sanding the side with his file.

"How long have you been working on that?"

He put the file down and turned his swivel chair in my direction.

"Mr. Llewelyn," he said. "Do I not employ you to work? Are you not paid to do something other than pester me with questions?"

"No, actually," I replied. "We are partners now and I am paid through the agency accounts, although you've been generous enough to see that I receive a steady salary since I am a married man. Of course, you never actually do any of the accounts, so in essence, I pay myself."

He looked grim. "Lad, I am doing fine work here. In answer to your question, I began this three years ago, though I have set it down for half a year at a time. This requires calm. If I make a mistake, I can ruin a month's work. I would appreciate some quiet, unless you have further questions."

"Just one," I said. "Our client, which is to say Her Majesty's government, expected us to take the real satchel, wherever it is, to Calais two days ago, yet here you are today settling down to rasp a block of hardwood for who knows how long."

"You do not agree with how I am running this enquiry?"

I was treading on dangerous ground here. I had to measure my words and not tell him he was fiddling while Rome burned.

"Not at all, sir, but I cannot do my work fully if I don't know what we are doing. Is there some task that I could accomplish instead of pestering you? Could I have at least a glimpse into your motivations?"

He lifted the hull he'd been cradling in his lap and laid it on its side on the desk. Then he stood and crossed to his smoking cabinet. There, he selected his most battered and yellowed meerschaum, its top blackened with carbon, its amber stem ground between his square teeth. It was the pipe he owned, I imagined, when he first captained the *Osprey*. The rest had been purchased in relative prosperity. He carefully stuffed it with his own blend of tobacco and carried it to the bay window. Then he took a vesta from a Swan match box and lit it as he watched the street.

"There is a gentleman on the other side of Whitehall Street. He is turned away, leaning against a gas lamp, but he has a cigarette case. I see a flash of light now and again. He's watching us through a mirror. Why don't you go ask him why?"

I jumped to my feet. "Thank you, sir!"

I began wrapping the scarf around my neck and reached for my overcoat.

"Not that one," Barker ordered.

The other hanging on the coatrack was what I jokingly called my "battle coat." It is of black leather and the capes in front contained thin sheets of lead, in the hope that they might stop a bullet. The pockets contain holsters sewn into the coat itself. I hate that coat. It is heavy, hot, and cumbersome. The leather creaks and I do not prefer caped coats. Reluctantly, I took it down from the rack. The latter seemed relieved to be rid of the burden.

I looked at Jeremy Jenkins, who tipped me a wink and returned to the penny dreadful he was poring over. I donned my gloves and took down my bowler hat instead of the crepe-covered topper, adjusting it on my head.

"That's me, then," I said, and stepped out of the door.

Once outside, I exhaled. My employer can be rather . . . what is the word? Gruff? Rude? Exasperating? Secretive? Ill-tempered? All of that and more. I began to suspect I was underpaying myself.

I crossed the street, but when I got there, he had disappeared. I took two steps before I realized I had been got round. Barker hadn't let me into his plans at all; he'd merely given me something to do. Ah well, I told myself. It's better than watching him scrape on that length of wood.

CHAPTER SEVENTEEN

When I returned, Cyrus Barker drew his ancient turnip watch from the well of his pocket and consulted it with the aid of his desk lamp.

"I believe it is time we looked into the matter of Mr. Heinlich, the atheist."

I recalled that he was on the list of suspects compiled by Hesketh Pierce, the Home Office man.

"We have just enough time to reach the Egyptian Hall," the Guv said. "His program should be starting soon."

We left Whitehall by hansom cab, intent upon Piccadilly, for there was no direct connection by Underground. It occurred to me that I had grown accustomed to such transportation in my work, and yet it was dear for me on my salary. Rebecca had an account from her late husband's estate, but I was loath to touch it, not having earned it. I had a picture in my mind of Asher Cowan looking over my shoulder disapprovingly if I spent a shilling on a book or a pint of bitter. The cab does that, you see; it leads one into abstract thoughts. Or rather, it did to me.

"Look at those lads, Thomas," Barker said.

I looked over in time to see two urchins successfully strip a man of his wallet and handkerchief while he told them the time. The Guv has compared the view from a hansom to the proscenium of a stage, offering entertainment and drama, and yes, even tragedy, in the mean streets of London town. We would have shouted out had we been closer, but I suppose in the grand scheme of things, the money would be carried home to feed many hungry mouths, whereas the gentleman had only the mild annoyance of purchasing a new wallet. He probably had two dozen pocket handkerchiefs at the moment in his dresser drawer.

"The atheist," I said, over the steady thump of the gray mare in front of us. The roadway was covered in two or three inches of snow.

"I assume he's not the only one, Thomas."

"The atheist speaker, then," I remarked. "An American, like Cochran. Is it a mere coincidence that his program should coincide with the camp meeting, or that they each arrived in the same city simultaneously? Do you suppose there is enough animosity between the two men to have one dogging the other's steps?"

Barker nodded, but did not speak until we reached our destination. Despite the fact that the columns and designs in the Egyptian Hall are not authentic, I find it quite satisfying, an Art Nouveau Thebes, if you will. The events held here were well attended and often controversial.

We found Karl Heinlich in a greenroom behind the stage. He was in front of a mirror darkening his eyebrows with some sort of wax. The man was in his early forties, clean shaven, with an average build. He looked a normal enough fellow. I saw no horns or a tail.

"May I help you?" he asked, his arm frozen in midair. "Sorry, my eyebrows are light and people in the audience cannot read my expression without some aid."

"Naturally," Barker said.

"Are you gentlemen from the press, or have you come to show me the error of my ways?"

"Neither, sir," my employer replied, looking grave. "We are enquiry agents. My name is Barker. This is Llewelyn."

I handed the man our card. He read it for a moment, digesting the information, then nodded his head.

"What may I do for you?"

"We have some questions. You have recently come from Germany, have you not?"

"Yes. From Heidelberg. We arrived three days ago."

Heinlich turned to open a small pot containing some sort of cream-colored concoction. He began applying it to his face. I'd heard of it before but never seen it. It was a new invention called "grease paint."

"While you were in Germany did you encounter a man named Hillary Drummond?" the Guv continued.

"No, I don't believe so. What's this about?"

"Mr. Drummond was found dead three days ago, having just arrived from Germany. Do you remember your arrival time?"

"No, I have no idea," he replied. "It was morning. Was he murdered?"

"He was killed with a sword. Run through just at Scotland Yard's door."

"In broad daylight?"

"Aye, sir. Just minutes after stepping off the platform. Witnesses say he was chased by several young men. With whom did you travel?"

"I travel alone, sir. My publisher books events in various cities and it is up to me to reach the venues on my own."

"Do you speak German?"

"Yes, I do."

I watched as he applied the cream to his face. It gave him a curiously flat appearance, like a painting. I noticed a small scar along his jawline.

"You have a scar just there, Mr. Heinlich," I said. "How did you acquire it?"

"You ask the most random questions. I fell out of a tree when I was seven, lacerating my cheek on a branch."

"While you were in Germany, did you notice any young men in uniforms?" I asked. "School or university uniforms, I mean."

Heinlich looked at us in the mirror. "There were none in the audience, but a group of them protested my speech once, even trying to stop me from entering. That was in Dresden, I think. There were long coats and caps."

"Blue?" I asked.

"No, green. They were not happy to have an avowed atheist in their city."

"How are you finding London?" the Guv asked.

"More civilized, I must admit, although we've been picketed here, as well."

"Was it the One True Church?"

"Funny you should say that. It was. However, they have protested our events often in the past, so I hardly notice their placards and chants."

"Were they the only ones to protest?"

"They were," he admitted. "I must be losing my touch. To some extent, my work plays on my notoriety, gentlemen. 'Come see the Avowed Atheist. Stop him before he corrupts your children.' Sometimes I feel like a freak in a sideshow, but that is part of the work. Frankly, if they read my book ahead of time, they might not come. It is occasionally dry, I must admit."

"Have you been following the One True Church?" Barker asked. "You say you have seen them often."

"Rather, it is the opposite," Heinlich said. "They have been following me. I believe someone has studied my schedule and made certain the tent revival always arrives the day before."

"Why have they chosen to bedevil you?" I asked. "Is it the allure of having a physical enemy to fight?"

Heinlich stopped applying the cream and sighed. "That might be part of it, I suppose, but more likely the reason is that Daniel Cochran is my younger brother."

"Ah," Barker said. "We attended his program last night. I noticed he made sport of people and races he finds inferior. Is this sort of behavior common for him?"

"Perhaps. I haven't spoken to him during this tour. I try to talk to him as often as possible, but now I'm being shut out, kept away by his supporters."

"What sort of fellow was he like as a youth?"

"At one time he was a wastrel. Aimless. Often drunk."

"What changed him?" Barker asked, settling into a chair.

"A girl, of course. He transformed himself for her. It was the single biggest achievement that he ever accomplished, but it did him no good. Her parents objected. Whose wouldn't? She married someone else, and in his despair, he threw himself into an evangelical tour across New York. As luck would have it, it was successful. He had to hire a larger tent and convince a few of his more fervent converts to come with him on the circuit. Eventually, it led to a European tour.

"I assumed he had forgotten the girl. Maud was her name, as I recall. When we last met, he asked if our mother had said anything of her. As it happened, she had. Maud had just given birth to twins. I didn't tell him. I hadn't the heart."

"Was your relationship always adversarial?"

"He was jealous of me to some extent. I received honors early, and won a scholarship to Yale, while he rarely applied himself. For years, he was casting about for a purpose in life, and never finding it. I worried about him. I still do."

"Do you consider preaching a futile endeavor?" the Guv asked.

"No, actually, I don't. Sometimes I wish I could have the comfort it brings. I tried, but I cannot. It isn't easy, what I do. People are easily offended. I have nearly been tarred and feathered twice. I was beaten once. I've lost count of the number of times someone has spat on me in the street or thrown an egg. Many of them are from my brother's flock. I was a theology student at Yale, Mr. Barker. It was there that my doubt overcame me."

I cleared my throat. "Is it your brother's obsession to prove he has succeeded in doing something you have not?"

"Perhaps. I don't believe he schemes to harm me. Occasionally he is spurred by a particularly laudatory report of one of my speeches in the press. I'll admit to you gentlemen that I also have a spy in the enemy camp. Our uncle is a kind of caretaker who keeps me abreast of his doings. In my defense, I'm speaking of his health. My brother taxes himself too much and he is excitable."

"Do you believe his religious sentiments are genuine?" I asked.

"I cannot say. If, for example, this entire enterprise should come crashing to the ground, would he pick up the pieces and try again or would he attempt another endeavor to prove he is better than me? To tell you the truth, I wish he'd find another nice girl and settle down, and build a small chapel to do some good."

"And you, sir," the Guv asked. "Should the physician not heal himself?"

Heinlich chuckled. "Very canny, Mr. Barker. Yes, I've proved to myself that I can impress people and orate with the best of them. I'm tired of travel. The last few months I've been spurred along by my publisher. I'd like to go home and build a house in the Berkshires. Perhaps a nice woman will come along then. I've proselytized long enough."

"Amen," Barker said.

A corner of Heinlich's mouth curved upward. He appreciated the irony.

"Mr. Heinlich, your brother's sermon yesterday was highly focused upon the Jews and Catholics and any other minorities that were not Aryan."

"The Aryans were originally Indian, and I'm sure he doesn't believe they'll enter the kingdom of heaven. Or the Greeks, or the Italians, or the Spanish. Not even the French. He holds salvation as if there were little of it, only worthy to be given to a small handful of European countries and America, and only a small portion of that, I should imagine."

"Has he always held such beliefs?"

"No. We come from a very progressive family. Our father, also a preacher, helped establish the Underground Railroad, which transported slaves from the Deep South to freed status in the North. We were not taught that one man was better than another. Far from it, in fact. We were to help our unfortunate brothers."

"How then do you account for your brother's behavior?"

Heinlich stood, stretched, and walked behind a screen to change his clothing. He continued to speak to us over the top of it.

"My brother is susceptible to whatever influences are around him. He's always been easily led. He writes his sermons at the last minute, taking in all he has read or heard since the last one. I've cautioned him about it, but he is mercurial."

"Can you suggest a reason why he should be so intolerant of other races and religions?"

"I can. Several reasons. First of all, I suspect he is saying what other people want to hear. Knowing what they want and seeing that need in them, he echoes what they always suspected. Also, he just came back from Germany, which has become increasingly nationalistic. Not long ago, I heard him espouse that the so-called white race was not related to other races at all. We are somewhere between angel and man. Have you ever heard such nonsense?"

"Do the two of you meet often?"

"I don't see him for half a year at a time, then we both return to Schenectady for the winter months. He feels it is his biannual duty to convince me of the need for grace. Every year his polemics grow stronger and stronger, but in spite of our religious differences, we would talk. Yet he continues his inflammatory rhetoric. Daniel loves to cause some sort of reaction in his crowds. He's not above showmanship. The less educated people who attend his meetings want a show. They want to see him exhort and sweat and rant about the need for salvation."

"Has he always been pious?"

"Not especially. He was spoiled as a child. Daniel is basically lazy, then angry at the world if things don't come easily to him. When he couldn't get into Yale, he began attending a minor religious college in Connecticut, but he left after the first year."

"How does he preach, then?"

"He founded his own church and named himself a clergyman by divine intercession. He holds no doctorate of divinity. He changed his name to Cochran to avoid association with me and opened a church in a former general store. My family assumed he'd fail, as he had at everything else he tried. Instead, he was a success. My father is gravely disappointed at his shifting beliefs. It's a bad situation and I don't know what the future holds for him. I am not jealous of my brother, Mr. Barker, but I truly wish he were not so successful."

Barker lifted his hand. "Come, Thomas. This gentleman has been patient with us. We should let him get on with his day."

Outside the Egyptian Hall, I sidestepped a frozen puddle.

"Do you believe him, lad?" Barker asked after he had filled and lit a pipe in a doorway, away from the wind.

"You've trained me well enough not to believe a suspect without examining his actions or motives," I said. "Is it time for lunch, sir? We could go to Le Toison d'Or. What do you suppose Etienne is serving today?"

My employer grunted. "Something with sauce, I should imagine."

CHAPTER EIGHTEEN

Thomas," Barker said two hours later, after we left Le Toison d'Or. "Let us discuss Rabbi Mocatta."

"By all means."

The Guv was in his cavernous chair, a scalpel in his hand, sawing bits from the block of wood again, layer by layer. The shavings littered the glass atop his desk. He looked content. Either that, or he was discontent and this helped relieve it. The case was weighing on him; in particular the death of Wessel. That innocent scholar would plague him for months if not years.

"How should you prefer we go about it?" he asked.

"You're asking me, sir?"

"He is your father-in-law, lad. We can run roughshod over him if required. We can uncover what hijinks he's been getting himself into, and where and why, or we can slap his wrist and let him infer that we can do more, which we can."

"But we don't know what he's done, or why he's done it. That is, unless you've had some of your urchins following him about."

"I've had one tyke watching him, but only to see where he goes. So far he lives a blameless life: the synagogue, his home, and the Board of Deputies. He is a solemn man."

"He was not unkind to me the few times we met. I've wondered if he was influenced by my mother-in-law. She's a fierce old bird. However, I cannot picture her writing Rebecca off the way she has. Forgive me, sir, I do not mean to throw my private life into this case."

"That cannot be helped. There are few rules in enquiry work. Pollock's list did not give the reasons why each of the suspects was considered. There is much to do this week. I don't have time to waste on a Johnny-come-lately to our list. What do you suggest?"

I cleared my throat, thinking furiously. Barker rarely asks my opinion, but when he does he expects a logical and well-considered one on the spot.

"Well, I don't believe the roughshod approach is necessary, although we might hold it in reserve if all else fails. However, the slap on the wrist is too gentle, I think. I want him to know I am serious. My opinion would be to go at him directly and clinically."

Barker nicked himself with the knife and pressed his thumb to his lips. Boatbuilding of any kind is rarely accomplished without spilling blood. He sniffed, as if disappointed at his own skills, or lack thereof, and put down his blade.

"That seems logical enough. What happens if this should delve into family matters? How would you proceed?"

"Cautiously, of course. Sir, I do not believe the one can be separated from the other. If you wish, I can handle the matter myself."

Emotional conflict is anathema to my employer. He gets highly embarrassed by discussing feelings, whether his own or someone else's. I've seen him bolt from a room in which a woman is crying, or worse, a man breaks down in tears.

"No, no, Thomas, I must be there. You are the scalpel," he said, holding up the instrument. "While I am the mallet. You suggest we confront him and see what happens, then act accordingly."

"Yes, sir."

"That is not a plan at all."

"Not much of one, I'll admit," I said. "But as far as I understand, in our work that appears to be our standard modus operandi."

Barker's mustache widened to contain his cold smile.

"Touché, Mr. Llewelyn. The point is yours. Very well, we shall see what the rabbi has to say."

"Bring your mallet."

"Believe me, Thomas, I intend to."

Mocatta was to be found at a small and recently begun synagogue in a former warehouse on the very eastern edge of London. We rendezvoused with a round little street arab with short hair that stood on end, and a mouth circled with jelly. He nodded toward the converted warehouse and I gave him two shillings for which he must have worked for most of three days.

"Your work is finished here," Barker said. "Off with you."

The boy gave us a gap-toothed grin and waddled off. We entered the makeshift synagogue. There were various signs and hoardings written in Hebrew and a good amount of new woodwork, none of it finished. A carpenter was adding a rail to some wainscoting and I asked him where the rabbi could be found. He pointed down a long hall. When Barker and I reached the far end, we found a door with the rabbi's name on a pasteboard sign tacked to it. It was a temporary assignment, not a permanent one. The door was open.

The rabbi was seated at his desk, elbow deep in volumes of the Talmud, a pair of semicircular spectacles resting on his nose. He raised his brows when he saw the Guv, but he did not lose his composure until he saw my face. Perhaps I was defiling his office.

"Good afternoon, Rabbi Mocatta," my employer said, bowing.

I did likewise, save that I did not greet him. A pair of Gentiles in his synagogue and we had him pinned to the wall, or at least trapped. He could not avoid escape.

"And you, sir," he replied cautiously. "Thomas. Have a seat, gentlemen."

"Thank you, sir," I said, trying to sound as natural as possible. I would not lose my temper. Not yet, anyway.

"What brings you to my office? It must have been difficult to find me."

"Not at all," the Guv said. "Tracking people is part of what we do for a living."

"Of course. How may I help you?"

"You'll scarcely credit it, sir. A list is circulating in government circles concerning radical extremists. An agent of the Crown was assassinated this week, or so I've been told. Various organizers are being closely scrutinized and you are on that list."

"I, on a list?" Mocatta asked. "Who made such a list?"

"The Home Office."

"So we heard," I put in. The idea occurred to me to embellish a little. "I believe it was created by Special Branch at Scotland Yard. They are usually the ones who deal with radicals."

"But that's ridiculous. Let me see it!"

"We were not permitted to retain it," Barker said. "To be frank, we had not full permission to see it. Thomas was concerned about the family and insisted we come here immediately to warn you."

Apparently the Guv was embellishing a bit as well. It made my father-in-law anxious so I saw no reason to stop. I'd have pitied him if he had not been a beast to my wife. As far as I was concerned, his chances of ever seeing her again depended on what occurred in that room then.

"Have you been approached by any anarchist organizations?" my employer asked.

"None. That is, none who admit it. They know the Board of Deputies would have no truck with violence. We monitor our more revolutionary brothers closely."

"Have you yourself attended any demonstrations, protests, or rallies?" Barker asked. "There has to be some reason you are on this list, even if it were a mistake. Such lists are carefully compiled and closely scrutinized."

"There are rallies here all the time. One stops, listens for a moment or two, then moves on. The East End is in perpetual need and one group or another believes they can fix all its ills with speeches and temporary funding. Yet the East End continues to be, long after these organizations run out of funds and shut their doors."

"Are there any new organizations that are causing unrest here?" the Guv continued. "Are any young gangs causing trouble? Is the underworld flexing its brawn?"

"No," the rabbi said. "That is, I don't believe so."

The conversation was dying. We had been stopped at every turn. It seemed likely the old man was being deliberately thick. It was possible someone was influencing him. He might be aided or enticed, or even threatened. It had to be one of those three. One does not casually get on a Home Office list. One has to work at it.

My eyes darted around the room. For all I knew, Barker's were as well. There must be some sign in this makeshift office he was using to show us what we wanted to know. I glanced at books on the shelves and stacked on the desk, papers spread out or fanned across tables. Then I saw something, a piece of pinkish vellum stuffed in a book, save for an inch protruding with a letterhead across the top. Upside down, no less, I deciphered it.

"What about the London Society for the Conversion of Jews?" I asked. "I'm sure they've been causing a good deal of trouble."

Mocatta's features darkened immediately.

"They have been demonstrating for weeks now. There was a rally last week, with speakers proclaiming the need to convert every Jew in London to Christianity. Yet if you listen carefully to their message—that is, to all the speakers' messages—you would understand that while they want us converted, we from whose loins your Jesus sprung would not be accepted into Christian congregations. Can you imagine an Anglican church opening its doors to a flood of Jews newly baptized?"

"So, what have you done, Rabbi?" Barker asked. "How have you fought against the attacks upon your faith?"

"Gentlemen, a son of Levi fights with his tongue. I confess I have protested at rallies, I have heckled speakers. I began writing speeches, and when I wasn't at synagogue, I spoke in parks and on street corners. I have been arrested twice, but set free. You could say I've grown to be something of a crusader."

"Very good," Barker said. "The East End needs one, especially the thousands of Jews in and around Whitechapel. As I recall, the London Society for the Conversion of Jews has been around for years with little or no effect. The fellow in charge was so unassuming, little conversion occurred. Is the man still alive?"

"Brother Simmons. Yes, he still does what he considers 'the Lord's will.' However, he's got an evangelist who has been preaching and marching the last two days. Something of a firebrand. Of course, he's painted us so darkly I cannot understand why such a fellow would want me as a brother."

"Has he been preaching the usual drivel about the old blood libel and Jews being Christ killers?" the Guv asked.

"Yes, but with drive and conviction. He's gaining converts all over town. Christians, I mean, anxious to cause mischief. No Jew I know has joined his congregation. Fortunately, this young evangelist will be returning to America soon, although not soon enough for me."

"Would the young man to whom you refer be named Cochran?" Barker asked.

"Yes! That's the fellow!"

"We have met. I assure you, we hope he leaves soon, as well. He's causing no end of harm."

"He's been fomenting trouble. I don't mind the proselytizing if they treated us with respect. I enjoy a spirited debate as well as the next man, Mr. Barker. What I object to is a poorly trained layman being condescending, then growing angry when I try to reason with him. This American, what is his name again?"

"Cochran."

"Yes. He's creating problems within the community again after we'd made such strides. We'd gone months without having our windows broken."

"Aye," my employer said with finality. "Condemnation is a terrible thing."

Mocatta saw that the wind had changed and shifted in his chair.

"Thomas here has become a partner in the agency."

"Has he?" Mocatta asked. "Congratulations."

I nodded. Silence was probably best until I saw where this was going.

"That means he shall be instrumental in the next case, should we be called upon by the Board of Deputies."

"Is that so?"

"He's fully trained now. I can teach him little these days. He could start his own agency, and that is why I made him a partner, lest he work in competition with me."

Barker let the silence unfold, causing a vacuum in which the rabbi had to speak. I'd seen the Guv do this with a hundred suspects and witnesses. Was it churlish of me to watch my father-in-law squirm?

My employer grasped the handle of his stick. "He's making a good salary and has put some money by."

"No doubt with my daughter's dowry," Mocatta said.

That stung, but then I expected it.

"Actually," I said, "I haven't touched the dowry and have no intention of doing so. It belongs to Rebecca and the house remains in her name. She used it until every one of her friends began to shun her for marrying a Gentile. There is no need for a home at all without social calls from her friends. It's almost humorous that I currently have more Jewish friends than she."

"Is that so?" the rabbi said weakly.

"Indeed. She has been so embarrassed that her family and her people have publicly shunned her, that for a time she went to Camomile Street to sit in her empty residence in the faint hope that her mother or her sister might come to visit. Of course, she waited in vain. You might not know this about your daughter, Rabbi, but she isn't the sort to feel sorry for herself, nor to sit in her residence lording over a maid and doing nothing."

Mocatta's shoulders slumped.

"Tell me," I continued. "Did my mother-in-law and sister-in-law stop coming of their own volition or did they fear they would upset you?"

"I did not order them to stop seeing Rebecca."

I glanced over at my employer. He gave a short nod.

"Rebecca has told me that she is your favorite, that your wife and eldest daughter have been very close. She's talked about sitting on your lap as a child while you read to her. She told me about how proud you were at her wedding to Asher. I didn't like hearing that, but I would not take away her time or her memories with him. He was a fine MP and an excellent orator. I heard him speak once."

The rabbi nodded and looked as if his throat were constricted.

"And certainly," I continued, "I did not take possession of his house or his belongings, despite the fact that I had full legal right to take them. She lives with me in Mr. Barker's house. He has opened it for her, going so far as to give us the entire first floor, renovating it for us during our honeymoon out of kindness. It has been difficult for him, having a woman underfoot; he likes his routine, yet he has been kind enough to adjust to her and she to him. After all, to whom would she go since she could not go to her own father?"

Barker cleared his throat and I settled back in my chair. Only then did I discover I had been perspiring.

"I find it ironic," the Guv said, "that Cochran's zeal, which has caused such concern and discomfort in your community, has been met with a similar zeal of your own. Now, I'm certain the Gentiles in the City and East End have little interest in what you had to say. There could be no conversion on their part. According to Thomas's treatment, they are not welcome, except in name only. You may extend an offer to them, but neither will your congregation welcome them nor will they treat the spouse who had brought the Gentile into the fold as anything other than a ravening wolf."

"Here now," the rabbi said. "That is not so. The synagogue is not that way."

"I agree," I replied. "It is not. I have experienced only kindness. Certainly, they have been shy; they don't know what sort of fellow Rebecca had married, and they never would because we don't feel welcome. It's odd, because I found their greeting to be genuinely warm and generous at the time of our marriage. I assume therefore that it was you who made us unwelcome."

I tried that trick of Barker's, not going on as I generally would, but accepting the silence. It was not easy. It took perhaps half a minute for him to respond.

"You are correct. I have been punishing the Gentiles and only succeeded in hurting my daughter."

"She cried, sir," I remonstrated. "You of all people should have known what pain you caused your youngest child, the apple of your eye."

He frowned over his spectacles.

"That is all I have to say," I said, rising.

Barker stood as well.

"Inform the Board of Deputies that the Barker and Llewelyn Agency shall no longer offer our services to them. Come, Thomas."

CHAPTER NINETEEN

The final suspect from our original list came to us unbidden. I much prefer it that way; there is less shoe leather and fewer cab ride expenses. We heard a stomping in our outer office, presumably to remove the snow from a pair of boots. Then we heard a rough, flat voice ask to speak to us.

"Mr. Cyrus Barker?" he enquired of the Guv.

"I am he."

"I'm Peter Naughton, Lord Grayle."

"Your reputation precedes you, sir."

"As does yours."

"Won't you sit?"

He took a seat in one of the visitor's chairs. Naughton had thick, bushy brows with a pair of pince-nez spectacles nesting in them. His hair was gray and he was small and stocky. For a man with a pedigree and fine clothes he reminded me of someone one might see giving odds at a horse race.

He, in turn, watched us. He studied Barker, then me, then

looked about the room, sizing up the coat of arms on the wall behind the desk, among other things. He took in the books. Finally, his eyes came to rest on one of the most commonplace things in the room, at least in comparison to the others: a photograph of Rebecca and me on my desk, standing by a ruin in Nineveh during our honeymoon.

"May I help you, sir?" my employer prompted.

"Yes, Mr. Barker. I broke my fast this morning with an old friend, Count Arnstein, a wonderful fellow with a nose like a pointer when it comes to finding religious relics. I've visited a shop he owns in Jerusalem several times. He's got the most wonderful treasures there, from Palestine, from Cyprus, Turkey, even Egypt! I bought a piece—"

"How does this involve us?"

"Oh, I do beg pardon. You are busy men. Professional men. Too busy to hear me prattle on."

"Not at all, sir," Barker replied. "What did Count Arnstein have to say?"

"He said he'd had the most wonderful manuscript in his possession, possibly the best find of his career. He offered it to the Kaiser or maybe to one of his cabinet members, I'm not certain which. Anyway, they bought it from him, paying some ungodly amount. He came here to London intent upon using the money to build a dam near his estate in Styria. He comes from a very old family in Austria, you know. Anyway, somehow the German government lost his manuscript, or it was stolen, I think. Now he claims he's being hounded by German agents. They sacked his room at the Albemarle. Bad sports, I say. They lost the bloody thing, he didn't."

"You've known the count for a long time, then?" I asked.

"Oh, a donkey's years, at least."

"How did a landowner in Austria become an antiquities dealer in Jerusalem?"

"His father was something of a treasure hunter, back when the family had money and prestige."

"Habsburg?" I asked.

"You noticed that, did you? Spitting image of Charles the Fifth, isn't he? The last of a noble family and all that."

Barker sighed. One could almost say he looked bored.

"Tell me, Your Lordship, have you purchased antiquities from the count yourself?"

"Dozens of them, young fellow. Bought enough oil lamps to light this entire office. Potshards, coins, manuscripts, statues. I bought an entire sarcophagus once. I've got the collector's mania, I'm afraid. There are more treasures in my mansion than in the whole of Jerusalem, or so I'd like to think."

I understood Barker's frustration. It was difficult to keep this fellow on course.

"Have you known Count Arnstein to have difficulties with forgeries?" the Guv asked. "Has he ever been accused of anything?"

"Of course. That's part of everything. Arnstein is a busy man and must rely on local workers. Antiquities are found by herdsmen or farmers. I must know everything, where it came from, who found it, and under what circumstances, who authenticated the work, putting their reputation on the line. What of the people involved? Were they trustworthy and reliable? It all depends upon a man's reputation, you see, and it fluctuates. If something from his shop is found to be a fraud, it does not necessarily make him one."

"What of manuscripts?" Barker asked.

Grayle waved a hand in the air.

"Worst of all. Let us say a manuscript is found. An expert is called in to authenticate it. He publishes his conclusions, then anyone with some sort of reputation must publish an opinion himself. Even if nothing is obviously wrong about it, either in writing, history, ink, or parchment, some biblical scholars will cry fraud just to step away from the pack and be noticed. Some of these fellows will cross a street to avoid the others."

"How would one recognize a forgery?"

"A layman couldn't. Only a serious scholar could, or an expert forger."

"Are you saying that serious scholars may be biased?"

"That depends upon whom you trust. I would have recommended a fellow to you, but he died two days ago. Some sort of vehicle accident. Terrible thing to happen."

Barker winced and looked away. Even I felt it in the pit of my stomach. Wessel's face was in my mind's eye.

"What do you think of the Vatican as far as manuscripts are concerned?"

"I cannot fault their scholarship, I'll say that. They are stingy with their manuscripts, by which I mean they will not sell any to me. If I had any criticism, it is that they move very slowly. Important manuscripts can be archived and then forgotten."

Barker nodded.

"Do you know something?" His Lordship asked.

"About what?" the Guv asked innocently. He can look innocent when he needs to. Innocent enough, anyway.

"About a manuscript! Did you mention the Vatican in relation to the Vatican archives?"

"I have no idea what manuscript you are referring to, sir," Barker insisted.

Lord Grayle gave a howl. "You do, sir, and I must have it. It shall complete my collection. I swear I would sell everything I own to possess a gospel written before the year 100. They are the rarest things on earth. I would sell the Koh-i-Noor, I would sell the Crown Jewels, I would sell Big Ben if I could lay hands on the actual words written by a first-century follower of Jesus Christ."

"Why?" I asked.

"Because nothing is so important or rare. So perfect."

Collectors are all mad, I thought. It doesn't matter if it is snuffboxes or the Word of God.

"Why not content yourself with the words only?" the Guv asked. "Copy them down and give the original to a museum."

"No, that is just the knowledge. I need to see the letters on the parchment, the stains, the holes left by worms. I need to know its provenance. Where did it come from? Who found it and under what circumstances? Who authenticated the work, thereby putting their names on the line? What were the reputations of the people involved? Were they trustworthy and knowledgeable? I must know everything."

"Excuse me, Your Lordship, but I expect you would purchase it, anyway."

Grayle laughed, then blew his nose with a large handkerchief.

"I would, at that, Mr. Barker. Fakes have their own charm. Often the man committing a fraud has worked harder than the man whose work he faked or the man who authenticated it. Some of them are works of art. Many are still debated over by experts: 'Did they get it wrong? I must see it myself.'"

"Does it matter to you whether it is real or not?"

"It does, but understand, I can read fiction and I can read history or biography, but I prefer to know which is which."

The Guv looked puzzled. This was a kind of fellow he had never encountered.

"I believe I can guess what you are thinking, sir," the fellow continued. "My collection seems to be full of false antiquities and spurious tales of biblical times, a jumble if you wish to use that term. But every inch of my mansion is well lit and the objects well displayed. You would take it for a wing of the British Museum. However, only I know about each item's personal history and the tale behind it. The tale is part of its charm."

Barker nodded, as if he understood better now. "It's yours. You can buy as you wish. You can display as you wish. You possess enough to study for the rest of your life."

"I do, indeed, sir. I enjoy them. I purchase them to please myself. I care not a whit about what a museum curator might say about my duty to the world, wanting me to display my collections to people who do not know or care about anything but being seen looking at something artistic and historical."

"There must be people you approve of who wish to see the works you own," I said.

"And they never shall. Some men, those with impeccable

reputations, I might allow to see or study one or two items, but no more than that. I am the curator of my collection, and I am the only patron as well. The rules are my own."

Barker pushed his chair back from his desk and stood. He walked to his smoking cabinet and retrieved a pipe, which he stuffed with tobacco and lit. Then he dropped the vesta in a beveled-glass ashtray on his desk.

"You hope we have the manuscript."

Lord Grayle leaned forward expectantly.

"I do. I very much do. Have you the manuscript?"

"No."

"Are you sure? It isn't in your house? It's not in this room, hidden away? Is it in your bank? Do either of these gentlemen possess it?"

"They do not."

The Guv sat back in that green leather chair of his and smoked his pipe. It was as if it had slipped his mind that we had a guest.

"I can give you money," Grayle continued. "A good deal of it. I can write you a check on the Bank of England. Name your price. I'll pay it. Yes, name your price and I will pay it!"

My employer looked up at a corner of the ceiling and blew smoke at it.

"I do not have it and if I did it would not be for sale to a collector."

Grayle leaned forward still and I caught a look in his eye that I had not seen when he entered. It was not madness, although it was close. It was not avarice, for he did not give a fig about money. It was the need to possess. The mask had slipped and his true and naked face was before us now.

He turned and regarded me. "What about you, young fellow? I understand you are recently married. You'll need something in the bank. Women want things: houses, jewelry, a private coach. You could keep her happy."

"I do keep her happy," I said. "And I don't need your money. You make a generous offer, I'm sure, but no thank you."

"Very well."

"I don't know how you came to the knowledge of my private affairs, but I assure you it does not sit well with me. You have overstepped your bounds."

Grayle uncrossed his legs and crossed them again in the opposite direction.

"I apologize, Mr. Llewelyn. Yes, I do overstep in my haste to acquire something I have decided I must own."

"How often are you successful, sir?" Barker rumbled from within the grasp of his chair. It magnifies his voice, I suspect.

"More often than not," His Lordship answered. "I have many friends, some of whom are in important positions. And my pockets are deep."

He reached into one and retrieved a folded paper that he placed on the Guv's desk. My employer reluctantly took it from the edge of his desk, opened it, and read it. Then he tossed it on down again.

"Lad, remind me what a million is again. Is it a hundred times a thousand?"

"A hundred times ten thousand, sir," I replied.

One can scarcely credit that there was a time when a million was a new concept. People were intrigued that there was a number that was very nearly too high to count. It was a term used in government circles in terms of spending. One would never run across such a thing as a million anythings, unless one were on the shingle at Brighton Beach.

"A million pounds?" I asked. "For a few strips of leather?"

After a moment, I realized what Grayle had done. He had tricked me into admitting I'd seen the manuscript. Barker looked down and placed the flat of his palm against his forehead. Meanwhile, Lord Grayle's face creased into a grin.

"You may be assured I am serious, gentlemen. I must have that manuscript. You must give it to me."

"It is not mine to give, sir. Besides, it is gone and out of our hands, is it not, Thomas?"

"It is," I said, chastened.

"There, you see. I fear we cannot help you."

The Guv flicked the bank check back across the desk to the edge, where our visitor tore it in quarters. A million pounds. Not a princely sum, but a kingly one. I never knew how much money Barker had; he had several accounts, and a list of charities he supported, mostly in the East End. I could not conceive of having a tenth of that money. It would require moving to the Côte d'Azur and learning to play baccarat. Rebecca would be weighed down with diamonds.

Too much money is a curse. Its possessors are rarely happy. Like Grayle, they flit from one desire to another. They know the cost of something, but have no idea of its value. The manuscript would satisfy His Lordship until the next thing he valued began to tantalize him. Tell a millionaire he cannot have something and see what he will offer you.

Grayle stuffed the pieces of the check into his trouser pocket. Then he searched for another paper inside his morning-coat pockets, which seemed to function as a mobile desk. He set it on Barker's glass desktop and slid it toward him. The Guv smiled. This was better than courier work.

He read the letter slowly. From what I could see, it was a full-sized document of some sort. My employer held it up and read it fully, his head tilted back. When he was finished I came to the desk and took it from his hand. Once in my seat again, I lifted it as he had and began to read.

In legal terms, it was a bill of sale. Count Arnstein of Styria relinquished full legal rights to the Ancient Scroll for the sum of seven hundred and fifty thousand pounds. There were red seals on it, coats of arms stamped with what I assumed were rings. I didn't like it. The more legal terms and Latin that were thrown about, the more solicitors were trying to bury something ripe.

"As I recall," Barker said, "Arnstein had given up the right to the manuscript. He was already paid for it by the German government. Now he would be paid twice."

Lord Grayle shrugged his rounded shoulders. "I don't care

about that. It is his concern. I only want clear title to the manuscript."

"Then you should get it from Germany," Barker replied.

"It is no longer theirs to give."

"Try convincing the Kaiser of that," I said.

"There would be a legal trial of some sort," the Guv pointed out.

"That's fine. I am in the midst of three already. What concern is another?"

"You must want the manuscript very badly."

"It shall be the pinnacle of my collection."

"A pity then that I do not possess it," my employer said. "A million pounds would keep one warm through the winter."

"I want the scroll!"

"You are a mere showman, not a scholar," I said. "The late Mr. Wessel was twice the man you are."

Lord Grayle sat back in his chair and raised both hands, imploring calm.

"I do not wish to cause a scene between us, Mr. Llewelyn. I'm just a humble collector. I want the scroll. Should you choose, I will buy it from you. Many people want it, I am certain, but they will not offer so high and round a sum. This is a business transaction, nothing more. Let us allow cooler heads to prevail. Consider my offer and tell me your answer tomorrow."

Now it was Barker's turn to be calm. He sat back in his chair and laced his fingers across his waistcoat. We watched him take in a bushelful of air and blow it out again.

"Your Lordship, this item you see, it may be a fake. It may be what the Council of Nicene deemed apocryphal. It may be the oldest gospel known to man. However, the one thing it will never be is yours."

Grayle jumped from his chair. "They said you were a stubborn man but I was willing to believe the best of you! I came in here offering a fair price and you became hostile. I have money, but I also have many friends. Powerful friends. Important ones. Get in my way and I shall crush you under my boot, and all you possess. You are not the Home Office. You are not the government. It was a mistake for Salisbury to choose one man!"

"Two men," I said. "Get out of our office."

"You will regret this," he said.

He took his glossy top hat and his kidskin gloves and his wand-like stick and marched out. Belatedly, he returned and pulled his coat off the rack.

The Guv still sat, while I came round to the bow window and watched His Lordship leave.

"Very good, Thomas, but I believe we have just made a powerful enemy."

I looked out at the traffic and the snow.

"He'll have to get in line with the rest of them."

CHAPTER TWENTY

Barker sat and smoked. He carved wood. I sat. Jenkins sat. I watched the Guv suck and blow smoke for a while, then I stood to get something. He immediately put up a hand. I was interrupting the flow of his thoughts. I returned to my desk. Running out of things to do, I oiled my Webley revolvers. The possibility occurred to me that someone could burst into our chambers, and there I was with my weapon in pieces, but that didn't happen. My pistol was fully functional before someone burst in.

My mind had barely registered the entry when our visitor stood in the doorway by my desk. He wore a close-fitting coat to his knees, a priest's collar, and a gold cross on a chain. Snow was dusting his shoulders and his dark hair, which curled back over his ears to his collar. The lower part of his face was covered in a mustache and short beard. His nose was thin and pronounced, his eyes vulpine. A stage Mephistopheles, I said to myself. Or perhaps Cardinal Richelieu.

"Mr. Barker," he said. "I am Monsignor Bello."

"Won't you have a seat?" the Guv offered. "What can I do for you, sir?"

"Let us not be coy. It is unbecoming. I want you to retrieve the manuscript, and give it to me."

Barker nodded his head thoughtfully, as if the suggestion had not occurred to him.

"Why would I wish to do so? We each have our part in this little drama. I deliver the manuscript to Calais, and you take it to Rome. This was worked out by the archbishop himself. Why would you have the impertinence to order me to give you what I was hired— nay, ordered—to deliver by Her Majesty's government."

Bello entered and looked about our chamber as if it were a hovel. All was shiny and new, with the best of craftsmanship and furnishings. Barker's desk and chair were built for him alone. The Persian carpets were of the highest quality. Our rooms were the envy of every detective in London, and not a few barristers.

"This is all you have to protect so priceless an object?"

"True, Monsignor," Barker said. "There is little gilt work here, but what there is has not been wrung from the sweat of generations of peasants."

Bello looked stricken at the remark. He gritted his teeth and his black brows pressed down upon his Roman nose. Then just as quickly, his features smoothed again. Barker gave him a cold smile.

"Droll, signore. Very well, forgive me. I did not intend to insult your offices."

The Guv nodded. He was being magnanimous.

"When do you intend to deliver the manuscript? Today? This evening?"

"Sometime this week, Monsignor. I have matters to attend to."

"This week?" Bello asked. "This week! But my men are waiting in France!"

"That is your concern, not mine."

"Do you not realize how important this manuscript might be?"

"Of course I do, though I doubt it shall ever see the light of day."

Bello shook his head. "I knew it was a mistake to hire you. I warned the Church not to hire you!"

"Sit, Monsignor, please. We need not be adversarial. In fact, we are supposed to work together. What caused you to find the arrangement unsatisfactory to the point of coming here today? You strike me as a very serious and competent administrator. No doubt you have arranged the journey from Calais to the Vatican meticulously. Is there a particular reason why you felt the need to come to London?"

"I know every kilometer between Calais and Rome. I do not know you."

"Then ask me questions, sir. I shall attempt to answer them competently. You cannot trust me if you do not know me."

Monsignor Bello looked at Barker as though he were attempting a ploy. Surely it could not be this simple.

"Has the archbishop told you what the satchel contains?"

Barker shrugged. "Some sort of manuscript. It doesn't particularly matter what it is. My duty is to deliver it. To you, in fact."

The monsignor smiled. "I am here now. Give it to me."

"Alas, I cannot. I'm sure your associates saw me place it securely in Cox and Co. Bank."

"They did. Take it out again."

Barker leaned deeper into his chair and tented his fingers together. "I could, but I won't. It is my duty to help Her Majesty's government whenever I can, and they have hired me. We have made a contract. Also, I like to get paid."

"No, I think not. The Society of Jesus has compiled a file on you just this morning. You are privately wealthy, though so far we haven't been able to learn how you obtained your wealth."

"I am, sir, but that doesn't mean I won't charge a fee. I cannot do so if I give the case over to you."

I raised a brow, knowing that Barker had already told the Prime Minister that he wouldn't take remuneration for this assignment.

Bello gritted his teeth in frustration.

"Have you attempted to open it?" he asked.

"I studied it before putting it in the vault. The lock mechanism has been filled with either lead or silver. It cannot be opened with a key. The lock would have to be cut off, then replaced and filled again in order to see whatever was inside without alarming the interested parties. Are you an interested party, Monsignor Bello?"

"Only insofar as maintaining its safety."

"We are agreed then."

"But it is preposterous! You are but one man! Granted, our file says you are a former soldier and a detective well-known to Scotland Yard. But really, Mr. Barker. Giving the manuscript to you alone while the whole of the Home Office appears to be delivering it themselves. It is highly dangerous. It is a mistake on your Prime Minister's part."

"It was a decision made between both archbishops and the Prime Minister. You may argue the matter with them. I am but a humble courier."

"But one man!"

"Two," I said, wondering if I needed to pull the Webley from my desk again.

Bello snorted. "One man and a clerk."

"My name is over the door, sir."

"Mr. Llewelyn," my associate said. "I believe Monsignor Bello is unimpressed with you. Prove to him otherwise."

"How would you prefer I do so, Mr. Barker?"

"I don't know. Rummage around in your desk and show him what weapons you have."

"Just my desk?" I asked.

"Well, anything within arm's reach."

"Very well."

I leaned forward and pulled the two Webley revolvers from cubbies in my rolltop desk. These I laid carefully on the carpet behind me because they were loaded and ready.

Then I reached into a pen cup and retrieved a Sicilian dagger

I keep there for opening letters. I purchased it because it closely resembled one Barker had. I laid it beside the pistols.

Beside my chair stood the hat stand, with my walking stick in the rack. I retrieved it, gave it a small thump in my palm, then twisted it and revealed seventeen inches of good Sheffield steel. These two pieces I laid on the rug as well.

I opened what I considered my miscellaneous drawer. It contained seven or eight knives of various sorts and countries of origin, a pair of brass knuckle-dusters, a weighted money knot, three throwing blades I bought from a circus performer once, a pair of iron caltrops one would not want to step on, and a whetstone that could easily brain a fellow. I pulled out the drawer and spilled the contents of the pen cup over that, since I could use any nib or pencil inside to stab an eye or a jugular vein. Lastly, I reached under my desk and set my Hammond typewriting machine on top of the pile. Granted, bringing it down on someone's head would damage the keys, but that would be of little consequence to the chap whose head I stove in.

"Bravo, signore," Bello said. "A nice little collection you have here. You are obviously a bloodthirsty young fellow. You will forgive me, I hope, for having insulted you."

With a look at Barker, I nodded. "Are you in any way mollified, Monsignor?"

"Would that I were, sir. I mean you no disrespect. I could send a telegram and have fifty men here in this office by vespers."

"Priests," Barker said dismissively. He was a trifle rude, but they were having a war with words, and one uses such weapons as one has on hand.

"Not merely priests. Many are former soldiers. No doubt you know that the Jesuits are the military side of the church. That is simplistic, of course, and we hope not to spill blood, but if necessary we are willing to die for the greater good. That includes safeguarding an important manuscript."

"Which you will do," Barker assured him. "From Calais."

"As I said, I can have fifty men here."

"In Calais, perhaps. Surely you have not brought an army with you."

"Bah!" Bello said, rising to his feet. "You'll find how quickly they can come!"

"Pray have a seat, Monsignor," the Guv said, trying to sound patient.

"I don't know why I am wasting my time. I came hoping to talk some sense into you, but you are obviously a Scotsman and cannot be reasoned with!"

My employer picked up a pen that lay on his glass-topped desk, the only object thereon, and began to tap it quietly on the glass. It was a harmless gesture, but it had meaning for those able to see it. His temper was rising, too.

"There is no need for insults about my heritage, Monsignor. I have been polite so far. I would offer you wine if we kept any. I could send our clerk over to the Silver Cross nearby and have him bring a worthy vintage, I suppose. I would not know about such matters."

"You are trying my patience, Mr. Barker. I have stated I have men who will take what you will not give."

"I wish you luck, sir. It is at Cox and Co., the only bank in London responsible for the payroll of Her Majesty's army and navy. The Admiralty is across the street. The Horse Guards, as well. They might have decided opinions about foreign priests trying to break into their vault."

Bello sat and raised his hands in a spirit of calm. "Let me make an offer to you that might be more agreeable."

Tap, tap, tap went the pen on the glass top of the desk.

Two arguments with strangers within an hour. One could see how one's nerves would fray.

"I'm an agreeable man," Barker said, his speech clipped.

"Very well. We will accompany you. That would satisfy your contract, would it not? We would be your bodyguards. We would keep you safe to live another day, to take the next case. I would be assured the manuscript is safe in order to complete my own mission. What say you?"

The tapping stopped.

"An equitable arrangement, don't you think, Mr. Llewelyn?"

"Some would say," I muttered.

"There is but one problem with it."

Bello looked about ready to jump to his feet again.

"What? What is the problem?" he demanded.

"Monsignor, I cannot allow a foreign army in this country."

"You? You can't?"

"I can't. You are not in Jesuit territory. You are in England. This is Templar territory."

Monsignor Bello blinked.

The Guv raised his left hand. There was a ring on his little finger, a plain, flat band of dull gold. There was a simple design on the ring, a cross in a crown with a legend that read *"in hoc signo vinces."* In this sign thou shalt conquer.

"Is this a joke?" Bello asked. "I am a serious person."

"I could call my own fifty men and escort you to Rome if you wish."

"I . . . I don't . . ." Bello said, or tried to.

"Surely you don't think they would entrust just anyone with so precious an object."

"No, no."

Bello's eyebrow was raised, an unasked question on his lips. He had been assured he was in possession of all the facts, but now he was not so certain. He tried to read the Guv's expression behind those glossy black lenses of his, but I am a past master and even I find it difficult. I would not expect a total stranger to make head or tails of it.

"Very well," Bello said, but he was treading water.

"If you have no further business, the lad and I have a good deal of planning to do."

"When shall you be leaving? Tonight?"

"Not tonight, and perhaps not tomorrow. If you can provide me with an address in Calais, I shall keep you abreast."

"Thank you."

Barker stood and bowed. Still at sea, the monsignor did likewise, then backed away.

"It was good to speak to you, sir," I said, and nodded also. We watched him turn and leave.

"Do put these things away, Mr. Llewelyn. We cannot have our chamber cluttered with open blades and pens."

"Certainly not, sir," I said, and began to put the objects back in my drawer.

I began collecting knives and pens and what-have-you from the floor, while he sat in his chair and cogitated. There was still an unequal division of labor between us, but I was not going to quibble about that. After all, I wasn't going to have a man with a metal brace on his leg get down on the floor and pick up trinkets.

The next I knew, the monsignor was pointing a pistol at us. My own Webley, in fact. "Gentlemen," he said. "You give me no alternative. I have tried to reason with you, but you are thickheaded. No, Mr. Barker, keep your hand away from that drawer! I will take that valise, please."

"You are welcome to it. It is in the vault next door."

"Sir, I am no fool. I believe you have it with you. I imagine it is between your feet at this very moment."

Barker shrugged and pulled his chair back on its casters. He lifted the bag and set it on top of his desk. Cautiously, Bello came forward and raised it.

"Be careful. It is sealed in glass," the Guv warned. "Very fragile."

"I know. Move your chair back, Mr. Barker. Farther. No, young man, keep your hands where I can see them! I am taking this away with me. It was never yours to protect. The archbishop has gone senile. What was he thinking, hiring two men for a matter this important?"

The truncheon caught him square on the back of the neck. Some can withstand a solid blow to the cranium, but a thump to the base of the skull and the nerves therein, that was too much for any man. Monsignor Bello slumped, and I leaped and caught the satchel just before it could hit the floor.

"There are three of us," Jeremy Jenkins told him. "And don't make remarks about clerks."

"Lad," Barker said. "Summon a cab we can bundle the monsignor into."

"Yes, sir. Where did you get the club, Jeremy?"

He lifted the Metropolitan Police regulation truncheon.

"I borrowed it from an obliging peeler, Mr. L. He didn't seem to need it."

CHAPTER TWENTY-ONE

The next morning, Cyrus Barker was whittling on that blasted block of his again. Calais beckoned. Even with blue coats chasing us, it seemed an easy matter. One boards a train. One boards a ferry. One gives the satchel to someone else, making it his problem, then boards the ferry and train again. I work for the most stubborn man in the world, I decided, or perhaps he didn't like Jesuits.

"What are the Jesuits like, sir?" I asked. "I must admit I've never met one. I read a book once about Jesuit assassins, but I could not trust the source."

"Who was the source?" Barker asked.

"Well, it was Jeremy, sir. He leant it to me."

"Consider the source."

"It was a good book!" our clerk called from the other room. "It was very factual."

"No doubt," Barker muttered.

Scrape. Scrape. Scrape.

Surely there must be another suspect to interview or a statement one could verify. I was about to perish from inactivity. Normally, the Guv is the energetic one and I am the chap who needs to be prodded.

The door opened and a man entered in a dove-gray coat that nearly came to his ankles. He wore an alpine-looking hat with a fanned feather in the brim. He actually clicked his heels, and handed a message to Jenkins before marching out again. Jeremy delivered it, but our employer did not look up from his ship. Our clerk looked at me, and I looked at him. We shrugged our shoulders at the same time. Jenkins lifted the message from the salver and set it on the edge of the desk.

The Guv chose to ignore it for five entire minutes. Never think that there is no bravado in him. He knew what effect ignoring the message would have upon my nerves. Somewhere in the City there must be a businessman who feels no need to torture his partner.

Finally, he leaned forward and opened the message, which was folded inside a small envelope. He read it and tapped the edge of the desk with his other thumb in thought.

"We are wanted at the German embassy. Hatzfeldt has canceled an appointment just to see us."

"Could we take the Underground?" I asked. "Hansoms are drafty and there is never a brougham about."

"Very well," he said. "However, I believe it is merely another chance for you to ride in a train."

"This from a man carving a toy boat."

"It is not a toy," he said. "It is a miniature replica."

"My mistake."

When we arrived in Holland Park, we were left waiting for twenty minutes. Perhaps Hatzfeldt was truly working on matters of great importance to his country, but it has been my experience that when one is left waiting it is to show them they are a subordinate and are having a favor bestowed upon them.

"Gentlemen, come in!" the ambassador called from his office. "We have much to discuss."

He waved us to a seat. Our host stood and bowed as we entered. When we were last in his office, Hatzfeldt displayed a certain air of bonhomie. Now he looked stern.

"Thank you for coming in response to my note. I have a message for you directly from the Kaiser himself. He says you must turn over the manuscript forthwith or you will engender an international incident."

I glanced over at Barker. His brows were nearly to his hairline. Even he had not anticipated such a response.

"Berlin has not discovered whether you stole the manuscript yourselves or are merely adventurers hoping to sell it for profit. Either way, our source claims that the manuscript has been brought to London hidden in a Gladstone bag. Do you own such a bag?"

"Sir," the Guv said. "I do not have your manuscript. I very much doubt it is in England, and the only bag I currently own houses the equipment for a ship model I am building."

"Do you think this is humorous, Mr. Barker? I assure you, I do not. You cannot estimate how much this manuscript means to my country. For years, our best scholars have postulated that there is an unnamed testament from which the books of Matthew and Luke were written. After years of searching, it was finally found in a mean little shop in Jersusalem. Unfortunately, the owner of the shop knew of our country's scholarship and quoted an outrageous price. We had been fooled before, and were made to look gullible in the European community. The Kaiser ordered the government to pay a princely sum, provided it could be authenticated by the best ancient-language scholar in Germany, Professor Gunther Bischoff. There was rejoicing in the palace that night. However, the manuscript was stolen that night from Bischoff's hotel room and he was found murdered by a complete scoundrel, a thief and murderer, and probably a spy for another power. Tell me, Mr. Barker, are you that scoundrel?"

"No, sir," my employer replied. "I can honestly say that I am not your scoundrel. I have not been in Europe for years, and then only in France. If you believe I have your manuscript, you shall be sorely disappointed."

"You, sir," Hatzfeldt said, rounding on me. "Are you an adventurer?"

"Sir, you must look far and wide to find a man less adventurous than I."

"Are you members of the Foreign Office?"

"If we were members of the Foreign Office, we certainly would not tell you," Barker said. "And if we were not, how would you know the difference? The only thing provable is that we have had a private agency for ten years in Whitehall, and there does not seem a likely reason why the Foreign or even the Home Office should concern themselves with the workings of so small an agency."

"Do you know who currently possesses the manuscript?"

"We do not."

"Do you know where it is?"

"We do not."

"Why were you interested in it?"

"We were hired by Drummond's parents, as we told you."

Hatzfeldt pointed an accusatory finger. "Liar! We have questioned Drummond's parents. They never heard of you!"

"Sir," Barker shot back. "If you know who brought the manuscript to England, why have you accused us of stealing it?"

The German ambassador sat down again, and examined Barker with slitted eyes, his arms crossed, his head tilted to one side.

"You will recall," the Guv continued, "that we came to you about our investigation. Would we have shown ourselves to you had we been guilty of subterfuge?"

"I would imagine, Mr. Barker, that subterfuge is your stock-in-trade."

"It is a useful tool, Ambassador, I'll admit. However, we are not spies. I have no respect for them. In theory I see the need, I suppose, but it is not an activity in which I would involve myself. It is the underbelly of government. It stains one's character. A man should be aboveboard, don't you think?"

Hatzfeldt looked at us as if unsure how to answer. Perhaps he was being tricked.

"Espionage has its uses," he said. "And it has been done throughout history, but I will admit it is not a profession I would like to see my son undertake."

"There you are, then."

"I wish I knew what was in your mind, sir, I must admit. You are as blank as a stone wall."

"An enquiry agent must hold his own counsel until every fact has been wrung from an investigation."

"We did some investigation of our own, gentlemen. Mr. Barker, your reputation is spotty. Some we have asked consider you the best detective in London."

"Private enquiry agent," I corrected.

"Just so. Some consider you a hammer to swat a fly."

"They should try to hammer a nail with a rolled newspaper," I replied.

"That is an excellent point. You yourself are an interesting study, Mr. Llewelyn. A failed scholar, with eight months in prison."

"I did not fail. The sentence merely got in the way of my studies."

"Recently married to a Jewess."

One can imagine that got right up my nose.

"Do you have concerns about Jewesses, Your Excellency?"

"Good heavens, no. They make up a tenth of my country's population. They are industrious, thrifty, and have a calming effect in our communities. I was merely trying to illustrate that you had a roundabout way of becoming an enquiry agent."

"Had I known the future, perhaps I would have planned more wisely."

"Oh, dear. I have insulted you twice over. My apologies, sir."

I nodded, though I was not fully mollified.

Hatzfeldt stood and began to pace with his thin arms akimbo. He was no longer the urbane fellow we had spoken with on our last visit.

"I did not mean to insult either of you. You appear genuine enough, although I have not placed how you are involved in this matter precisely. Understand this. A piece of German property was stolen and one of our citizens murdered. If it can be proven that the English government has conceived and executed this plan, then there is a breach between our two governments. It may rupture our relations and void our treaties. The Kaiser is incensed. In his current state, it might lead to war. Wars have been started over far more trivial matters. Do I make myself clear?"

The Guv pulled himself forward in his chair so that both hands rested on the knob of his blackthorn stick.

"Yes, Your Excellency, you do. I am concerned, naturally, but only as a citizen. I cannot enforce policy. I am not a member of the British government."

"For whom do you work, Mr. Barker? It is not for the Drummonds."

"I make it a part of my enquiries not to disclose the name of my clients. However, I am certain to be able to find a witness to prove Mr. Llewelyn and I have been in this country for the last week or more."

Barker can parse words with the best of them. He always tries to tell the truth, but often he gives himself room to maneuver. Indeed, he had not been hired by the British government to investigate the case. He was doing that on his own. He'd been hired to deliver the manuscript to France. The trick was to avoid the question while making it seem that he had answered it.

"Mr. Barker, you are a seasoned professional. That is a fact. I will not be able to trick you into some kind of confession. You say you have a client, but I have a suspicion who really hired you."

"Certainly, you are entitled to your suspicions, sir," the Guv rumbled.

"Thank you. I have no further questions. You may go."

We left the embassy, walking under the German flag with its two-headed eagle.

"He was less than cordial," my employer remarked.

"I suppose losing a million-dollar artifact would make one that way," I replied.

"His government would like him to conjure the manuscript out of thin air, a trick he can never accomplish."

"Do you think it's true about the Bischoff fellow being murdered?" I asked.

"It is highly likely, if what Hatzfeldt says is true, but he, too, may be covering for his government. It is what he does for a living."

We had walked a street or two, heading toward the Underground.

"Someone is following us," Barker said.

"From the embassy, I presume."

"Not necessarily. He could have been hired by Lord Grayle."

"Do you believe his threat to be credible? Friends in high places?"

"I'm not concerned," the Guv answered. "Our friends are higher yet. We may even have the same friends, which shall make it interesting."

We found our seats on the Underground and the man following us took a seat in the next carriage. I got a good look at him. He was about thirty, blond, with no obvious scars.

"Very German-looking," I said.

"What makes him German-looking?"

"I don't know. Blond. Stern-looking."

"Could he not be Danish or Swedish?"

"I suppose."

"Try to be precise, Mr. Llewelyn, and do not make judgments based upon personal prejudices."

"Yes, sir. In any case, he can join the others following us about. They can lunch together."

"You do talk rot sometimes."

We returned to our offices. As expected, Barker found the hull of his miniature ship and began filing it. It was like a dog gnawing a bone. I entered our expenses, such as they were, in the ledger.

"I don't know why it is necessary for me to keep an account when you so often offer our services for free," I said. "In theory, this is supposed to be a profitable enterprise."

"It is necessary if for no other reason than to tell us the fare to the German embassy."

"Apparently, there is still much I do not know about private enquiry work."

He took the file and began sanding the deck slowly.

"Enquiry work is like Chinese boxing, lad," he murmured. "When one has become a partner, or an instructor, one has officially begun the work. One is no longer an apprentice, but one is still just a beginner."

"Thank you, sir," I said. "That is comforting."

"Not at all," he replied. "Anything to help."

He never understands sarcasm.

CHAPTER TWENTY-TWO

It felt good to be home early after all the threats we had recently endured. After dinner, Mac shooed us away from Rebecca and I climbed the stair and entered our suite. We spent an hour or two reading on either side of the fire. She did not ask me about the case and I did not tell her. The two of us agreed early in our marriage that she would hear all about a case when it was concluded, but not before. However, a small part of it involved her personally, so I told her about it.

"You went to see my father?" she asked. "Both of you?"

I explained in detail all that was said while we were in the rabbi's office. She was surprised that the Guv would entertain the thought of giving up so important a position as the Board of Deputies.

"I think I shall go to Camomile Street tomorrow and see if anything has changed."

She looked expectant and happy. I must remember to defend her more often, I thought.

"By the way, I think you should know that Harm and I are now the best of friends."

"What?" I exclaimed. "Impossible."

"Not impossible," she replied. "I found his weakness, and I must admit I have exploited it."

"What is his weakness?"

"Chicken livers. I gave him a few this morning and a few more this afternoon, and he's hovered nearby ever since."

"I wish I'd known that when I first came to this house."

The following morning, we met Pollock Forbes at King's Cross Station to see him off. I realized I did not know how long he had lived in London, or even why. Barker was tight-lipped about him; perhaps he did not know much about his reasons, either. Had the Templars been as important before Forbes became master, or was it all due to his efforts? I would probably never know.

Forbes wore a coat with a fur collar, his throat swathed in a plaid scarf, the Forbes tartan, no doubt. His top hat was glossy and he did his best to appear as if nothing were amiss. He did not cough, his flesh was not slick with sweat, and though his face was pale, the feverish red blooms on his cheeks were gone. Only the few of us who had visited him over the past week were aware of his true condition.

"It's nice of you gentlemen to see me off," he said. "I know you are fully occupied."

"What sort of friends would we be if we let you leave London without saying farewell?" Barker asked.

"I would understand if you couldn't be here. Has the package been delivered?"

"I have every confidence it shall be there directly."

"I'll hold you to that. How do the new reins feel?"

"Few are aware the leadership has changed hands," the Guv said. "They shall learn soon enough."

A man appeared at my elbow then, placing a pair of tickets in his pocket. It was the young man we'd met at Pollock's flat.

"Mr. Charles," I said.

"Just Charles," he replied. "Charles Putnam, actually. I'm Pollock's secretary. You're Llewelyn, aren't you?"

"Thomas, yes."

Barker and Forbes were discussing some point of business, so I plucked Putnam's elbow and we both moved back a step or two.

"How is he?" I asked.

"He couldn't stand this morning. I must admit, I don't know what's holding him up. Form, perhaps. He hates being pitied."

"Most of us do. Can he travel?"

"I'll find out soon enough. We'll be stopping at Edinburgh tonight, where I have a room ready at the Waverly, with a doctor waiting. Pollock wanted to travel through to Aberdeen, but I insisted. London has been sucking the life from him. The damp, the soot, the sewage, the food. Now I wonder if six months in the country will do him well. The Sandwich Islands may be his only hope for survival."

"I shall miss him," I said. "Barker and I both will, not to mention a thousand diners at the Café Royal. Tell him if he does not improve I shall come to Aberdeen and trounce him at dominoes."

Putnam whistled. "Brave words. I'll warn him."

"Will you have discharged your duties once you reach Aberdeen?"

"I shall be there to the end, no matter how long it takes."

"Excuse me. This must be a blow."

"I've been expecting it for years. Still, it is harder than I anticipated. I've seen the man every day for a decade. I cannot imagine what life will be like if he does not recover."

"Is there hope, then?"

"One doctor is optimistic, another pessimistic. One thinks the cool air in the Highlands will do him good, another suggested that someplace called 'Arizona' would roast the moisture right out of him. Where is that? Do you have any idea?"

"In America, I believe, near Mexico. It's full of cowboys."

"Oh, jolly," Putnam said. "We shall fit right in."

I pulled my watch from my waistcoat pocket and inspected it. We still had a quarter hour before the train arrived. Barker took Forbes inside, while we stood on the platform awaiting the engine that would take the two of them to Edinburgh.

"Does he confide in you?" I asked.

"Sometimes. Why do you ask?"

"I was wondering if it took him long to decide that Mr. Barker should be his successor. He seems an unusual choice, if I may say that about my own employer."

"He's had a long time to consider. I've seen at least one list in his room."

"I'd have thought he would have chosen an aristocrat. Is it because Barker is Scottish?"

"No, there is at least one other he considered who was a Scot. You look concerned."

"I am, rather. It could cause all sorts of changes at the agency."

"I'm sorry, old man. I don't believe he took your feelings into consideration, any more than he did mine."

I decided I liked the fellow, or at least I sympathized with him. Being dragged along behind an important man and having to constantly cope with changing circumstances was something I found familiar.

Eventually the express engine to Edinburgh steamed forward, changed tracks, and eased back until the couplings locked. She was a beauty, the Scotch Express, sleek and black, picked out in red. She had raced the Western Line a few years before, a race in which I'd have given my back molars to participate.

"Here comes Pollock," Putnam said, and I turned and watched as he and Barker returned. I began to get a lump in my throat. He came up to me and shook my hand without speaking. There was nothing I could think of to say. He patted the Guv on the sleeve and turned. The two of them had already said their adieus.

Forbes and Putnam boarded the train, the latter raising his hat to me. I caught a glimpse of them as they took a seat in one of the carriages. Then the steam whistle blew and Cyrus Barker and I watched the train pass out from under the canopy into a gently falling snow.

We left without speaking, both of us in our own sad thoughts. I vowed I would never play dominoes again if it couldn't be with Pollock, and though I didn't stop visiting the Café Royal now and then, it was never the same again. It never could be.

We took a hansom from the station, still without speaking. There were blankets inside the cab and we covered ourselves in them.

"You couldn't say no, could you?" I asked.

"No, I couldn't. Could you?"

I shook my head. "What shall we do? Do we now work exclusively for the Templars? Shall it be government work from now on?"

Then he spoke the words I thought I'd never hear from his lips.

"Thomas, I have no idea."

Jenkins had banked the fire in the grate well enough that one felt the heat as one entered. We doffed our coats and sat, thinking. The Guv's last remark had shaken me. I could not leave it alone.

"Why don't you have an idea?" I finally said.

He inhaled and then blew his cheeks out. "There are too many variables, and I'm still considering my options. We're playing with the hounds now and we cannot afford to be timid."

"Or wrong," I added.

The telephone set on Barker's desk jangled, making me jump. At that moment I couldn't think of a single good thing that might occur if I answered, merely catastrophes. Still, one mustn't let down the side.

"Barker and Llewelyn Agency."

"Inspector Garrick, please," a voice said.

"There's no one here by that name."

"Garrick, hello. It's Poole. The Old Man's on his way, just as you predicted. Batten down the hatches and all that. Meet us there if you want to hear fireworks."

"Thanks," I said.

"Cheerio."

I placed the receiver back in its cradle. "Munro is coming again and no doubt tearing up Whitehall as he comes. We must prepare."

"Mac," Barker said, looking up. "Take a stroll."

"Yes, sir," he replied from the other room.

I scooted my caster chair into the waiting room, where our butler now occupied a desk behind Jenkins.

"Hello, Jacob, old fellow!" I said. "Didn't see you there."

He hates when I call him "Jacob," at least to his face.

"Thomas."

He was busy stuffing a large folder full of the correspondence that had recently arrived. I noticed he was out of his uniform. His silver waistcoat had been replaced by one in a subtle check. Going to the stand, he took down a bowler much like mine, in place of his customary homburg hat. He donned the bowler and stepped out the door, then disappeared in that way he has that made him a prince among butlers.

Munro arrived no more than a minute afterward.

"Barker!" he bawled as he entered the door the second time since the case began.

"I am right here, Commissioner. There is no need to shout."

"Don't tell me when to shout and when not to shout. Clap him in darbies, gentlemen. And the little cheeky one, too."

"How nice," I said. "Did you miss me?"

He smacked me for my trouble.

Barker stood and held out his wrists. The metal bracelets barely fit around them. I, on the other hand, could practically pull my hands through.

"What do I do with him?" one of the constables asked about our clerk.

Jenkins sat impassively. Even a room full of constables didn't fully concern him.

Munro waved him away, then leaned across the Guv's desk

to stare him in the eyes. He was getting fingermarks all over the polished glass.

"Where is it, Barker?" he demanded.

"Where is what?"

"You know what. The leather bag."

"It's next door in Cox and Co. in a vault."

"Don't try that with me! It won't wash."

Between the cold air and his hot temperament, Munro's face was red as a tomato.

"I'm sorry you don't believe me, sir," Barker said. "I shall say no more."

"Good. Take the place apart, men. We're hunting for a leather valise, old and scuffed. It will be heavy. Treat it very carefully."

They were none too gentle. A fall from over six feet does not agree with the spine of a book or its brethren. They tossed our waste bins about, and rifled in the drawers of Barker's desk. I'd have made a caustic remark, but I had already been slapped once and I did not require another.

"Here, sir!" one of the constables cried. He wasn't much older than the blue coats that had tackled me.

Below the Barker crest and cutlasses was a table containing a tray of glasses and a bottle of brandy for those clients of ours who needed fortification. Beneath that was a small bookcase, which actually wasn't a bookcase at all. It was a safe made for the agency by Chubb and Sons. It had a combination lock, a series of tumblers that needed to be turned in order to open the safe.

"Open it," Munro told Barker.

My employer lifted his shackled wrists and shrugged his shoulders.

"You, then," he said, turning to me.

"I forget the combination," I said. "A room full of peelers makes me nervous."

He stormed into the waiting room and lifted Jeremy from his chair. No one was as surprised as our clerk.

The commissioner escorted him to the safe and pointed. "Open it!"

Our clerk looked over his shoulder at the Guv. He nodded. I'm a partner and I expect to be pushed around now and again, but there's an unwritten rule: you don't harm a clerk. Apparently if it isn't written, Munro feels he need not abide by it.

Jenkins put a hand over the lock to stop the officers from seeing the combination, then he turned the long handle and it opened soundlessly. There in the safe was the satchel, disreputable as always.

"In the bank at Cox and Co., my blessed mother!" the commissioner hooted. "We have what we came for. Take them!"

We were led to the front door, where our coats were thrown over our shoulders and hats pushed down low on our heads. Then we were rudely pushed outside into the cold. The constables wore their sturdy coats which came up to their throats and down to their knees. I hopped over an icy puddle and then was jerked into the traffic of Whitehall Street. People looked at us on the street or in cabs as we were trotted down the road in irons. Nothing in my eight months in prison was more embarrassing than that very moment, being prodded with truncheons and pulled by the wrists, the better to display to everyone in London that we were criminals.

I assumed our destination was Scotland Yard; it seemed to be the obvious choice. However, we were dragged past the Met and farther south down Whitehall Street, accompanied by a squad of ten officers. Aside from the commissioner, that made eight men to protect London from Cyrus Barker, and if I may flatter myself, two to take on Thomas Llewelyn, Esq. We formed our own parade, a parade of shame, if you will, arranged by Scotland Yard for our benefit.

I tried not to look anyone in the eye, but sure enough one caught mine, a young man in a long coat leaning against a building, scowling. He didn't wear a blue coat. It was Soho Vic, and he was angry. Perhaps he had always admired Cyrus Barker before, but would not admit it. Perhaps he understood where he would be and what he would have been if not for the Guv. Seeing Barker shackled and humiliated was the first time I'd ever seen Vic display any emotion. Certainly, I was part of the humiliation, but later it seemed to me that he felt it deeper than I. The unimaginable had happened: Barker captured. Disgraced.

I looked over to see how my employer was enduring Munro's torture and as I should have expected, he was calm, his back ramrod straight, walking as if he were taking an afternoon constitutional. My employer nodded at Vic and passed on. He did not appear to be angry. That was for his satellites such as Vic and myself. We had more than enough anger between us.

Why weren't we going to Scotland Yard? I asked myself as we passed the old Banqueting House, one of the few parts of the Palace of Westminster that was finished. The Houses of Parliament were just ahead on my left, Westminster Abbey at the foot of the street, and to the right, the combined Home, Foreign, and Colonial Offices. Before that, however, was Downing Street. Ah, yes, Number 10 Downing Street, the home and offices of a certain public servant who was certain to be unhappy at that moment. We were a pair of flies with wings that needed to be plucked.

Munro turned and paced to number 10 where a young constable stood at such exaggerated attention I expected him to fall over. Munro marched us in the front door and down a hall: the commissioner, Barker and me, ten constables, and our old friend Swithin, who didn't like people moving about without being escorted.

Eventually, I recognized the door to the Prime Minister's office. Munro threw it open and led us up to the Prime Minister's desk. We were pushed down into the same chairs we had occupied during our first visit. Salisbury sat at his large desk, still flanked by all those books. One would think that owning such books would make a man happy, but the Prime Minister was not a happy man. Not by any stretch of the imagination.

CHAPTER TWENTY-THREE

Gentlemen, you are sacked!" Salisbury thundered. "Truly sacked! You shall never be more well and truly sacked! I've never met a pair of more incompetent asses in my entire life. I don't know why I took counsel about finding a suitable courier for the satchel, can you, Munro?"

The commissioner was caught flat-footed.

"I? Uh, no, sir."

"I should have made the decision myself. A random nanny and her three charges could have successfully delivered a satchel to the Dover ferry in half a day, including time for rock candy. You bumblers could not accomplish it in four days. In that much time, you could have wagged the satchel under the Kaiser's nose and still made the trip to Calais before now."

I wanted to slide into my collar as a turtle does its shell. We'd never been sacked before, and I hadn't received such a tongue-lashing since I was in grammar school and had spilled an inkwell on the headmaster's desk. Even the judge who sentenced me to nine months in Oxford Prison for theft had not subjected me to such abuse, and it was only starting.

"Let me explain your duties to you again, Mr. Barker. They are not onerous. You take the package to Charing Cross Station. You board the express to Dover. In Dover, you transfer to a ferry bound for Calais. Arriving in Calais, you deliver the satchel to Monsignor Bello. He should not be difficult to find. He is the one surrounded by priests, who has been waiting several days for the satchel. The monsignor is a busy and important man. He does not have time to sit about on his hands. Likewise, the staff at the Vatican Library has been awaiting the delivery of the manuscript."

He fumbled in his pocket for a handkerchief and wiped the sheen from his forehead.

"There, you see? You have tricked me into revealing what was inside the satchel. It was my intention not to reveal the contents. Very well! It was a book. Well, parts of a scroll, actually. An ancient scroll. You were supposed to safeguard it! The Vatican has promised to hold it safely in their vaults for Great Britain. It is a national treasure. What have you dunces been doing with a national treasure? Practicing curling?"

I glanced at Munro, who was now sitting in a chair enjoying the show. From his expression, he seemed to find the entertainment first-rate. Looking back, I found the Prime Minister's eyes boring into me.

"Mr. Barker! Mr. Llewelyn," he said, sitting down in his chair and trying to calm himself. "You are not trying to disgrace England, are you? Tell me that you are not working for a foreign power. Tell me you have not been employed by the Labour Party in order to sabotage my government!"

"Certainly not, Your Lordship," Barker said. "I am a loyal Conservative."

I closed my eyes and inhaled. It had not been a question. Barker was only making matters worse, if such a thing were possible. Was there some kind of punishment for what we had done, or rather, hadn't done? Was the Prime Minister able to throw us in a cell for however long he thought sufficient, even it were years? Would I still be free at the end of the day, or would Rebecca find herself married to a prisoner? Would Barker's solicitor, Bram Cusp, be able to free us from such a situation? Would he even try, and damage his own reputation? Worst of all, was there some way we could just disappear from the earth having thwarted a plan of the most powerful man on earth? My word, how did we get ourselves into such a mess?

Salisbury leaned forward and folded his hands together on the blotter in front of him.

"Mr. Barker. Would you be so kind as to tell me why you have not delivered the manuscript?"

"Your Excellency did not inform me there was a particular day or time by which you wanted the satchel delivered," the Guv said.

I turned and regarded him. There was no sheen on his forehead. He seemed calm and self-contained. He was not flustered by having a man shout at him for five solid minutes.

"Do you not understand the word 'immediately'?"

"I do, sir," my employer replied, "but you did not use it. What you said was 'as soon as possible.' There is a good deal of difference between the two terms. It was not possible for me to deliver the satchel."

"Not possible or not convenient?" Munro asked in a low voice.

"Yes, Mr. Barker, Private Enquiry Agent. What have you been doing with your time?" Salisbury demanded.

"Thomas and I have been attacked twice by the same young men who killed Hillary Drummond. They knew of our involvement within an hour of our taking possession of the satchel. I think it likely someone here in Whitehall Street is working against us. That is, against you, sir."

"Brass!" the Prime Minister shouted. "Have you any witnesses?"

"Dozens, sir. By my calculations, I have been followed about by CID men, Home Office agents, members of a German fencing club, a German agent and at least one suspect. We attended Drummond's funeral yesterday and it seemed as if half of the mourners had followed us there. Tell me, were you the one who ordered us followed? Were we being spied upon by Her Majesty's government after we were hired?"

"You obviously didn't do the work," Munro said.

"Perhaps, but you did not yet know this when your men began following me about. I assumed the Prime Minister has not told you until this minute what the satchel contained."

"Of course not," the commissioner said.

"May I have these darbies removed, please?" I asked. "I promise I will neither attack anyone nor run away."

The Prime Minister looked at the commissioner. The commissioner looked back at the Prime Minister. Munro began patting his pockets.

"I'll get that, Thomas," my employer said, unlocking my restraints with a key from his waistcoat pocket. He did not remove his own.

"Where did you find that key?" Munro nearly shouted.

"This one?" the Guv asked. "I always carry it. You might consider checking a fellow's pockets before you parade him in front of heads of state. I have a pistol, a nine-inch knife, and a number of sharpened coins. Do you still have your Webley, Thomas?"

"I do, sir."

"There you are, then. Had we been working against our country's interests, the commissioner here would have escorted us through this building to your very desk at your mortal peril."

No one spoke for a moment. The Earl of Salisbury was trying to take it all in. The head of the Met was a little red about the face. Barker seemed to be enjoying himself. The Prime Minister took another tack.

"What is all this about the professor—Wessel, wasn't it?"

"Yes," Barker replied. "A friend and a capital linguist. I hold myself responsible for his death. I don't know who the University of London will find to take his place."

"Why did he meet you in that hovel in Limehouse?" Munro demanded.

"What hovel in Limehouse?" Barker asked.

"Don't play the innocent with me. You were seen entering and leaving a tearoom of special interest to Scotland Yard."

"So, you admit you were following us, then?" my employer asked.

"It was necessary to protect the manuscript."

"But you didn't know there was a manuscript. You didn't even know there was a satchel."

"You were a person of interest. Wessel was dead."

"Your chronology is off. Wessel died later."

"Because of you, Cyrus Barker. Death follows you like a shadow."

"I run an enquiry agency, Commissioner, not a sweetshop. The work we do is dangerous."

"You are dangerous!" Munro insisted. "You sent that poor scholar to his death."

"I sent him back to the university in a hansom cab. I presumed he was safe since Limehouse was bristling with plainclothesmen, who were no doubt Special Branch detectives. Did none of you think to follow him?"

Munro looked away. Apparently, no one had.

"Mr. Barker," the Prime Minister asked, once more taking over the conversation. "Can you please tell me what you were doing in the middle of the night in a questionable district of London with the manuscript with which I entrusted you?"

The Guv shifted in his seat. It was hard wood, probably to discourage long meetings, and he was still in his bracelets.

"Prime Minister, the manuscript was locked in the vault of the Cox and Co. Bank at the time. The bank manager will attest to that."

"Swithin!"

The Prime Minister's winged servant appeared at the door. "Sir?"

"Bring tea."

"Sir."

The door closed. Salibury pounced. "Mr. Barker, one last time, for what purpose were you and Mr. Wessel in Limehouse?"

He was caught there, I thought. He had wriggled and explained and argued as well as anyone could, but eventually one is called to account. My employer reached up with his bound hands and removed his bowler hat. He laid it in his lap and brushed it with a hand. He looked diminished, somehow.

"Prayer meeting, sir. We were having a prayer meeting."

"Prayer meeting?" Salisbury practically shouted. "In the middle of the night in the blackest, most godforsaken part of London?"

"No place is godforsaken, even in the East End."

The PM regarded a piece of paper on his desk, looking for a passage in it. "A prayer meeting in a tearoom run by an Asiatic known for his association with eastern criminal organizations known as 'triads.'"

"Yes, sir," Barker replied. "And that 'Asiatic' is my oldest friend. He was my first mate when I was the captain of a merchant vessel in the China Sea."

"You appear to have led a colorful life."

"Not intentionally."

"You—damn it, man, you've got your own key. Remove those restraints!"

My employer reached again into his waistcoat pocket, removed the key he carried there, and unlocked his own manacles. His bowler was still on the edge of the desk, as he stood and crossed to where the commissioner sat. Munro leaned back as if fearing some attack, but all that happened was a pair of darbies were placed in his lap. We all watched as Barker pulled the coat from his shoulders and donned it properly. He brushed it with a hand, straightened his tie, and sat again.

"You were saying, sir?"

"The prayer meeting," Salisbury prompted. "You expect me to believe you were having a prayer meeting at two o'clock in the morning?"

"I do, sir. I am—was—a deacon at the Baptist Tabernacle. Professor Wessel was a scholar in ancient languages. What else should we be doing? It is not a public house or a low den. It is a tearoom. We drank tea and read Scriptures."

Sometimes I'm in awe of the man. We did drink tea, and he was reading the Scriptures. It was a simple answer because it was true.

"Why not do that at home?"

"It was not safe, as can be proven by the professor's murder. There are men out there armed with swords, waiting to kill people for whatever is in that satchel."

"Are you in the habit of having late prayer meetings, sir?" Salisbury asked.

"I am, although not generally with the professor. Most often it is with Robert Anderson."

Salisbury had been scratching his long beard, but he stopped and looked at the Guv, and then over at Munro.

"Robert Anderson, the former spymaster general?"

"Aye, sir."

"The current assistant commissioner of the Metropolitan Police?"

"The same."

Munro rubbed his face with his hand and sighed. "I cannot control with whom my subordinates do or do not associate."

I coughed. Munro frowned at me.

"I'm just a layman," my employer continued. "I needed an expert to parse several words that have always troubled me. For instance—"

"I don't need your 'for instances,' Mr. Barker. Why didn't you just deliver the bloody satchel and have done with it? You could go on to your next case and I could concentrate on things of national interest. At least the manuscript is finally on its way, although I'm sure the Home Office has a few choice words to say to you. You were supposed to coordinate with them."

"Sir, Mr. Llewelyn was attacked in the street. Then I was confronted in my office by two youths armed with swords. Then Wessel was killed. When would I have time to coordinate with the Home Office?"

"Confess, Barker," Munro said. "You were investigating the death of Hillary Drummond, which is Scotland Yard's duty."

"How well are you coming along?" I asked.

Very well. Perhaps that was not the most politic thing to say. Munro seemed to think so. He sprang up and had a hand clamped around the back of my neck before I could think. He moved quickly for a man with too many social banquets in his system.

"Pray, don't hurt my assistant, Munro," Barker said.

"Partner!" I corrected.

"Insolent pup," the commissioner replied.

"Woof."

Barker gave me a murderous look.

"Have you been investigating the death of Drummond?" Salisbury asked. "You admitted attending his funeral."

"I may have questioned a person or two," my employer said.

"Such as the German ambassador," Munro said, like a schoolboy informing on a classmate.

That was one too many, apparently. The Prime Minister shook his head, stood, and began to pace in front of all those wonderful books I coveted the last time I was here.

"The German ambassador," he repeated. "You've brought Hatzfeldt into this?"

"Merely to ask if he could find information about a British national who died upon arrival on English soil."

"Then the two of them disrupted a public event run by an American," Munro cried.

He ripped a newspaper clipping from his pocket and placed it on the desk. Salisbury didn't want to look at it. He waved it away. I leaned forward.

"Is my name in it?" I asked. "Did they spell it right?"

There was no sign what newspaper or journal the article had come from. It was a humorous column written by a waggish fellow whose hand I hoped to shake someday. It told how Cochran and his camp followers had descended upon London like a plague of locusts, how he had become a social climber in order to bring socialites and stevedores alike to his tent revival. I began to read.

Then after a rousing sermon of which London has not seen the like since Charles Wesley, a demonstration was done to prove the superiority of the so-called Aryan races, who, Cochran says, were actually the remnant of the Ten Lost Tribes of Israel. The demonstration involved a youth from the reverend's camp followers and a volunteer from the audience performing physical culture exercises on the horizontal bar. It went awry, however, when the volunteer, a stripling of a Welshman named Timothy Llewelyn, proved superior on the bar. This broke up the audience, and eventually the camp meeting itself.

"Stripling?" I asked. "Timothy?"

"Quite, Thomas," Barker muttered.

"Mr. Barker," the Prime Minister said. "This is a sad ending to a bad business. I should have known better than to accept the offer of a man to work for free. I have received what I paid for. You may bluster and you may explain, you may turn logic on its ear, but the fact remains that you failed to do a very simple task and you are sacked. I never want to see you in this office again. You shall not be hired by any agency of the government again in any matter. You have proven yourself unsatisfactory and your work inferior. You are sacked. I am done with you both. Go."

We went. The worst part was the look of triumph on Munro's

piggish face. I would have dearly enjoyed poking that snout of his, but we were disgraced.

"At least we aren't in jail," I said, as we exited Downing Street.

"That is cold comfort, lad," Barker growled. "Prodded along in darbies on my own street. I was willing to show mercy, but not now. The gloves are off."

CHAPTER TWENTY-FOUR

While our return to Craig's Court was more sedate than our leave-taking, it was no less embarrassing. I assumed every eye I felt on me had seen us being dragged down Whitehall Street in restraints. The Guv and I had been arrested dozens of times since I had begun working with him, but never had I endured such public humiliation.

Barker's face was set; he was no longer the logical and humble fellow who had tolerably answered Salisbury's questions. His blood was up. As he said, the gloves were off. It was a phrase he had uttered only once or twice since I'd met him. I had no sympathy for Salisbury, and even less for Munro, but I wondered what my employer would do.

Sacked.

Sometimes a case was unable to be solved and we returned the retainer fee to the client, but that was far different from being sacked.

I watched as he stoked that pipe of his, retrieved the block of wood that would eventually become a model of the *Arrow*, and began carving again as if nothing had happened. The fellow has nerves of iron.

"We've been sacked!" I said, hoping to get some response from him. Any response was better than none.

"Mmmm?" he said gruffly, then turned to his task again.

"What now?" I asked. Sometimes it was necessary to state the obvious. "What do we do?"

"I am doing something," he said. "Jeremy!"

Our clerk put his head into the room. "Mr. B.?"

"Be a good fellow and nip over to the Shades for a few sandwiches. See if they have any fried potatoes. And some ale, of course."

"Righto."

I opened my wallet and gave Jeremy a sovereign and a stern look. He wiggled his eyebrows and hurried out into the snow. I moved to the fireplace, added coal, and banked the embers.

"Damn and blast that Salisbury!" I said.

"He was well within his rights as a client to dispense with our services," Barker said. "If that has not occurred before, we can count ourselves fortunate."

A boy came in with a note, and I gave him a sixpence. We were just tucking into our sandwiches a quarter hour later when another entered, stamped the snow from his feet, and laid a few more notes on our clerk's desk. Jenkins offered him half a sandwich and he snatched it and ran off like a squirrel with a nut.

I was casting about for something to do to look occupied and then stopped the attempt. If the Guv could not be bothered, then why should I? Still, it rankled me.

"The Prime Minister has a point, I should imagine," I said. "We promised to take a manuscript to Calais and we failed to do so, as you said. We deserved what we received."

Barker held up his finger, carved a tiny splinter from the wood block, and blew it away.

"Succinctly put," he said, not bothering to look up.

"We could have taken it there at any time."

"No doubt."

"It's only two hours by train. Or is it less?" I asked.

"It's less, I'm sure of it," Barker replied.

"And the ferry to Calais, that would take half an hour, perhaps?"

"If that."

"So, it would have taken two and a half hours to get there and an equal time to return."

He nodded.

I tried. I wanted to, but when the time came I found I could not ask him the reason for not doing as we had been instructed to do.

"At least tell me the satchel you gave him was the right one."

He puffed his pipe. He carved the block.

"You didn't give the manuscript to the Prime Minister?" I exclaimed. "Are you mad? Have you lost your reason?"

"Not that I am aware."

The outer door opened again, bringing another tyke. His arms were full of notes. He pulled off a sock he was using as a mitten with his teeth and laid the stack on the desk beside the others. He received another sixpence. He examined its authenticity with the few teeth in his mouth and headed out into the cold again.

Mac caught the closing door and entered, looking neat as a pin. He hung his hat on a hook.

"Gentlemen," he said, pouncing on the letters. His timing was impeccable, but then it always is, drat the man.

Another boy came; another note; another sixpence. I emptied my pockets of coins and put them on the corner of Barker's desk and the Guv did the same.

Then an older boy arrived, looked about as if Scotland Yard would lay darbies on him at any moment, then removed at least ten notes from his coat. I gave him a full shilling and he tugged his peaked cap before leaving. I noticed he wore an actual coat and he had new shoes.

"One of Vic's urchins?"

There was no response but the fall of wood shavings on the floor like snowflakes.

"That's an awful lot of letters," I remarked. "Especially for weather such as this."

For the rest of the afternoon it continued like that. Snow drifted outside our door and notes drifted inside. Some were in envelopes and others merely folded scraps of paper. Mac recorded the information from the notes into his notebook. Barker carved. Jenkins nursed one of the bottles he had brought from the Shades, and I complained. It was one of my better skills.

There was a gap between visits long enough for Mac to set down every note in his notebook. Eventually, he rose from his ersatz desk, and took the notebook to the Guv. If he was expecting a word of encouragement, this was not the day for it. Barker harrumphed and returned to work. Jacob Maccabee did not seem especially offended.

Several other letters arrived, one carried by a professional messenger boy in a serge suit with buttons. He removed his pillbox cap, his manner most professional. He looked about eleven years of age. Jenkins had to sign for the note. I gave him a shilling though he brought but one note.

One can only be outraged for so long. The Prime Minister had sacked us. We were persona non grata at Scotland Yard. The Home, Foreign, and Colonial Offices would have little to do with us, but did it really matter? The agency was still open. We still had the money to pay messengers. Rebecca would still be there when we arrived home, provided we could find a cab in the snow.

An hour went by. Two. I'd have read a book if there were a novel on the shelves, but all we had there were reference materials: atlases and almanacs, dictionaries and directories. I'd have read Bulwer-Lytton at that point. I stepped out into Craig's Court and felt the air whistle about me. The heat inside had been stultifying, but it was dangerous outside. I looked for blue coats. I didn't see one, but there was a man watching me from an alley across the street. I couldn't make him out due to the falling snow. He appeared to be wearing all black, like a stage villain, and wore a hat with a wide brim. I stepped forward with the intent to cross the street, but as I did, I noticed another sentinel down the street near the Admiralty. By the time I looked back the first had disappeared. It could have been my imagination. Anyone standing in that dazzling snow would look dark. The second man evaporated as well. I looked in both directions to see if there were more keeping watch on our chambers. The next I knew, I was nearly bowled over.

"'Ello, Egg-Face!"

"Vic!" I exclaimed. "You gave me a turn. What's in the sack?"

Soho Vic carried a cloth sack over his shoulder like Father Christmas. Normally, he tried to present a kind of East End toughness, but I'd never seen him look so excited before.

"Hold the door and see for yourself," he said, swinging it open for me. "You have a future as a doorstop."

He walked to Jenkins's desk unbidden, upended the sack, and poured papers and envelopes all over the surface.

"I didn't expect your new position would produce so much correspondence," I remarked, staring at the pile in front of me.

"Cor, those aren't for the Guv. They're from Downing Street."

"What?"

"We bottled it, didn't we? Whitehall's our territory now. Any boy from anywhere else is paid off or warned off."

"You mean, these letters are not for us? They're for other people?" I said, shocked. "But some might be important!"

"They should have thought of that before they sacked Old Push. Sorry, I mean Mr. Barker."

"Vic," I said. "Boys bring messages from all over London and you stop them just before they reach the door of Number 10?"

"S'right," he answered. "You have a talent for stating the obvious."

"Did you do this on your own?"

Barker cleared his throat but did not stop working. "I thought a show of force was in order."

"No messages going in," I said. "What about out?"

Vic waved a hand at the desk. "There they are, all in one bunch."

"You stole them!"

"No, we didn't. We paid for them. The messengers made it all the way to Downing Street, didn't they? They deserve payment. Most don't care if a message misses the front door by a foot or two. They'd accomplished their mission, they supposed. If they argued, they'd trade their note for a kick in the knee and a bloody nose."

I was appalled. Barker's plan could disrupt the government. No one could say what was inside each one or how momentous it all was. I wasn't certain it was even legal. We were taking an awful risk.

"What about the professional messenger boys?"

"Nice little chaps," Vic said. "Very helpful and generous. One of them gave us the very trousers he wore out of the goodness of his heart. Another of them wanted to show us how far he could glide on the ice on his stomach. He traveled over a dozen feet on the paving stones of Whitehall Street."

"I see. And what of the commissioners? They are retired soldiers and former officers. Surely you couldn't humiliate them."

"Oh, no? They changed their tune after a Shadwell snowball."

I put my hands on my hips and glared at him. "And what, pray tell, is a Shadwell snowball?"

There was no response from Barker, whose chair was turned away from us. Jenkins looked at the ceiling, ignoring the question, while Mac studiously recorded the messages that in fact we were not privy to.

Victor Soho, as he styled himself, grinned.

"It's like a real snowball, only instead of snow, there's—"

"Night soil," Barker supplied, ahead of Vic's response.

"You're joking."

"Naw," Soho Vic said. "Very careful of their uniforms, they are. Can't stand a bit of horse dung on their nice gabardine trousers, lucky for us."

"I think I'm going to be sick."

"They've got to learn some respect," Vic went on. "They has to know the Whitehall Street Boys are here now."

"Ah," I said, turning to the Guv, or at least the back of his chair. "This acting as a benefactor was merely for my benefit. You were actually forming a gang!"

"It's tragic how disorganized the messenger business is here in Whitehall," Vic answered. "Truly a crime. Everyone coming and going, messages traveling hither and yon and everyone accepting that they reached their destination until proven wrong."

"Wait. What about the postman?" I asked.

"Of course, we would not interfere with Her Majesty's postal delivery," Barker said. "Now that would be illegal."

Vic nodded in agreement.

"We're not savages," he said. "But an ordinary messenger is fair game, either here or in Whitechapel, get me?"

"I 'get you.' These notes were all destined for Downing Street, then. Or coming out of it."

"Most of them," Vic replied. "Some were meant for the Foreign Office. And the Home Office. And the House of Commons. Then there's Scotland Yard, of course."

"You stole these notes from all over Whitehall?"

"'Course we didn't. Said I paid for them, didn't I? Coin of the realm? They weren't legal messengers, anyway, and really, who can tell one street arab from another?"

"What are you going to do with them?" I demanded.

"Record them," Barker called to Mac in the waiting room.

"Yes, sir," Mac answered.

"Jeremy, do you have a box large enough to carry these to Downing Street?"

"I believe so, Mr. B."

"Then send them on their way in an hour or two."

Sir," I said. "That sounds foolhardy, if I may say it. Salisbury won't swallow such an insult lightly."

"What would he do? Sack me?"

"I . . ." I began, but I didn't know how to answer.

"When one travels with the pack, one must learn how to bite," he said.

I sighed. I was trying to save us from being arrested again, and he was quoting aphorisms to me. I shook my head.

"I'm certain this cannot be legal," I said. "And I'm a married man now. I'd prefer not being arrested when I can avoid it."

Barker actually put down his boat and turned toward me, which was fine. I was growing tired of talking to the back of a chair.

"You're not involved in this," he said. "You knew nothing of it until now."

"I don't believe the Prime Minister of England, Scotland, Wales, Ireland, Skye, Manx, and whatever bloody islands I've forgotten shall strain so fine as to believe me innocent in this, whether you say it or no. And what about Mac? He just walked in the door!"

"I can argue for myself, thank you," Jacob Maccabee murmured, but I suspected he was worried as well. He had aged parents who might be inconvenienced by a stint in jail.

"If they're mixed together, how shall we know what went where?"

"We're not idjits," Vic said. "Penciled the name or address on the back, didn't we? And we bundled these together."

"You've cordoned the area, and disrupted the government!"

"Mr. Llewelyn is correct," Barker said. "We've gone far enough. Pull your boys out of Whitehall, and scatter across the river."

"You're the boss, Push."

"This never happened, as far as you are concerned."

"Never heard of it," Vic said, holding up his hands. "I was in Wapping, eating mussels."

"Good, then."

Jeremy came from the front room with a stationery box in his hands. We separated the folded notes from the envelopes, then divided them between Whitehall and other locations. Then we put the Whitehall messages in the box. Jenkins had to press down to make them fit. Then he found some string and tied the box closed. Meanwhile, Soho Vic tucked the ones to be delivered elsewhere under his arm, and carried the box.

"I'll deliver these in the morning straightaway," he said, "and I'll leave this box on the Prime Minister's doorstep tonight."

Barker reached into his waistcoat pocket and pulled out his watch.

"Five thirty-five," he said. "Jeremy, don't you have someplace to go?"

"Crikey!" our clerk exclaimed. It was five minutes past the time he normally left and therefore he was five minutes late for an appointment with a pint at the Rising Sun. It might even be sitting on the counter at that moment, awaiting his arrival. Without another word, he grabbed his hat and ran out the door.

"Since we are without benefit of client," the Guv said, returning to the matter at hand. "The three of us are at loose ends. I think we have deserved a night's rest."

CHAPTER TWENTY-FIVE

Y ou look worried," Rebecca said to me over the book she
was reading.

We were in my old bedchamber, which had now been
turned into a study. There was a snug coal fire humming in the
grate. I was in carpet slippers and a dressing gown, with a book
in my lap looking out the window at the frozen garden below.

"Hmmm?"

"What are you thinking about?"

"Nothing. Well, Juno, actually. The stable is cold and her water
is liable to be frozen. I've been so busy, I haven't thought of her
until now. Does she have enough hay? Is her blanket dry? The
old duffer who owns the stable is forgetful sometimes and the
stable lad doesn't really care about another man's horse."

"Are you thinking of going out in this weather?" she asked. "I'm
sure there isn't a hansom to be had in all London!"

"I can walk," I replied. "It's less than half a mile, and there are
no drifts in the road."

"Thomas, that isn't a good idea," she said.

"She's dependent upon me. It's my fault if she freezes or gets sick. I'd never be able to live with myself if something happened to her."

Before I married Rebecca, I sometimes wondered if anyone would ever bond with me as well as Juno. She was my girl and at times it seemed as if she understood me perfectly. She accommodated me so much it was as if she could read my very thoughts. Now we were without a case, the weather was terrible, and frankly, I had forgotten about her. She gets nervous when left alone for too long and will kick at the stall doors. She could injure herself, I reasoned. There was no getting around it.

"I have to go, I'm afraid," I answered. "I won't be able to sleep otherwise."

I changed clothes and met her at the top of the stair.

"At least let me see you out," she said. "You would be this solicitous if it were I in the snow and not Juno, wouldn't you?"

"Only if your water was frozen."

She smacked my arm. "You're terrible. I don't know why I agreed to marry you."

"I'm still mystified about it, myself."

In the hall she wrapped not one but two woolen scarves around my throat and pulled a thick tweed cap with flaps down over my ears. Then she made me change my shoes for my stoutest pair of boots. Mac came out of his pantry, looked at me, then looked through the window beside the front door to see the weather. He, too, thought I was mad, but it wasn't his duty to see to it that I was safe.

There was a creak of the stair and Barker came down from above, dressed in his gold-and-black Chinese dressing gown. He looked at the three of us suspiciously, as if we were youths at some sort of prank. Mac slunk off. Even Rebecca looked a trifle guilty.

"What the d—" he began. "I mean, what is happening here? Where are you going?"

"I must see after Juno, sir. I forgot about her."

Juno was the Guv's horse before I bought her from him, and though he no longer owned her, he expected me to do my duty by her, to make sure she was brushed and blanketed, that the farrier and the veterinarian saw her regularly. But now, like Mac, he looked out the front window.

"Cannot it wait until morning?" he asked.

"I'm concerned that her water is frozen."

"It's dangerous out there, Thomas, and I don't merely mean the weather."

"If any blue coat follows me he can keep me company."

"A wit to the end. Take precautions. If the snow becomes heavy, stay close to a fence as you walk. Don't wander off the road. Mrs. Llewelyn and I do not want to find you frozen in a drift somewhere. It's not good for business."

"Or marriage," Rebecca added.

For once, they agreed on something.

"I shall be exceedingly careful," I said.

With a nod from Barker and a peck on the cheek from my wife, I stepped out into the cold. To be truthful, it wasn't that bad. There was no breeze at all, and the air was still. The moon overhead cast blue shadows onto the whiteness, reminding me of the sentimental images on Christmas cards of houses covered in snow and bedecked with pine boughs. But it wasn't December, it was the cold, harsh reality that is January.

It was very quiet, unnaturally so for London. I heard nothing but the crunch of my boots in the alleyways. There was a layer of snow, perhaps an inch or so, but beneath I felt frozen ice, hard as iron. Before I was married, I used to take long walks at night to combat my insomnia, but that had greatly abated since marriage. Now that I was out in it again, it all came back to me, the feeling that everyone in the world was asleep but me, the belief that all London was mine and I was its night watchman of sorts. Sometimes it is best to get out from among people, even ones you love, and clear one's thoughts, or at least that was the lie I once told myself.

My hands were in my pockets, my collar pulled up around my face, and that absurd tweed cap with the hanging flaps was perched on my head. Whose cap was it? It certainly wasn't the dandy Mac's. It would not fit on the Guv's head, and I didn't believe Rebecca had brought it along with her from the City. Houses are like that: they acquire gloves, brollies, scarves, hats, and boots for which the owners cannot account. Anyway, the hat was unsightly, but it kept my ears warm.

I trotted the last few hundred yards and then pushed the livery door to the side, just enough to squeeze through. Inside, it was dark and cold. I lit a lantern. My advent caused some pawing and snuffling among the occupants inside. Plumes of warm mist rose from every stall. Finding Juno's, I squeezed between her body and the wall.

"Hello, baby," I said. "How are you tonight?"

She turned her head and rubbed an ear on my coat. She'd lean all her weight upon me if I'd let her. I pressed my cheek against her bony face and rubbed her neck. She was glad to see me, too.

Stepping back as far as I was able, I took stock of the stall. As expected, her water bucket was frozen. It took a strong kick with my boot to break the surface ice. She drank almost immediately, then she decided to find out how my coat buttons tasted. Juno is always interested in my coats.

I sang out for the stable boy, but he was gone. Her blanket was soiled and had not been put on properly. She looked as if she hadn't been curried in a month. Drat that lazy boy, I thought. No, drat this one for not taking proper care of his own horse. I rebuckled her blanket, brushed out her mane, and wrapped her left back fetlock, which I had been concerned over. I turned her hay, filled a bag full of oats and fed her, while telling her what a fine horse she was and how I would never neglect her again. I cannot say whether she believed me, or even understood me, but she liked the sound of my voice and my presence. When the bag was empty, I stroked her muzzle until she fell asleep. Coming to see her had been the right decision.

He was there waiting when I came out of the stall, blocking the door, one arm raised, holding a saber in front of him. Gunther Voss, my nemesis from the stage at the camp meeting revival. Instead of the trousers and singlet I last saw him in, he wore a coat and bowler, like the man at the funeral. Had he been one of the original three who'd stolen my bag that first day? I didn't know for certain. I hadn't seen their faces.

"Guten Abend, mein Herr," he said, holding the weapon loosely in his right hand. The blade gleamed in the light from a single lantern.

"Oh, it's you, Gunther," I said. "Back for more?"

He came forward slowly in a fencing crouch.

"Not very sporting of you, old fellow."

I looked about. There was a pitchfork. Barker had taught me to fight with a weapon called the "Tiger Fork," which was similar. There was a long-handled sickle against the wall, but by my calculation, I would be skewered before I reached it. I had promised Rebecca I would return, and I do my best to keep my promises.

I'd made another promise, this one to Cyrus Barker. I had taken precautions. I pulled my trusty Webley from my pocket and aimed it at his chest. I thumbed the hammer. He cried out and stepped back. I could tell he was going to back out and run, so I pulled out the second pistol.

"Stop. One more step and I'll shoot you dead where you stand. Do you understand?"

"You will not shoot," he replied. "You are English. Fair play and all that."

"I am Welsh, Gunther, and we don't care how the bloody English play."

He took a run of two steps before I cocked the other pistol and he stopped again.

"Don't tempt me," I said. "I don't want to spoil your looks with a bullet between the eyes, but I am perfectly willing. I won't lose sleep over it, I promise."

He slumped. He'd gambled and lost. His anger over being

humiliated had caused him to make a rash decision. He threw down the sword. He may have been ordered merely to watch the house, but the chance to get even with me had proven too great.

"That's wise," I said. "Now, move along. I'm taking you to see Mr. Barker. For your sake, I hope he shall be more patient than I. He'd believe you should live until your graduation. I do not."

The truth was that I had expended any animosity I had against Voss by beating him at the chin bar, but he need not know that. Questioning him would be more profitable if he felt one of us was more bloodthirsty than the other. Normally, that is the Guv's domain, but this time I appeared better suited.

I marched him through the snow to our front door, and had him rap upon the knocker. Mac opened it, saw the situation, such as it was, and let us in. Barker descended the stair in time to encounter Rebecca and the two came down together. At the foot of the stair, both regarded Mr. Voss, Mac, me, and the pistol in my hand as if we were some kind of tableau.

"I found him at the stable," I said, as if he were a stray dog.

"Thomas," Barker rumbled. "Take him to the basement so that we can question him. Mac, lock the door."

CHAPTER TWENTY-SIX

I ordered Voss down the stair at gunpoint, with Barker following behind us. Voss was watchful but trying to put on a brave
face. I set out a chair and was about to get the rope when someone slipped past my employer. I turned my head. It was my wife.

"Rebecca?"

"Mr. Barker, do you intend to question this man?"

"I do, ma'am."

"Then I shall be his advocate."

"I doubt he shall need one," the Guv replied.

"No? Are you not keeping him here against his will? Does he
have access to his consulate?"

"No, ma'am."

"Is he able to walk about? Will you offer him so much as a glass
of water?"

"That is not how interrogations occur, Mrs. Llewelyn," Barker
explained.

I'd seen Barker interrogate a man before, during my first case.

I feared he would kill the man. At one point, he'd kicked the fellow's chair so hard it came apart under him.

"Let me guess, then, if I may. Will he be tied to this chair, Thomas?"

"Yes," I admitted.

"And will you yell at him and threaten him and badger him until he offers you the information you require?"

Barker shrugged those monolithic shoulders of his. "If necessary."

"Will you threaten him with bodily harm if he does not give you what you demand? If he does not, what will you do then?"

"Madam," the Guv said. "This young man and his comrades have been responsible for three deaths so far. He tried to attack your husband, I presume. Did he, Thomas?"

"He did," I answered in a low voice. I did not want to side against my own wife.

"You could be a widow twice over were it not for his training."

"Now, that was uncalled-for," I said. I also did not want to side against my employer.

"Mr. Barker, this is a mere boy," she said. "A child."

"He is old enough to attend university or fight in his country's army."

"I admire you very much, sir," Rebecca said, stepping in front of Voss with her arms spread wide to protect him. "But these are not the methods of a man who respects civility and the rule—"

Voss jumped up then and seized my wife by the neck. He pulled a knife from his pocket and put it to her throat.

"Rebecca!" I cried out.

Barker moved forward, hoping to separate the two of them some way. He could do nothing. I could do nothing. One slice of that blade and she would be gone from my life forever.

She hit him in the chest with her elbow, giving herself perhaps an inch of space, in which she turned in his embrace. Then a voice came out of her mouth that even I did not recognize.

"What do you think you are doing, young man? I am bargain-

ing for your life and this is the thanks I get? Did your mother teach
you to treat women in such a manner? Does your father know that
you go against the rules of common decency and lay hands upon
married women?"

I've never seen a man's eyes go so wide before. His irises looked
like mere spots in the whites.

"Give me that knife, Mr. Voss! Sit!"

He sat. She handed the knife to Cyrus Barker.

"Anyway, I shall not have this boy subjected to physical mo-
lestation or harm. Do we understand one another, Mr. Barker?"

I slowly watched a smile spread across his face. I saw something
there I had not seen in many a day: respect.

"I do, ma'am. Forgive my behavior. We would be honored to
have you represent your client. Thomas, please find a chair for
your wife."

I did. She sat and gave me a smile of her own. She had hidden
depths. I must remember never to cause her to unleash such a
diatribe on me.

"Let us begin," the Guv said. "Thomas, can you take notes?"

"I can."

"Let us begin, then," Barker said. "Sir! What is your name?"

"Gunther Voss."

"And where are you from?"

"I will not say."

"Are you a student?"

"I am."

"And a Mensurite?"

"Like my father. And his father."

"How long have you been in this country?"

"Five days."

"And why have you come to England?"

Voss grinned. "To see the sights."

"Gunther!" Rebecca pounced again. "Do not be flippant! If
you refuse to answer, then say so!"

He sulked. "I refuse to answer."

"Who brought you here?"

"I refuse to answer."

"You see?" Cyrus Barker said, turning to us. "There is no leverage I can employ. Go upstairs, Mrs. Llewelyn. I have methods to make him more pliant and agreeable."

"I understand your needs, Mr. Barker, and I know that the stakes, whatever they are, are very high. I have seen the worry in my husband's eye. But we are civilized here in England, and if I allow you to employ your methods, how better are we than underworld ruffians in a basement in Whitechapel? It would be mere geography."

"You argue well. You would make a good barrister. However, we are not progressing, and we must progress. It is vital that we progress."

"Let me try again," I said. "Mr. Voss. Gunther, tell me, what do you study at university?"

"Chemistry and philosophy."

"Philosophy! A proper subject," I said. "I've read Kant and Schopenhauer and Leibniz."

"Kant is still relevant, but Schopenhauer and Leibniz are outmoded."

I stopped taking notes. I stopped writing as he went on about his subject. I had gotten his attention but did not know what to do after I had. I looked at the Guv and shrugged.

"Have you come to study philosophy in London, then?" I asked.

He frowned and sat back. "I refuse to answer."

Barker rose and began to pace. Rebecca and I looked at each other. We had reached an impasse. Voss had snapped shut like an oyster, and we had no way to pry him open again. The Guv consulted his watch.

"Ten thirty," he said. He turned to Rebecca. "I would like to keep him here for another hour or two."

"He has done nothing wrong, Mr. Barker."

"He menaced me with a sword," I replied.

"From what distance?"

"Well, fifteen, perhaps twenty feet."

"So, he was going to throw it at you? You drew your pistol?"

"I did."

"What happened to the sword?"

"He dropped it."

"Did you bring it with you?" she asked.

"No."

"Then how are we to know that he brandished a sword? You have no proof."

"Rebecca, I'm not lying!"

"I didn't say you were. I said you have no proof."

"Shall I go to the stable and bring back the sword?"

"She's got you, Thomas," Barker purred. "Confess."

"Hang it!"

"You were saying, Mr. Barker?"

"I would like to keep Mr. Voss here until someone more quali-fied can question him."

"Whom did you have in mind?"

My employer crossed his arms. "The German ambassador. One of his purposes is to protect the people of his country. He could not only question him properly, and elicit better answers, but also take him to the embassy afterward. I have no idea if the ambassador is able to come, but it seems the most likely solution."

"I agree. He may be the very thing. Call the embassy by all means."

He nodded and left, climbing the stairs and making a telephone call on the set in the hall. He'd closed the door behind him. Re-becca and I moved toward it.

"Was I too hard on you?" she asked.

"You were wonderful! I abdicate all arguments from now on."

"I shall hold you to that," she replied, turning to Voss.

"Gunther?" I said.

"*Ja?*"

"Would you like some beer?"

"Beer?"

"There are some bottles and glasses in the lumber room there," I said to Rebecca. "Would you get them? I've still got my pistol here, you see."

She rose and soon returned with the bottles. I opened one with Voss's knife and poured a glass for him.

"This is good beer," he said after tasting it.

Rebecca accepted a small glass. Voss took no more than a taste until he saw me help myself, and then he set to with a university student's thirst. Really, Mac makes an excellent pilsner. Barker returned, took a glass and sat on the stair.

"The ambassador is coming," he said. "I assumed it was impossible, but he readily agreed. However, he is hosting a function at the embassy, so it may be after midnight."

Rebecca held up a slender finger. "Two hours, you said, Mr. Barker. You must free my client at twelve thirty."

"That was arbitrary—"

"Nothing is arbitrary, sir. Words have meaning. Your word is your bond."

"Very well," he said, stoically. "I hope I have not summoned the ambassador too late."

It was 12:23 by my watch when the ambassador arrived. By that time, Voss was sleeping on a cot while I watched. Barker and Rebecca were upstairs waiting. I heard Hatzfeldt enter and speak to Rebecca.

"Not at all, madam. I must thank you. It was the third event I've hosted this week. What is wrong with society these days? Where are the witty conversationalists? Where are the Disraelis? The Melbournes? The Byrons? The only true conversationalist in this country, Mr. Wilde, sits in Reading Gaol!"

He came down the stair, a grand sight in his evening kit, and the governmental silk sash across his chest. His shirtfront was snowy, his collar so crisp it could cut paper. His bulbous head and weak chin were of no consequence in his element, the society event, where he could discuss the latest news and gossip, while at the same time forge alliances and change policies. Suddenly, Bark-er's fine home seemed dated with this bon vivant in our midst.

"My, Llewelyn," he boomed, coming down the stairs. "I have just met your lovely wife. What a lucky fellow you are. What is this room?"

"It is for physical culture," I explained. "There are mats and equipment, and a shooting gallery over there."

"Fascinating. And here is the fellow, eh? You have not injured him in any way, I trust?"

"Mrs. Llewelyn has played advocate for him," Barker explained. "I believe she alone has so much as touched him."

"I am pleased to hear it. What is his name?"

"Voss," I said. "Gunther Voss."

"Mr. Voss!"

Voss had sat up when the ambassador entered, but was obvi-ously not the type to snap awake at a moment's notice. He yawned. *"Ja?"*

Hatzfeldt began to question him in voluble German, so that I barely understood a word. Since I didn't understand what was being said, I noted his gestures and facial expressions. The am-bassador began with a hardy bluster, which was met with mono-syllabic responses. Then he began wheedling him, drawing him out, asking questions that must have required longer answers. What had been a suspicious young man suddenly became relieved and agreeable.

"Madam," Hatzfeldt said, turning to Rebecca. "Would you ob-ject if I smoke?"

"Not at all, sir."

He pulled a slim case from his pocket, inserted a cigarette into his holder, and lit it. Then he turned and began to question Voss again. The conversation was tenser this time, or so it seemed to be. The ambassador probed. The young man shrugged. He probed elsewhere, and the young man evaded. He pounced and Voss grew sullen. Finally, he came forward and patted the boy on the shoulder as if with a benediction and said something that made the boy look chastened, but relieved.

"I'll take him with me, I think. I'll get him to his proper destination, the little rascal. He's been getting himself into some trouble, I should imagine. These plowboys often do in a big city like London."

"No doubt," I said.

"By the way, I think you should find one thing of interest. Mr. Voss is not German. He is Austrian."

Barker and I glared at each other.

"Arnstein," I muttered.

"Valentine Arnstein?" Hatzfeldt asked. "Is he in London? I should have known he would be involved in something like this."

"You know Count Arnstein?" Barker asked.

"Too well, I'm afraid. He is a perennial nuisance. He causes problems wherever he goes. Berlin would very much like to speak with him. He disappeared as soon as our manuscript was stolen."

"We presume he was coming after Drummond," Barker said.

"But he'd already received the million pounds," I added. "I thought he wanted to sell it again to Lord Grayle if it could be found."

"You've lost me, sir," Hatzfeldt said. "To what million pounds do you refer?"

"The money for the sale of the manuscript to Germany, of course."

"He did not ask for money at all. He wanted our help to invade Austria-Hungary. He wants to start a new Holy Roman Empire, to return to power the last of the Habsburgs, which is to say, himself. We were having the manuscript authenticated when both he and it disappeared. No one thought it would be found here in London."

"I don't understand," I said. "How can one man make himself emperor?"

Hatzfeldt held up a finger.

"He can't unless he has help. Have you ever heard of *Die Heilige Fehme*?"

"It was a secret society," Barker answered for me. "The oldest in Europe. But it disbanded in Napoleon's time."

"Oh, come, Mr. Barker. You know a secret society never fully disbands, it merely goes underground. For the most part, it consists of aristocrats, and as long as money and power flow through them, societies like *Die Heilige Fehme* will flourish."

My mind grappled with the thought of a country, any country, run by aristocrats for aristocrats through a secret cabal. It wasn't particularly difficult.

"I have heard," Hatzfeldt continued, "that Arnstein has been traveling from university to fencing club to landowners' castles and ancient families. He is impressive enough, despite the one arm, and his entrée is always his Habsburg face. I think it ugly, personally, but he is a classic beauty as far as wealthy families in Germany, Austria, and Hungary are concerned.

"Do you have the manuscript, Mr. Barker?"

"No, sir. I am sorry, but I do not."

Hatzfeldt sighed.

"I suppose not," he said. "It did no harm to ask."

He turned and spoke to Voss. The young man stood. He offered a hand to my wife and she shook it. Her hand was tiny in his. He followed after the ambassador.

CHAPTER TWENTY-SEVEN

The next morning, I was thinking about the situation in Whitehall, wondering if the Guv had gotten us into even more trouble. There are probably no laws specifically against stopping in the south end of Whitehall, where many of the houses of government stand, but who could say? Those government chappies are very thorough and some laws deliberately vague. If there wasn't a law against what we had done there would be very soon. Once or twice I've wondered how strong a grasp of British law my employer has. I've also wondered if he cared in the slightest.

I didn't like this. Helping people on a smaller scale seemed what our agency did best: helping people find lost relatives, determining how and why someone was killed, safeguarding people who were being bullied. That was what Barker was born for and, just as possibly, I as well.

"What's wrong, Thomas?" Barker asked.

"What do you mean, sir?"

"You've been tapping your front teeth with your pen for a good five minutes now."

I put the pen back in its tray. "Have I? I've just been trying to work out what we shall do next."

"Not worrying, then?"

"Worrying? Ha. About what?"

"That's the spirit."

Our outer door opened and I nearly jumped, expecting another visit from Commissioner Munro, or perhaps the Royal Guard coming to take us to the Tower. Exactly how many years were the young princes held there? I wondered.

"No, no," a voice came from the waiting room. "That won't do. I have been expressly ordered to deliver this to Mr. Cyrus Barker personally."

"I am Cyrus Barker," my employer boomed through the doorway.

The man entered the room. He was a commissioner, of sorts, but merely the letter-carrying variety. He was perhaps five-and-sixty. His uniform was neat as a pin, his trousers creased, his boots highly polished.

Jeremy Jenkins was put out. The idea of someone delivering a note themselves, circumventing his authority, was crushing. He stood in the doorway, arms akimbo, clearly dismayed.

The Guv took the message and slit it open.

"Thomas, it seems the Prime Minister wishes to see us again."

"I can hardly wait."

"Mr. Llewelyn," Barker said, reading my mood. "They cannot sack us twice."

"May I say, sir," the old campaigner said, unbidden, "that we are all behind you, to a man. We would not cross the line unless requested directly."

Barker looked over the note. "Thank you, sir. What is your name?"

The man stomped twice on the floor and stood at attention. "Sergeant Alfred Tunney, sir."

"A pleasure to meet you, Sergeant. How are things in Downing Street?"

"Contentious, sir. Constables are still holding back a small crowd. Some lads have been throwing clods. I nearly got some on my uniform."

"I see. You are an official-looking fellow this morning, sir. Would you be willing to escort us south?"

"It would be an honor."

Barker put down the note and stood.

"Come, Thomas," he said.

"Yes, sir."

We bundled up and stepped outside, the sergeant at our heels. The snow was falling much more heavily than it had before. There was a knot of people at the end of the street, and people walking by were stopping to observe. I noticed a young rake leaning against a building, one boot against the brick. He tossed the fag end of a cigarette into the gutter. It was Vic, as nonchalant as ever. He brought his hand to the brim of his top hat as we passed.

I studied the crowd as we came to Downing Street. For the most part they looked like professional men. Some might have been from the House of Commons, in which case they were trained to dispute the constables trying to keep order. However, one officer's coat had been soiled with muck.

"This is your doing," I said. "Enjoy it."

"I shall."

Barker inserted his bulk between two men arguing in the crowd. The crowd parted as if the Guv were Moses. The people gave way and the constables moved aside. The Guv nodded to the sergeant beside us and we passed through.

There were men blocking the doorway to number 10. A constable stood on either side, but not just any constables: they were the largest and strongest the Yard had to offer, the human equivalent of draft horses. One held a clipboard and was consulting it while barking orders. Between them stood our old friend Swithin. His face brightened when he saw us.

"Gentlemen! You are expected! This way."

"Could we not walk a bit slower this time?" Barker asked. He tapped his brace with his sturdy blackthorn stick.

"As you wish, sir."

He led us down the familiar halls at a more sedate pace than our previous visit. There was no more trotting to keep up. Also, I sensed more respect in the halls as we passed through. People stopped to watch as we passed. The day before, we had been brought here in steel cuffs. Now we walked freely to the Prime Minister's door.

Swithin turned. "May I take your coats and hats, gentlemen?"

"That would be agreeable," Barker said.

"I'll bring tea."

"Do you have coffee?" I asked.

"I'll search the kitchen."

He opened the door and led us in. "Messieurs Barker and Llewelyn, sir."

Salisbury sat in his chair as we had left him, his fingertips pressed together. However, he looked far less thunderous than when we last spoke.

"Gentlemen, won't you sit?"

We sat. Barker rested the cudgel against the arm of the chair.

"Mr. Barker," he said. "You could have warned me."

"Warned you about what, sir?"

"Let us not be coy, sir. You should have said you were the new leader of the Templars. I am a member, though I do not attend meetings. You can imagine my distress upon hearing that I had dismissed a superior officer."

"I was not aware of your association," Barker said. "I have not received a list of the membership from Mr. Forbes."

"We have four telephone sets in the residence and they have been jangling nonstop since you left. We heard from the Admiralty and the War Office. Both thought you'd been treated shabbily. We heard from the Temple Bar and the Exchange. They'd heard I had slighted you in some way. The Conservative Party, that is, my own party, is discussing a vote of no confidence should the Templars throw their votes elsewhere."

"Mr. Barker donates substantially to the party," I said.

"It appears it is I who have bungled this business, sirs, not you. I freely admit it. I have made mistakes in the past. Every politician has."

"So has every detective and enquiry agent," Barker replied.

He was being magnanimous, I thought. By now, I would have roasted Salisbury's feet over hot coals without so much as an ounce of guilt.

The Prime Minister paused for a moment before speaking. "Tell me, Mr. Barker, are you responsible for the incident in Whitehall Street?"

"I am, sir."

"Did you hold back a few letters that should have arrived here?"

"A few? It is more like fifty, sir. And there were a like number for Scotland Yard."

"You realize you may have endangered important work. Certain projects here are sensitive."

Barker nodded. He looked as if he wanted to put a foot on the edge of the desk. Raising his limb kept it from throbbing.

"Of course," my employer replied. "I debated the matter thoroughly. It seemed the only way to get your attention."

"Well, you have it, sir. How was such a thing accomplished?"

"With the help of a dozen street arabs working to my instructions."

"You mean a few ragged boys nearly brought the British government to its knees?"

"I do."

"I was not aware there was such a breach in our flanks. I must be certain to correct it. When did you employ them?"

"That was—when, Thomas?"

"A few days ago, sir."

"You knew you were going to be sacked yesterday?"

"Of course, sir. I would have considered sacking me were I in your shoes."

"I must remember not to play chess with you, Mr. Barker."

Barker gave one of his wintry smiles. "I don't play chess, sir. The stakes are too low."

"Finally, I am beginning to understand what possessed Munro to suggest you for the assignment."

That stopped both of us cold.

"I was not aware that he suggested our agency," the Guv said.

"Oh, yes. He was rather enthusiastic. Naturally, he received the first dressing-down afterward."

I looked at the Guv, but he did not reply.

"You have guile, Mr. Barker," Salisbury said. "I misjudged you. You must forgive me, sir. I said some terrible things to you. I called you bumblers. Perhaps I didn't understand your reasoning. Would you please explain why you chose not to deliver the manuscript?"

"I fear I cannot," Cyrus Barker said. "Not yet. You shall get a full explanation in time, I promise you that."

"That will be an interesting story, I'm sure. You've come very close to ruining your career and spending time in jail."

"That is a constant danger in our profession, sir."

Swithin arrived with a large silver tray and set it on the table between us. He handed a cup each to Barker, the Prime Minister, and myself. I noted that he had found coffee somewhere in the Downing Street larder.

"I wish there were a better way for our business relationship to end, Mr. Barker," Salisbury continued, "but you admitted you would have sacked yourself under the circumstances."

"I did," my employer replied.

"Still, I regret that Mr. Pierce had to take the manuscript to Calais. He should be there by now with Monsignor Bello."

"Tell me, will the Jesuits open the satchel, do you think?"

"I would assume so. The monsignor will probably authenticate it before taking it to Rome, otherwise a simple courier would have done. Not that you are simple, mind you. Why do you ask?"

"The Jesuits will be most surprised. He will find the works of Cotton Mather in the satchel. Edifying, yes, but not what he expected."

The Prime Minister jumped from his chair as if he'd been stung.

"What? Are you saying Pierce is carrying a false manuscript?"

"The commissioner demanded that my assistant open my safe. I gave him permission. A constable took possession of the satchel inside, while I was clapped in irons. No one asked me if the satchel in the safe held the manuscript, and at that moment, I did not feel especially obliged to tell him. This was borne out when I was marched in darbies the length of Whitehall for all of London to see."

"Yes," Salisbury replied. "That was unfortunate. So, where is the manuscript? Is it still in the original satchel?"

"It is."

Salisbury leaned back in his chair, rested a hand on one edge of his desk, and stroked his beard with the other.

"Bello will be grinding his teeth," he said at length.

We did not inform him that Bello had visited us, I noted.

"No doubt Pierce will be less than pleased, as well," I replied.

"Can you deliver the manuscript to Calais as soon as possible?" Salisbury asked.

"That's how we found ourselves in this trouble before, sir, our interpretation of the words 'as soon as possible.'"

"I believe you will deliver it far more than I did yesterday. Very well, deliver it for me. For us. For your government. Get it out of London. We wish to have no more to do with it!"

"I will," my employer replied, standing. "Thank you for the tea. Most refreshing. Come, Mr. Llewelyn."

I nodded to old Swithin as we left. Outside, the snow had become fierce. Barker stuffed two fingers under his mustache and gave an ear-splitting whistle that echoed across the narrow street. I looked about and watched as one boy, then another stepped back from the crowd and wandered away. The loudest voices were silenced. The police looked about, expecting some sort of trick. Those who had been trying to get inside rushed to the gate where the officer with the clipboard stood.

"Let's go back to the office, Thomas," the Guv said. "Good heavens!"

We stepped out into Whitehall Street and were instantly swallowed up. A blizzard had started. The snow before had been nothing like this. We held our hands out to stop the wind from whipping our faces. I clutched my bowler to my head and turned north, the very direction it was coming from. We ducked our heads and moved into the teeth of the storm.

"Why did Munro press to have us hired?" I called out to Barker.

"To humiliate us when we failed."

"The man's a menace!"

We stopped speaking then. The storm made it too difficult to communicate. At some point we locked arms lest one of us wandered in the wrong direction. The snow was wet and heavy and already to the tops of our shoes. It stuck to our heels, making us stumble. I'd forgotten my scarf, so my only defense was to hold my coat up to my nose with my hat brim pushed down, leaving myself only a half inch or so to see through. It was utterly miserable, but there was one saving grace: our offices were not far away.

We passed Scotland Yard and I waved a fist at it as we went by. I could not make out which pub we were passing and felt relief when I saw the white marble of the Cox and Co. Bank ahead. We were nearly at our offices. Finally, we reached Craig's Court. And stepped into complete pandemonium.

CHAPTER TWENTY-EIGHT

A youth appeared out of nowhere, seemingly, a youth in a light blue coat and a matching cap. Perhaps he had just stepped out of the court, or perhaps he had been in front of us all the while, but we could not see him. He raised a sword in his right hand. In turn, I lifted my stick, as he raised his over my head, ready to strike.

The Guv had no time to dally. He parried the youth's attack, the blade biting deep into the wood of his stick. Seizing the boy's wrist, he chopped the knob of the blackthorn across his head. The boy fell like a stone.

Barker shouted something. I called out, but I felt as if a handkerchief were in front of my face. The sound of my voice was swallowed up. Somewhere ahead, I heard Barker bellowing, but his voice was heavily muffled.

Another young man came out of the alleyway, a sword in his hand. He swung it into my shoulder, cutting the fabric of my coat. However, I had the finest sword cane James Smith and Company sold, which I had purchased at great expense the year before. I didn't hesitate. I lunged and there was a spray of crimson blood in the snow. My hand came in contact with a hard surface. I recognized it as the wall of the Silver Cross.

I didn't feel any blood inside my sleeve. At one point I ran headlong into another body, a tangle of limbs, with neither of us able to use our swords. I managed to step on his hand, however, and stumbled on, hoping I was still going in the right direction.

They were all around me. I could hear the crunch of their boots and the sound of their voices. They were yelling in German. If I stopped moving I would be surrounded and they would make short work of me. Survival was my only thought. Instinct came to the fore.

How many were behind me? Two? Three? I hoped it was not more. Were any ahead of me? Were they behind? The flying snow was making them invisible. I wouldn't know until I met them.

I was nearly at our door when a figure stepped out in front of me, so close that I skidded on the ice and almost fell into him. My jaw hung open. He looked like a figure out of grand opera.

He wore a formal cape, black as pitch, and a wide-brimmed hat with a low crown. It made me think of the shrouded figures who had watched me the day before from the shadows across the street. I looked hard at him, but could not see his face. It was covered with a dark mask, the kind one might see at a festival in Venice. It was a crow's face, shiny and black. The eyeholes were round and covered in glass. The flakes glanced off the hard beak. He seemed unnaturally black.

We stared at each other for no more than a second. I tried to move past and he let me, but only to get to the youth behind me. He lifted a filigreed sword in his hand. As he moved forward there was a glint as I spied a cross around his neck and a dog collar. A wave of shock went through me when I realized what he was: a Jesuit assassin.

Our court was in the middle of a full-scale battle. Men in blue coats and men in black capes and gleaming coal-black masks. An owl. A cat. There must have been half a dozen men altogether in the alleyway. As I watched, Barker charged out of his office, a broadsword in his hand, and jumped down the steps into the path of one of the blue coats. The clash of steel upon steel was muffled by the snow, which was falling so fast that it was on my very tongue and in the back of my throat.

We were caught in a war between two factions: Catholic Jesuits and Protestant Mensurites. With whom would we side? The Austrians had tried to kill us, but the Jesuit leader, Monsignor Bello, had pointed a gun at us in our very offices. The decision was taken out of my hand. The so-called assassins were ignoring us, while the youths seemed hell-bent upon taking our lives.

I had an advantage over the Austrian boys. They had been trained in a rigid school. One could not move positions or stand back. One stood toe-to-toe and fought until someone bled. I was not constrained. I moved back, I stepped forward, side to side, whatever took my fancy. I, too, had been trained in this traditional style, but it wasn't my master.

Raising my sword over my head I lunged and my opponent met it with his blade. He could kill me, I realized. It wasn't like facing a pistol, which one could discharge from across a room. That razor-sharp blade could pierce a lung, a heart. It would be an excruciating way to die. I had too many things to live for now. Were it a matter of this university youth or me, there was no need to guess which side I would take.

There was a flash and a burn and suddenly my cheek was sliced. Blood seeped down my face. Some blighter had either forgotten or disregarded the rules. I turned on him, a tense young man who seemed to know what he was about. He was a solemn, silent opponent. He lashed forward again, revealing excellent form. The boy knew far more than I about fencing, perhaps more than I would ever know, but he had never faced a Barjitsuan before. I parried one blow over our heads and then buried a shin in his thigh. He fell screaming. There are bundles of nerves there and the skin is soft. Such a blow hurts like the dickens. I knew that, but had little compassion for someone who tried to lay open my cheek.

I bumped into a Jesuit, the owl, a small but lithe fellow who pressed his advantage against his opponent. Why had I not paid more attention in fencing class? He turned for less than a second and regarded me. I could see his eyes through the glass lenses in the mask. Perhaps he will turn on me, I thought, but he didn't. Instead, he returned to his next adversary and left me to mine, a pale-haired, tan-faced aristocrat. That blond hair had been passed down through generations and that tan acquired recently in Baden-Baden. He assumed the position, or tried to. I am an aggressive fighter and savor that first second when a bout begins. I jumped onto the step and caught him in the nose with the brass ball of my stick.

"Lad!" Barker cried. I turned and dared look at him.

He was standing near our front door, pointing into Whitehall Street. There was a vehicle passing. Not a hansom cab, but some kind of closed carriage. I saw Barker turn away, reaching into the rubbish bin beside our steps and lifting a satchel from inside. He shook the snow from it and began to run. As best I could, skirting men with swords intent on killing other men, I followed behind.

The satchel was in his hand. It had been in the dustbin, the dustbin the entire time. Anyone could have reached in and taken it. Scotland Yard had hunted for it, the Home Office had bargained for it, the blue coats were fighting for it, and there it was in plain sight, like Poe's Gold Bug.

Barker leaped, pushed off the carriage step, and sprang onto the board, beside the astounded driver. The Guv caught the man full in the chest with his shoulder, and he fell over the side with a yell, disappearing into the void, swallowed by the open maw of the blizzard. Meanwhile, I took my place on the step. A window of the brougham was pushed down in front of my face, and a man's voice came from inside.

"What the devil is going on here? Who are you?"

"Scotland Yard, sir," I said. "There's been another bombing attempt by the anarchists. I'm afraid we must make use of your vehicle."

A face appeared in the window. A fellow about my age, with a small mustache and a large monocle. He looked drunk. Drunk and rich, I'll be bound, to force a servant to go out in this weather.

"Oh, very well," he said, and fluttered a hand. "On your way, then. Old Perryman will get you there."

I didn't have the heart to tell him Perryman was in a snowbank and my employer had taken the reins. We passed Scotland Yard. Less gracefully than my employer, I made my way up into the seat beside him. He was clutching the reins, but had lost the whip. The cape of his coat was folded back over his shoulders, showing the gray silk lining. His teeth were gritted and his mustache was frosted with snow.

"The owl," I called over the clatter of the horses.

"What owl?" he asked, impatiently.

"The Vatican assassin in the owl mask."

"What about him?"

"It was Barrie, the little fellow from my fencing club."

"What of it?"

"He wasn't an assassin."

"Of course he wasn't. There are no Jesuit assassins. They are a myth!"

"You hired my fencing club to pretend to be assassins!" I cried.

He snapped the reins.

"I didn't hire them!" he said. "I asked them. Hutton jumped at the chance to do some actual fighting."

We careened around a corner and it was touch and go for a moment. We slid on a sheet of solid ice. We righted ourselves, however, and continued on our way.

"Do you think the trains will still be going in this storm? Or the ferries?"

"They'd better be," he growled. "I stole a carriage, I can steal a train!"

"I like trains," I said. "Always wanted to run one!"

"This may be the only chance you'll have."

"I say, Perryman!" a voice called from inside the brougham. "Have a care! You've spilled my champagne!"

"Sorry, sir!" I called.

CHAPTER TWENTY-NINE

It should come as no surprise for those who know me well that mathematics is not my strong suit. Should you require a quote from *Twelfth Night,* or the year Charles I was beheaded (1649), then I will gladly step in and be of service. Square roots and fractions, however, are akin to Urdu in this soft brain of mine. As a youth, I suspected my maths tutor had the system in his pocket. The square of an isosceles triangle changed from day to day according to his mood and he used it to inflict harm and confusion on those of us who eventually grew to become classics scholars, poets, and private enquiry agents.

Take London to Newhaven Station on the South Coast, for example. It is about sixty miles from Victoria Station, and as the London-to-Brighton express travels sixty miles per hour, one could expect to reach the ferry at Newhaven in an hour precisely. Dover, on the other hand, is but an inch on the map, yet somehow it is nearly ninety miles away. I presume their trains scoot along at nearly the same speed as the LBSCR, or else everyone would queue to go by Newhaven, unless they were going to Antwerp, and what cause does an Englishman have to go to Antwerp?

Anyway, it takes two hours, which somehow doesn't work out, unless the times table was calculated by my former maths tutor. Two hours, if one is traveling at sixty miles per hour. What about thirty miles per hour in a driving blizzard, with the snow drifting on the rails like sifted flour? The chances were more than even that the train would stop entirely.

Inside, Barker was pacing and growling to himself like a dyspeptic bear.

"Damn and blast," he muttered to himself.

We were perhaps halfway to Dover. I say perhaps because only the driver would know and I suspected even he was having trouble sighting landmarks. The thought of spending two more hours in the smoking compartment with Barker was insufferable.

"I wonder if the engineer requires a second fireman," I said. "This weather is exhausting, even to an experienced man. He'll be fairly knackered by now. Shall I see?"

"Anything to get us to Dover faster!" the Guv replied.

I'd have reminded him that we could have arrived four full days earlier, but sound reasoning suggested otherwise. I wrapped my scarf about my throat, then stepped out into the snowstorm, nearly blown off my feet in the process. I moved forward along the tender. My bowler was gone in the first minutes despite all my efforts, tugged out of my hand. Making my way to the cab, I offered my services, was gratefully accepted, and stepped up onto the footplate. This was the answer to a dream. Part of me has always wished to be a fireman or engine driver. Seizing the shovel, I threw a large scoop of coal into the firebox.

Cyrus Barker's boat, the *Osprey,* has a large boiler, and I have spent many an hour in front of it, feeding its eternally hungry maw. The cab on the express was as hot as Vulcan's forge, but from time to time a blast of freezing air and snow smacked into the back of my head and down my collar. I shoveled until there was a proper fire going, then I stood and looked out the front glass. Snow was striking it like arrows, and one mile looked precisely like another in weather like this. On the other hand, the view from the side of the cab presented the most beautiful sight, Kentish farmhouses covered in snow. I remember that evening, the tempest and the sublimity of the landscape, as if it were yesterday.

An hour went by, and shoveling began to lose much of its appeal. They never did close the line that night, but of course we were not to know that. The driver was much concerned about derailing due to the drifts or having a snow-laden tree fall across the tracks. Either one would certainly ruin Barker's plans, but it would take a blizzard covering half of England to do it.

The last hour was pure misery, my front singed and my back frozen. Then there was a squeal of brakes and suddenly buildings and platforms whirled by my head. I put down my shovel as the first fireman slapped me on the shoulder. Opening my mouth to speak, I was seized and pulled bodily out of the cab. My employer clapped one half of a pair of darbies around my wrist and locked the other about the handle of the satchel.

"You guard the manuscript, and I'll guard you. Let us see if our luck holds and the ferry is still running."

We fought our way through knots of passengers wanting to get to the Continent while buffeted by the weather, a tool in the hand of an angry god. Was there some sacerdotal force willing this manuscript to be stopped or destroyed? Was it never meant to see the light of day and Arnstein had ripped it from a well-deserved tomb? I had no answer. I'm no theologian, just a humble enquiry agent, blundering through a mammoth gale, one foot in front of the other.

There was no hope at all that we could spy Calais thirty miles away when we could not see thirty inches in front of our faces. We worked our way along the platform until we reached the ticket office. Behind me, I heard a man counting loudly.

"Is the ferry still running?" I asked.

"We'll know presently," the ticket seller said. "The bursar is counting heads. If there aren't enough passengers, there is no need to risk life and limb, in all this."

"Can we buy a ticket?"

"You can. I would recommend doing so. If you do, you'll be boarding ship immediately. If not, we'll refund your money should the ferry stay in port for the night."

"Two, please," I said, pulling the wallet from my coat pocket and counting the fare.

The ticket man looked dubiously at the steel bracelet on my wrist, but my money was sound. I could not tell from his expression whether he wanted the ferry to go or not. On one side, there was duty and reputation, and perhaps even extra money. On the other, a hot cocoa, or better yet, a hot toddy by the fire and no sleet in your face. It could go either way.

We boarded and stepped into the cabin, which was heated by the boiler and almost too warm. People were removing their coats and scarves. The windows were fogged by the heat in the room.

"Look about, Thomas, look!" Barker growled in my ear. "Do you see any blue coats? Any young men who might be concealing a sword?"

I looked about, face by face, to see if anyone was watching us or was acting suspiciously.

"No, sir," I said. "No one fits that description."

"They could be waiting on deck."

"If so, sir, we'll take them head-on as we always do."

"Good, lad! I was a little concerned that being married now you might shy away from a skirmish. You did well in Craig's Court."

"Thank you, sir."

It would have been nice to be sitting in front of a fire just then, Rebecca beside me, cocoa in my hand, if not the aforementioned toddy. But I would see this through, if only to protect the Guv from having to defend the satchel against who knows how many adversaries.

A young man pushed his way into the crowded cabin. Barker

reached into his coat, resting his hand on one of his pistols. The youth proved to be one of the crew.

"We's going!" he called.

The cheer the passengers gave was subdued, as if they suddenly realized for the first time what they were doing. Ferries sink. They capsize. They can be too small, too delicate for what the Channel demands of them. There was no guarantee that we would ever reach shore. We were steaming into the maw of a monster.

The vessel gave a lurch and I could feel the movement of the propellers behind the ship. I heard calls back and forth as the ropes were being untied and thrown into the boat. We're up against it now, I thought.

Barker looked ready to pace, but he saw the sense in staying where we were. No one would suddenly leap up with a sword and try to attack, hampered by dozens of people around us. It occurred to me in passing that the easiest way to attain the prize of the satchel was to cut off my right hand at the wrist. I was especially fond of that hand.

"Eyes open, lad. I doubt we are the only armed men on this ferry."

I agreed, but wondered to myself if the manuscript were real or if it mattered at all. Would it languish in a forgotten corner of the Vatican archive forever, after we'd risked life and limb? Did I particularly care? No, in fact. I did not care a hang, but Barker did, and after all, I was a private enquiry agent now, not a hired assistant. This was the work and I was here, so I might as well get on with it.

The journey was anticlimactic. The blizzard was doing its best to push us sideways until we swamped, but the thrust of the stout boiler was matching the attempt. It thrummed under our feet and were I not fastened to a holy relic I might have stepped to the boiler room and asked for another shovel. We moved ever forward. I wondered if we could see Calais yet, or whether it would overtake us as Dover had. Barker stood and broke into my reverie.

"Let's step outside, Thomas. These close quarters are driving me mad."

We pushed our way to the front door and stepped through it, provoking angry cries from the passengers.

"Blast, but it's cold!" I cried.

We pushed our way to the rail. There was no welcoming sight of Calais, only a gray sky whipping our faces with sleet. I looked down below at the sea and realized for the first time that we were surrounded by chunks of ice. Ice, as far as I could see in every direction. We could founder out here. It was almost as bad as sinking.

We saw two figures move to the rail at the far end and Barker reached for his pistol again, but it was only a couple of men gesturing at the ice below, as if one were blaming the other for their predicament.

"They are speaking German," the Guv said.

"This is the only ferry that can take one to Germany, sir. It's not unlikely."

"True," he said, removing his hand from his pocket. "I see a faint shadow over there."

He pointed south. I saw nothing, but he had those spectacles with the side pieces to keep the snow out of his eyes.

"How far?"

"It's difficult to gauge. I'd say we've come two-thirds of the way, at least."

We heard the sound of running feet, then. I looked over Barker's shoulder. The two men were rushing toward us. Too late, I realized one was carrying a pistol. The Guv's pistol barked once, twice. Then rough hands seized the satchel and tried to pull it away. The man strained, taking a step, then turned back, realizing for the first time that I was attached to the satchel, or it to me. I looked into his eyes and recognized Count Arnstein. This entire intrigue had nothing to do with Germany at all. He had used England's animosity toward Germany as a means to get what he wanted, a new Holy Roman Empire.

The count took me by the arm—his one-armed grip crushing on my biceps—and slammed me into the rail.

"You see that, Herr Llewelyn?" he said, looking down at the Channel, where I spied a small lugger bobbing in the water like a cork. "I hope you can swim!"

Then he climbed over the rail and jumped. I'd have gone over with him, but I had braced a foot against the rail. The weight was unbearable. He outweighed me by five stone. It felt as if a kicking mule were dangling from my arm. The metal bit into my wrist and I could feel my shoulder trying to slip out of its socket. I gritted my teeth and tried to keep myself from being dragged over the side. At that moment, it seemed inevitable.

An arm wrapped around me and I looked up to see the purser doing his best to save an endangered passenger. My employer tried to grab me also, but it was too late. I slid over the side. Arnstein was dangling, flailing about like a trout on a line. That was it, I thought. He was going to escape and take me down with him into the icy water.

At the last second Barker caught my ankle. Inexorably, he began to haul me up with the purser's help. Arnstein began to kick harder. Caught between the count below and the two men above, I thought I'd be ripped in half.

I felt the Guv seize my arm and drag it upward. As I looked down I saw my wrist was bleeding freely. Arnstein's jerking movements, had cut it open. Barker and the purser pulled me over the rail again and my employer fumbled with my wrist. The darbies were released and I fell back onto the deck as Arnstein dropped into the water. Barker had used his key to free me, but Arnstein had managed to get the satchel.

I pulled myself up just as the door to the ferry cabin opened and a crowd of men and women ran to the side.

"Man overboard!" one of the crew cried.

Arnstein came up out of the water, floundering a bit, then held up the satchel in triumph. Surely the manuscript was ruined by now, I thought. Or was it? We watched him swim toward the lugger.

"He's going to escape!" I cried.

The purser placed a blanket around my shoulders. "He'll never make it, sir. It's too cold."

Arnstein kicked off from the stern of the ship and began to swim, but it was difficult to hold the bag and swim with only one arm. He tried to swim, kicking his feet as he moved, but he was buffeted by blocks of rough ice. Triumph turned to panic. He seemed to be looking at no one but me as he flailed to get away. The lugger was so near I saw men on the bow waving to him. One threw a life preserver. It landed near him and he reached it, putting his arm through.

The satchel was no longer in his hand, I saw. It was halfway to the bottom of the Channel, from which it could never be retrieved. The leather scroll, created nearly two thousand years ago, was destroyed. All this work, all this effort, every stratagem that we had attempted had all been for naught. The relic was gone, the words of a long-ago saint, an apostle perhaps, destroyed, a mere pawn in a man's search for power and a birthright.

Arnstein gave a sudden convulsion then, and as we watched, he slowly slipped from the life preserver. He floated away from the boat, no longer thrashing about, until he was halfway between the two vessels. I saw no movement in his eyes. Slowly, his body rolled over on its side and then flipped over. Only his shoulder blades were visible. He had frozen to death in the frigid waters of the Channel.

Barker and the purser helped me inside. The heat awoke every nerve of my body. I gritted my teeth, but I was not going to cry out.

"We'll get you to a doctor, Thomas," Barker said. "We'll be in Calais soon."

"Rebecca will be worried."

"We'll send a telegram. In your condition, we will not be able to return to London tonight."

My employer was right. He's always right, blast him.

CHAPTER THIRTY

I do not know who has jurisdiction when a death occurs in the
English Channel. Perhaps it hadn't happened before. As enquiry agents, we have the kind of occupation that breeds pre-
cedents. We were closer to Calais than Dover, but I was not certain
that was a deciding factor. This was all academic, of course.
No matter who was in charge, the Guv and I were certain to be
blamed for Arnstein's death.

Both of the young men who attacked us had been shot, one
in the knee and the other in the thigh. Having been the obvious
aggressors, they had been disarmed by the male passengers. My
employer had offered his pistol to the captain and had removed
mine from my pockets, as well, before helping me into the sweltering cabin. I could not lift either arm.

The ferry was pushed into port by the snowstorm, where a
squad of gendarmes boarded as soon as we docked, or so I seem
to recall. My memory of the day was rather blurred. The Guv assures me that I was given a dose of laudanum from the medical

kit on board, but I do not recall having received one. Before we were allowed to leave the ferry, Cyrus Barker endured another questioning, followed by a terse interview with Monsignor Bello.

A few hours later, I awoke in a small bed in a seaside hotel in sight of the dock. The wind was still singing outside the window. Barker sat by the fire, staring into it like an auger.

"I lost it, didn't I, sir?" I asked. "The satchel is gone."

"Don't concern yourself, Thomas. Better to keep your arm than a few strips of leather."

"Sir, my arm is not worth a million pounds."

"It might be to your wife. I am more concerned about her opinion at the moment than Bello's or the Prime Minister's."

"After all our stratagems, we failed," I said. "Perhaps it would have been better to just let me go over the side with Arnstein."

"Again, I believe Mrs. Llewelyn would wish to be consulted in the matter. How is your arm?"

"Useless at the moment, unfortunately."

"You've done all you could. Really, everyone has. Are you hungry?"

"My stomach's off," I replied. "Could I have some water?"

Barker stood and poured water into a tumbler from a glass pitcher. He was in his shirtsleeves with his sleeves rolled to the elbow. He put the glass into my good hand and watched as I drank, to be certain I didn't let it fall.

"Get some rest," he ordered. "Save what strength you have for the morning."

The next I knew, there was light streaming through the window. I crawled out of bed, cradling my throbbing arm, and pulled back the sash. Calais had been blanketed under a foot or more of snow.

"At least the snow has stopped," I said, but when I turned, I realized I was alone.

I looked about and then returned to bed. Since my marriage, I'd had very little time alone. It was novel, but I had no idea what to do with myself. I couldn't shave. I could not don a jacket. I couldn't even don my suspenders, which were currently hanging from my waist. I had slept in my clothes.

Barker came in then with a doctor.

"I'm thinking of moving to Arizona," I remarked. "Or the Sandwich Islands. Someplace where cold weather is something one reads about in books."

"Back to normal, then, are we?" the Guv asked as the doctor lifted my arm.

I groaned in pain. The doctor, who did not speak English, shook his head and tsked as if men hanging by my limbs from boats was a habit I should consider quitting. He bathed my bloody wrist in iodine and wrapped it in gauze. I refused the offered laudanum and he tied my arm in a sling of white linen.

"Is the ferry running?" I asked my employer.

"Not yet, but the captain hopes that the sun will melt the ice in the Channel enough to travel later this afternoon."

"I need to send a telegram to Rebecca."

"No need, lad. I've already taken care of it."

"What did you say?" I asked, sitting up quickly.

It was a mistake I instantly regretted. My body protested.

"I said you were injured in the course of your duties but are under a doctor's care and we hope to return today, if possible."

"She'll be worried," I said.

"No doubt. Good wives would be, given the circumstances. However, a month from now this shall be a mere memory."

"As I recall, you made the same remark during our first case. My shoulders ached for six months."

"Yet here you are."

I could not argue with the logic, or didn't wish to. "What shall we do for the next several hours?"

"You will rest while I send a few more telegrams. Then we will be questioned thoroughly by Inspector Benoît of the Sûreté. In the meantime, I've taken the liberty of ordering breakfast for you."

"Thank you."

A minute or two later there was a knock upon the door. It was probably the breakfast, but one must be cautious in our occupation, so Barker pocketed his pistol before he opened the door. A man was leaning against the doorframe.

"Barker," Hesketh Pierce of the Home Office said in greeting.

"Mr. Pierce! Come in, sir. Mr. Llewelyn would rise, but he is currently recuperating from an injury."

"I know. I've been staying with the monsignor since I delivered the false manuscript here at some expense. Cotton Mather?"

"It wasn't a criticism, sir. It merely came to hand."

Pierce slid into a chair and glared at us.

"So, it is gone, then?" he said. "The manuscript, never to be seen again."

"Gone, sir. Long gone."

"All that subterfuge, and the killer lost it in the drink."

"The satchel was chained to Mr. Llewelyn's wrist. Count Arnstein seized it and leaped over the side. It was either the satchel or his life."

"You know what decision I would have made."

"Naturally," I said.

"Barker, you made me look a fool."

The Guv crossed his burly arms. "How so, Mr. Pierce?"

"The bloody false manuscript."

"You were retained to deliver a parcel, were you not?"

"I was."

"And you did so. Were you ordered to look inside it and verify the contents? No. That was Bello's task. You were a courier, therefore no blame should fall to you. Do you know who will be blamed?"

"You will," Pierce said.

"Precisely. Are you and I friends?"

"Far from it, I should imagine."

"Then this should not concern you. Who else will be blamed?"

"I suppose Munro, for assuming the satchel contained the manuscript."

Barker smiled. "Are the two of you cronies?"

"What, Munro? The man's a bounder."

"Then you and the Home Office are out of it. Move on and work on something else. If anyone questions you, tell him what I told you."

"It's a thought," he said.

"Aye."

Pierce crossed his legs. The man had the suavity that can only come from good breeding. A third son of a noble family, indeed.

"Bottom of the Channel, then?" he asked. "All out of tricks?"

"I did not say I was out of tricks," the Guv replied.

"That's the spirit. Keep them guessing to the last. You know, you should join the diplomatic corps."

"That, Mr. Pierce, is the one thing I would never do."

"Tell me, Barker, what did you say to Bello that shut him up? I thought he'd tear your head from your shoulders last night, but he left on the first train to Paris this morning, quiet as a lamb."

"I will not say he was happy, but he was less angry," Barker said. "One must be philosophical about such things. Once the manuscript so much as touched the water it probably dissolved. There was nothing to authenticate and deliver, so he left as soon as possible. As the titular spear of the Jesuits, I'm sure he has much to do besides worry over the fate of the manuscript."

Pierce nodded in agreement. "You do realize the lions are gathering in London."

"I've already been sacked once," Barker said. "What can they do to us further?"

"I shudder to think. Have you gentlemen heard? No, of course you haven't. The archbishop passed away last night. He was eighty-three, and he had been ill, I thought you should know."

That was it. It was too much. I lost the manuscript. My arm was injured, if not forever incapacitated. We faced an unfathomable future due to the unsatisfactory results of our mission. Now that sweet old man, that giant of English theology, was dead. I had liked him. He had treated us very kindly.

Pierce stood. "I'll leave you to your fate, gentlemen. Someday when this has blown over and you are no longer pariahs, I shall stand you a drink. Mr. Llewelyn, take care of yourself."

He slipped out the door and was gone.

"Pierce seems an agreeable enough fellow for a Home Office man. I suppose we can risk one pint of stout," the Guv said.

My food arrived a few minutes later, croissants and jam, two eggs and coffee, and it was an interesting experiment. I was hungry now, I could spear the food, but it took all my effort to bring it to my mouth. I had to lunge at it and take my chances.

"You do realize we're going to be roasted alive when we return to London," I said to the Guv.

"If so, the heat from the fire will be mainly upon me."

"Oh, believe me, there will be enough heat to roast everyone, for all your assertions."

"Do you need help eating that?"

"Thank you, no. I can manage. A prisoner deserves a final meal."

"Has anyone told you that you have a touch of melodrama to your character?" he asked.

"Only everyone I've ever known. Was there any mention of last night's event in the morning newspapers?"

"There is, but my French isn't good enough to translate it. As far as I can make out, you were mentioned only as a passenger who tried to save the count."

"I suppose Arnstein was eulogized."

"Not yet. He was still unnamed at the time of publication. I have no doubt it will be corrected in the afternoon edition. It is news. People falling from a ferry is rare."

"I say, I could use some help with the coffee. The cup is heavy."

He lifted the cup to my lips, coming near to knocking out my front teeth.

"Thomas, do you suppose your wife will be angry?" Barker asked. "If she has any reservations about your continuing our partnership, I would like to know. I would not want the future of the agency endangered by this incident."

"This is a rather small injury compared to some that have occurred during our other cases. I am certain it can prove as an object lesson. Still, I probably won't be much use lifting a pistol for a while, sir."

"Believe me, lad, if I can limp through the Prime Minister's office behind that madman Swithin, you can lift a pistol when necessary."

"Yes, sir."

I gave up on breakfast. I had managed most of one egg and a croissant with very little jam. The knife had been uncooperative.

That morning, we visited the gendarmerie. Our interview with Inspector Benoît was hampered by our poor French, and his poorer English although perhaps I made it seem a little worse than it was. We were asked the same dozen questions a half-dozen ways. When one has been dressed down by the Prime Minister of England and the Commissioner of Police, one aggravated Frenchman is of little consequence. We did not admit what was in the satchel. We were couriers; we had no idea what we were delivering. It was a standard delivery. No doubt it was insured. We did not know why someone would give his life to obtain whatever was inside it.

We left the police station in time to reach the harbor and board the ferry. The temperature had been higher than expected. I envied Barker's dark lenses. The snow reflected the light in every direction. I looked over the side into the water, thinking of Arnstein. Ice, ice, everywhere, in chunks large and small. They scraped along the bow.

"Was his body recovered?" I asked Barker, who was standing near the foredeck looking toward the white cliffs ahead.

"I have not the vaguest idea," my employer replied. "I saw men with boathooks from the lugger, but I was occupied."

"And what became of the lugger?"

"If the occupants were fortunate, the blizzard beached them. If not, it was a small vessel in fierce winds. It may have sunk."

"Those poor boys," I murmured. "What of the two that you shot? You did shoot them, did you not?"

"I did."

I thought of those ten or twelve young men in their blue coats, scions of important Austrian families, dedicated to their master, to their hereditary king of sorts: a local landowner, a great man to these people whose fathers and grandfathers going back many generations had served the Habsburgs. They had willingly sent their sons with him on a holy quest of sorts, to retrieve a relic stolen from him. A relic he would use to restore his family to its former glory. All of it had come to naught. Rather like our own plans.

Scotland Yard was awaiting us in Dover, a half-dozen men and an inspector. The inspector was Terence Poole.

"Well, well," he said in greeting. "You two have certainly got yourself in a spot of bother."

I held out my arms for the darbies. Well, one arm, actually.

"We can do without the hardware, I think," Terry Poole said. "You're in no condition to bolt. Cyrus, can I have your word that you will accompany me in a calm fashion?"

"You have it," the Guv said. "Is it possible to stop in Newington?"

"No. Your house is an arsenal. But, as I recall, you keep a change of clothes in Craig's Court and only a minor arsenal there. It is less than a quarter mile from our destination."

"Downing Street," I said. "I hate Downing Street. If I ever ran for public office, I'd fear I'd find myself there."

"Don't worry, Thomas," Poole said. "That would never happen. Who would vote for you?"

We boarded the express to London. Every roof, every hedgerow, every field under a heavy blanket of snow, a rare sight for the south of England. We eventually reached London, where the blinding whiteness of the snow had already mixed with the soot.

I feared we would be delivered by Black Maria, but instead, Poole ordered two hansoms, the other four officers going their own way. I knew then why Poole had been sent to fetch us: if

Barker escaped or cut up rough, the punishment would fall on his old friend's shoulders. I had to hand it to Munro. He knew how to manipulate men.

The cabs rolled through the snow-filled streets. In the sunshine, everything had begun to melt. Water dripped off icicles, gutters were full of slush and water. We turned into Whitehall Street and came to a stop in front of the Prime Minister's residence.

I was helped down and was being led toward the door when the constable at my side gave a cry and turned about in the opposite direction.

"What happened?" I asked.

"Some snot-nosed brat just threw a clod of muck on my oilskin cape! Now I'll have to wash it off!"

Somehow, it was comforting to know that Soho Vic still protected our flank.

CHAPTER THIRTY-ONE

Being called on the carpet a second time in one week in front of the Prime Minister of Great Britain is not something I would recommend. Salisbury's mood was so dark he was taking small pills for his digestion as if they were sweets. How much power did he have, I wondered, and how far could these powers extend? Could they close the agency? Could we be tossed in jail, or rather, prison? I'd already experienced the latter and had promised myself never to give cause to go there again. Being married made me want to avoid it even more.

Over and above our circumstances there was something that made our situation even more wretched. Commissioner Munro had come to gloat. It was difficult for him to hide the glee from his face, which was just as well; he did not have the face for it. He probably did not smile from one year to the next and those particular muscles had atrophied.

"I don't know why I let you continue with this little charade, Barker," the Prime Minister said in a low voice. "Knights Templar or no, I should never have trusted you. You have caused an international incident. You are complicit in the death of an Austrian aristocrat and their embassy has asked for an investigation."

"I'm certain—" Barker began.

"Don't interrupt!" Salisbury thundered. "You've damaged our reputation with the Vatican and the Roman Catholic Church. The Archbishop of Canterbury regrets trusting you. Munro here regrets suggesting your name for the assignment."

"Had I known," the commissioner said, "what a blunder you would make of a simple trip across the Channel, the work of an hour or two, I'd have had one of my own men take responsibility for it."

"You have sullied the name of the Knights Templar, if such a thing were even possible," Salisbury continued. "And Her Majesty's government is considering making charges against you. Against both of you. I hear, Mr. Llewelyn, that it was you that dropped a priceless antiquity into the Channel."

"Yes, sir," I said. "It was."

It was easier just to agree than to argue over the circumstances or make a vain attempt to explain what had happened.

"Mr. Barker, your incompetence has been a disgrace to our country. Do you have anything to say for yourself?"

I'd been so absorbed with my own misery since we'd arrived that I had not taken the time to look at the Guv. However, at that moment, the man was relaxed. There was not a shred of anxiety in his entire body. It was if he'd been thinking of something else entirely during the tirade, such as needing to get some new tobacco, or whether he might visit our barber for a shave.

"Well?"

Barker snuffed as if aware just now that some answer was required of him. Then he rummaged around in the inside pocket of his coat until he found an envelope.

I'd seen it in his hand right before the battle in Craig's Court. He placed it on the very edge of the Prime Minister's desk, teetering there, so that it had to be snatched from the farthest corner.

Salisbury pulled it open with enough ferocity as to nearly rip it to shreds. I saw the Prime Minister blanch as he scanned it and then sit back in his chair. He read the letter, then he read it again, then a third time just to be certain the wording had not changed since the second. At last, the paper fell on his blotter. Heedless of protocol, Munro pounced on it like an old tom and began to read it.

"You posted it?" Salisbury exclaimed. "You posted the manuscript?"

"Aye, sir," the Guv answered. "It seemed the best method to get it to its destination safely. I trust Her Majesty's postal service, even if you do not. As for the Continental mail, I thought them capable of managing to get a simple package to Vatican City without incident, which is precisely what happened."

"But the satchel was quite heavy. There were so many sheets of glass."

"Ah, there was. I consulted an expert in the matter and he assured me that the entire manuscript could be pressed between four panes only. He arranged them very carefully—carefully enough for the manuscript curator at the Vatican Library."

"So the other sheets of glass—"

"Remained in the original satchel."

"And the copy in the Home Office's possession was a fake."

"Aye, sir. When it was taken from my safe, no one questioned its contents."

"I see. What, then, is this business with the silk hose?"

"Silk hose?" I cried, tearing the letter from the hands of the Commissioner of the London Metropolitan Police Force. My eyes took it all in.

Mr. Cyrus Barker
7 Craig's Court
Charing Cross, London

Dear Mr. Barker,
   This is to inform you that the manuscript you sent to us has arrived safely. It has been stored carefully in the vault and is

pending a decision from Cardinal Bettini and the other officials as to when and where it will be translated. I was surprised when the package arrived in a manner contrary to what we expected, but was gratified that it was received in such excellent shape. Neither damp nor handling has affected the text in any way that we can see.

I must admit yours was one of the most unusual packages this library has seen. These eyes have witnessed a hundred things used as packing materials, from wool, fleece, wood pulp, and wads of cotton, but this is the first time we have encountered silk hose as a means of cushioning a priceless article. It was satisfactory, but you might consider something more practical should you find another item to send to our vault.

> *In Christ's name,*
> *Cardinal Russo*
> *Vatican Library Curator*

"Hose," I moaned.

"It came to hand, sirs, and seemed a plausible way to protect the delicate manuscript."

"You waited several days to receive word from Rome?" the Prime Minister asked.

"I did, sir. It was my attempt to keep Arnstein and his conspirators occupied, unaware the actual manuscript was hundreds of miles away."

"When did you post it?" Munro demanded.

"First thing on the second day."

"But it was in the vault of the Cox and Co. Bank that morning!"

"It was, for a while, and then it wasn't. Should the day ever arrive that I cannot outwit a band of CID men I shall close my offices and retire."

"The man's impossible!" the commissioner boomed. "Let me arrest the scoundrel now!"

Salibury frowned, considering what to do next.

"Your order was to take the satchel to Calais." The Prime Minister sat back in his chair and regarded my employer. "You got round me, Mr. Barker, didn't you? You irritated me until I gave you permission to do it your own way. You tricked me."

"I would have refused the offer if I had not had enough room to maneuver. As a rule, I don't care for courier work. There are too many restrictions."

"So, gentlemen, you managed to both deliver the package and find the killer of Hillary Drummond. You may have thrown a bit of mud on the Home Office's shoes, but you avenged the death of one of our best agents."

Barker shrugged his shoulders in reply.

"What about your interference with the messages that come in and out of Whitehall? Will there be any more assaults?"

"There is no reason. I merely needed a show of strength."

Barker stood and cracked the muscles in his neck. We had in no way been dismissed yet, but he pulled his coat about him and began to button it.

"If there's nothing else, we have potential clients waiting."

"Ummm, yes."

"Oh, and be certain to send for us if we can ever be of service to you again."

Salisbury's jaw fell open and then he burst into laughter. He was still laughing when we left his office. Munro was at our heels, pulling a particularly dour face.

"Commissioner," the Guv said. "Will you walk with me? There is a matter we should discuss."

We left by the front door at last, that famous black door with the ornamental lamp hanging over it. We were an odd trio, two private enquiry agents and the Commissioner of the London Metropolitan Police Force. I walked behind, having no way to know what would happen next.

"We don't like each other, do we, Commissioner?" my employer asked Munro.

"We most certainly do not."

"Nor were you a favorite of Pollock Forbes."

"Are you gloating?" Munro asked. "If you do, I would prefer to walk alone, thank you."

"Pollock Forbes did not trust you. He gave the helm of the Knights Templar to me, to do with as I will."

"You are beginning to irritate me, Barker. Say what you have to say."

"We do not get along, but I believe you to be an honest man. Even trustworthy in your own way. Forbes convinced me to take over the Templars, and yet I do not want it, not all of it, anyway. There may be pertinent information that Scotland Yard might not only need, but need in a hurry. I have a small practice here, precious but small, and were I fully invested in the society, I would have to give it up, which is something I would never do."

Munro frowned as if he were certain he was being tricked, only he wasn't certain how.

"We shall lock horns a great deal, but I suggest we share the duties of running the Knights Templar."

"In exchange for what?" the commissioner asked.

"In exchange for not having to run the blasted thing myself. I am not accustomed to the kind of frivolities enjoyed by many societies, for example. Nor do I care for the rituals."

Munro stopped and stared, bushy brows meeting in the middle.

"I'll never get you, Barker, as long as I live."

"No, Commissioner, I don't think you will."

"Why join a secret society if you do not socialize or enjoy rituals?"

"Because it brings together men of importance in order to do the most good."

"You want power, then."

"No, I most definitely do not want power. Do you? Have you plans to take the Prime Minister's position? Have I misjudged you?"

"All I want is to have an efficiently run police force and to see it safely into the new century."

"I want that as well."

"You're still sore about my turning you down for the constable's position all those years ago!" Munro cried, laughing.

"It rankled for a time, I'll admit, but if you had not refused me, I would not have opened my offices."

"And become a thorn in my flesh."

"A messenger to harass you and keep you from becoming conceited."

"Second Corinthians 12:8. Only it is a messenger from Satan, as I recall."

They walked in silence for a while, lost in thought, as I dogged their steps.

"How will I know what is best for us to do?" Munro asked. "It would be so much better if you would just turn the society over to me fully. I have the men to do what needs to be done."

"I prefer a system of checks and balances," the Guv said. "You will not get what you want all of the time, and neither will I, but we will get some of it."

"Do not think I will promise not to throw you in a cell just because we are working together. I shall not accede to that."

"I would not ask. My solicitor is on retainer. He needs to earn his keep."

"Let me consider the matter and get back to you."

"No," my employer said, shaking his head. "You must decide now, or the offer is rescinded."

Munro blustered. His face turned red and his hands balled into fists.

"You are the most infuriating man in all of London. Of England, in fact!"

"That is a high compliment, sir, and is corroborated by many in this town."

"Very well," Munro said. "I accept, the Lord help me. We shall divide our duties later. Do you require men to transcribe messages?"

"Perhaps later, although I have a man working on them at the moment. I will see that they are sent to you personally."

"Scotland Yard, sir," I said.

"What?" the Guv asked.

"We are here. Scotland Yard is right there."

"Thank you, Thomas."

"Come to my office tomorrow afternoon. I shall clear my schedule."

"Two o'clock?"

"Fine."

"Good day, Commissioner."

"Barker."

We parted company. The air was cold and crisp and dazzlingly clear. I tucked my stick under my good arm and slid my hands into my pockets.

"Thomas," Barker said, with an air of disapproval. "Pray take your hands from your pockets. It reflects upon the agency."

"Oh, good," I said. "At least one thing hasn't changed."

Barker raised his blackthorn and a cab came to our feet. Slowly, we crawled aboard.

"Newington, driver! I'd say we've earned a day off, don't you?"

CHAPTER THIRTY-TWO

Y ou posted the manuscript," I said, shaking my head. "And did not tell me."

We were up in Barker's chamber, which runs the length of the house. To call it a garret would be a trifle modest. We were sitting in two large leather chairs, sharing an ottoman in front of a crackling fire. The snow had blown south across the Continent and we didn't miss it. I hoped we had received our allotted amount of snow for the winter.

The Guv had one limb stretched out toward the fire. The trouser leg had been rolled up past the knee and his foot was bare. The brace had been removed at last. It was still too early, really, but no one could convince him of it. His calf looked like a map of a war zone. A jagged line of sutures meandered down it, like a river of blood. There were angry welts from where the metal and leather had pressed repeatedly against the skin. The limb looked pale and unhealthy, but all that didn't matter. The brace was off

after almost half a year. No more could he be pitied for his infir-
mity. No more would he be less than a threat to whoever crossed
our path. He flexed his toes toward the warmth of the hearth, a
small and personal victory.

"Aye, I did. Or rather, Mac did. He was quite put out that I sent
the socks to the Vatican, however. I told him better they than I."

"And you saw no need to inform me?" I asked. "I can understand you not telling me when I was an apprentice, but now I am
a partner."

"You are a partner, true, but I still have a thing or two to teach
you. If I tell you everything you cannot develop your own powers
of logic and observation."

"I see the observation, but not the logic."

"Look, a man asks me to deliver a package to Rome. Very well.
I put it in a box, add postage, and send it on its way. In what way is
that illogical? The postal systems of Western Europe are the envy
of the world."

"What of Jeremy's counterfeit manuscript?" I asked.

"It begins realistically enough, but toward the end, I'm afraid
he became creative. It was destroyed."

"It would have been nice to see Monsignor Bello's face when he
realized what he had," I remarked. "From a distance, of course."

"He was certainly inventive with his language when we finally
spoke in Calais, and he a man of the cloth. I might have told him
what I had done with the manuscript had he not aimed a pistol
at my head in my own office. I tend to take such matters personally."

"When did you first suspect Arnstein?" I asked.

"Now, lad, you know I suspect everyone at the start of an enquiry. In his case, he discovered the manuscript, or possibly even
forged it. Yet the German ambassador said that no money had
been paid for it, which he would most certainly not have said
if Arnstein had been paid and they had no manuscript for their
troubles. He wasn't concerned about the count, he was angry
about Drummond stealing the satchel and killing the translator.

He believed not only that the Foreign Office was behind it, but that the British government had possession of it, which of course they did. At that point, the satchel had become a liability, should it be proven to be in our possession. This is why Salisbury was so anxious for us to get rid of it, to get it off our shores as quickly as possible."

"Whereas you had already posted the manuscript and were awaiting confirmation, while trying to determine who had killed Drummond and Wessel."

"Aye. We had only a small window of opportunity."

I stared into the fire, letting the questions I had inside me come bubbling up.

"Did Arnstein kill Wessel because he was the translator?"

"That seems logical, does it not? More likely, however, it was the blue coats. I believe he had difficulty managing so many young men who would willingly die for him. They killed Wessel and his driver, hoping to find the manuscript themselves."

"What will become of them, do you think?"

"If they were in the lugger and did not capsize, then they returned to Dover and took the next ferry to Antwerp. I presume the lads I injured were handed to the Austrian embassy."

"What about Cochran? Surely he was involved."

"Only peripherally. I don't think possessing the manuscript would have added much to his tent revival. He was doing very well without it. Even more so now. Have you read the newspapers? Of course you haven't. He was shot two nights ago by a released mental patient. He wasn't hurt, but he was grazed, enough to make his believers think that atheists and liberal socialists were trying to kill him. His camp meeting was more than full last night. He performed an impromptu second service for those who couldn't get in."

"Why do evil men prosper?"

"I don't know that I would call him evil, just opportunistic. Remember, if there is suitable punishment in this world, what is left for the next?"

"If he were innocent, or mostly innocent, how did Voss come to join his flock?"

"Likely the boys of the academic school were told to lie low until needed. Perhaps this was where Voss chose to be. He could have heard him speak during Cochran's German tour. I would have questioned him further, but Hatzfeldt spirited him away. Name another suspect."

"Karl Heinlich."

"Of every story I heard this week, his appeared to me the most plausible. He cared about his brother, he was tired of touring. He'd lost his faith as a youth while attending a progressive university. Every word he spoke seemed true. If the man was guilty of theft and murder, I'd have been glad to expose him, but he was innocent."

"And Grayle?"

"Ah, His Lordship. He'd heard from Arnstein that the manuscript was somewhere in London. It was too rewarding a piece of gossip not to impart to the most famous collector in Britain. It was an open secret, despite what Salisbury said. Grayle didn't care about theft or murder or national machinations. He merely wanted to own the manuscript. It would be his new bauble. I wonder what he will try to purchase next."

"Why do you think the German government, that is, the Kaiser, did not send a squad of their own men to London to find the satchel themselves?"

"I am only speculating, Thomas, but the manuscript was stolen, a beloved scholar was murdered, and the Germans were humiliated once more. Tensions are so high between England and Germany now it would be dangerous to send a dozen agents to London. Also, the manuscript might simply have been too much trouble to bother with, especially if their scholars believed it to be a fake gospel, which is still possible."

Mac arrived with the iron pot and tiny cups Barker used to drink gunpowder tea. I drank some with him but only to be polite. The drink is almost tasteless, and what taste there is noxious.

"Is there anything else?"

"We can add the Home Office and the Jesuits to the list of organizations that do not trust us."

"I did not become an enquiry agent to make friends. I'm here to right wrongs and help people find justice."

I laughed. "What are the Templars but a group of friends and acquaintances, albeit well-connected ones?"

Barker put his thimble-sized cup back on the tray and lifted another. "I see your point and shall not argue with it."

We sat and listened to the fire while I considered the case.

"Was this Pollock Forbes's plan all along?"

Barker laughed and actually slapped my knee. "Now, see, you are coming along after all. Aye, it was all Forbes's maneuvering. When he told us he wanted me to take the reins or he'd have to choose someone else, he meant someone in particular."

"Munro."

"Indeed. It was Forbes himself who suggested us for the assignment, but Munro pressed Salisbury, hoping to embarrass us."

"Which he did," I replied.

"But Forbes knew we would carry a card or two up our sleeves."

"Yet you gave the society over to Munro. Why, if you think him a scoundrel?"

"He may be a scoundrel, and petty, and mean-spirited, but he is an able administrator. The new building was built under his direction, the regulations he created have produced better constables and inspectors. He would not be my first choice for Master of the Templars, but who would be? Certainly not I."

"You weren't tempted? I thought you were for a time."

A second empty cup was set beside the first.

"The temptation was there. The thought of so much information at hand was tantalizing until I realized that less than a hundredth of it concerned my work. Why should I care that a Lord

Mayor has a mistress or the Chancellor of the Exchequer has a gambling problem, unless it has to do with a specific case, and what are the chances of that? As high as a manuscript arriving in Berlin, that proved a notion an academic had theorized recently."

"You believe it to be a fake?" I asked.

He shrugged. "It doesn't matter to me or my faith, and I doubt it will be proven either way. It is a permanent conundrum. The British government was wise to send it away. They might have even suggested to the Vatican that the manuscript is dangerous, and should never see the light of day again."

"It's a shame. I'd like to believe it was real."

"Ever the romantic, Mr. Llewelyn."

"Guilty, I suppose. But, another gospel!"

"It would be like Krakatoa, lad, spewing ash and fire all around the world. Best let it slumber."

I pointed at him. "You're siding with Salisbury and Munro."

"Am I? It's possible. Just because I think them heavy-handed doesn't make them any less competent at their occupations."

"You think them competent?"

"I do. If there were a better, younger, and more able man for the position, I believe we would know who he is."

That was twisted logic, but I wasn't about to get into a political debate. I'd never told him I was a liberal socialist, but I'm certain he suspected it.

"Ah," I said, which is always vague enough to make a good bookmark in a conversation, since it sounds agreeable while meaning absolutely nothing.

"Did you have further comments?" the Guv asked, pouring himself a final thimble of tea.

"I suppose my mind tried to connect Cochran to the German government and Arnstein to Lord Grayle. After the Pritchard case last year, I am suspicious of conspiracies among our suspects. The thought that Germany had nothing to do with this case save as a victim astounds me."

"I'm sorry, but I cannot change events to please your theories."

"I suppose not. A pity, though."

Barker nodded.

"Sir, do you think a country can become an imperialist nation like Great Britain, without having to do the kind of things Drummond did, such as theft and murder?"

"No, Thomas, I don't. There will always be a need for spies and informants. Drummond was given his orders and he performed them to the best of his abilities. Momentarily, at least, that poor little German scholar in the hotel room was England's enemy. How Drummond felt afterward is mere conjecture. He may not have had time to even think about it before his own demise." He paused for a moment. "Thomas, could you bring that case on the mantelpiece, please?"

I retrieved it for him. It was a black pipe case I had not seen before. The leather was shiny and new. He tripped the tiny lock and opened it. Inside was a new snowy-white meerschaum. At some point in time, it was lying in a reef somewhere in Turkey. Now it was carved in the likeness of its owner, Cyrus Barker, including his bowler hat and a minuscule pipe in his mouth. He had one just like it when I was first hired, smoked until it was the color of honey, but it had been shot from his mouth while we were working on an enquiry in the Scilly Isles. Now a version of it was back again. It was a spot of vanity in a man generally without it.

He lifted the pipe, ran his hand over it, then opened the jar that read TABAC on the side, and stuffed it full of his private mixture. He lit it and lay back. Then he pulled a small cushion from behind him and rested his foot upon it.

"How do you suppose," I asked, "Arnstein's private academy happened to be in Germany in time to follow Drummond?"

"Were I in his position, I would not go into negotiations with the German government alone. It would be too easy for him to suddenly disappear, rather than be paid the million pounds. The man needed foot soldiers, and he just happened to have some."

"They were children," I said.

"To their mothers, perhaps, but in most countries in Europe,

the majority of them were old enough to join the army or be con-
scripted into it. Also, the chances are excellent that these little
aristocrats have fathers and grandfathers who began the same
way. Military families can place a heavy mantle upon a young
man."

"Was Arnstein paid? He claimed he had been, but Hatzfeldt
implied otherwise."

The Guv was busy smoking his pipe, testing it, gauging its draw
and suitability. He seemed to ignore the question for a minute.

"The fact that it was in a hotel, being valued, was proof that
Arnstein had not yet been paid. I think it likely that Drummond
had followed Arnstein from Vienna, having received word from
an informant where he was going. I'll admit I was trying to prove
to myself that Drummond was traveling in Germany with Cochran or Heinlich, but I could not make the pieces fit."

"Thomas?" a voice carried from below. "Are you coming?"

"Yes, Rebecca, in a minute or two!" I looked at my employer.
"Do you intend to quit the Templars?"

"I fear I cannot now. I must look after Munro and make certain he stays out of mischief."

"How will you do that?"

"Checks and balances, lad. I have a few spies of my own."

"Shall we still find our offices inundated with messages?"

"Eventually, I'm going to suggest Munro assign a constable to
type the messages for both of us. They may arrive a day late, but
one cannot expect more than that."

"Have you put Mac out of his situation? I thought he enjoyed
working in the office, and he certainly had nerves of steel to step
out of our chambers just before Scotland Yard's arrival."

"Mac is always competent. However, I do not want to place
Mrs. Llewelyn in the position of having to cook for the household,
especially when our plans often change hourly."

"We could hire a cook. For the evenings, I mean."

"No, no, that would be worse. We would feel obligated to be
home at a specific hour for dinner. Mac is far more flexible."

"I suggest we keep the messages in our office, have Mac set them down, then send a copy of the list and the originals to Munro's office. Mac can work half a day and get back to his duties at home, unless for any reason we find we need his services on a particular day."

Barker puffed and considered. "That seems like a sound enough suggestion. Let us put it to Mac and see what he says."

He exhaled the last scraps of smoke from his pipe.

"What of Mrs. Llewelyn? Would she object to being freed of the obligation to cook?"

"Not at all, although she might decide to continue to learn from Etienne."

"Most men would make the decision for her," he remarked.

"Are you suggesting I should?"

"No. Your wife is a very intelligent woman, and the two of you must work out your decisions together."

I looked at him with some degree of doubt. "You think her intelligent?"

"Of course. You made a fine choice, Thomas, and may I say that if the Mocattas choose to continue to ostracize their daughter over so trivial a matter, it is their loss and our gain."

"You do not mind having a woman in the house?"

Barker gave one of his rumbling chuckles. "You make her sound like a broom or an iron. There is more than one sort, you know."

"I do, yes," I said. "But I didn't know you did."

"Well, I am certain we can all agree on something. You got far better than a rascal like you deserves."

"Wait!" I said. "You had the satchel, and Jeremy removed enough glass to protect the manuscript. Then he put poor old Cotton Mather between the glass sheets. Munro took possession of the satchel, Pierce delivered it to Calais, and Bello had apoplexy when he found out what was inside. Am I correct?"

"You are, in all essentials."

"But there was another satchel, the one in the dustbin that you locked to my wrist. What was in there?"

"There were a few books I put in for ballast, but for the most part—"

"Don't tell me! It was your ship model!"

"Aye," the Guv said, looking glum. "Three years' work at the bottom of the Channel, along with my best tools. I will have to start over again."